THE KING STREET AFFAIR

Also by Jon Sealy

The Whiskey Baron

The Edge of America

The Merciful

So You Want to Be a Novelist

The King Street Affair

A Holy City Novel

Jon Sealy

Haywire Books

HAYWIRE BOOKS

Cover design: GetCovers

ISBN: 978-1-950182-08-4

Library of Congress Control Number: 2024903074

For Barbara Sealy
In memory of Otis Walter Sealy
and Carl Sealy

They had been corrupted by money, and he had been corrupted by sentiment. Sentiment was the more dangerous, because you couldn't name its price. A man open to bribes was to be relied upon below a certain figure, but sentiment might uncoil in the heart at a name, a photograph, even a smell remembered.

—Graham Greene, *The Heart of the Matter*

Part One

Chapter One

CHARLESTON, South Carolina. The gray slush of a January day in an election year, another disastrous period in a long string of disasters for the United States of America: drone strikes and protests, cyber espionage and volatility in the stock market. Wars and rumors of war. Showboating politicians. The palms in Marion Square slashed sideways in the wind. Temperatures had dropped over New Year's and now locals, unaccustomed to the bone-chilling weather from the north, huddled in bars and cafés and waited for the foul weather to pass.

From a window table in the Swamp Fox restaurant, sharing a late breakfast of French toast and bacon and luke-warm coffee with a woman he'd spent the night with, Wyatt Brewer watched the wind toss the palms, a black Lincoln peel into traffic on King, a taxicab's glowing taillights on Calhoun. He'd slipped last night and shared a bottle of wine with the woman across from him, but it was too soon to tell whether the damage would be permanent. There was no roadmap for middle age.

From the mist out the window, a young woman emerged like a phantom from *Wuthering Heights* and paused on the

3

corner to wait for the light to change. Around twenty, beautiful, a waterfall of blonde hair whipping around her face. She kept her head down and, although she held a black umbrella at an angle in front of her, the gusts had nearly turned it inside out.

Wyatt watched her struggle, and his heart clenched for the way she resembled Mary Grace, God rest her soul. It occurred to him that he might be spiraling into another depression, where time and memory seized hold of his faculties and played tricks on his senses. Now on the other side of forty, Wyatt was at a precarious age where he could almost believe in metaphysical forces: Mary Grace returned to her youth and plopped on a modern-day street corner.

When the light changed, the girl pressed against the wind with a headstrong and oblivious gait. Then she was gone, a wisp in the wind lost amid the rain and the palms.

Ten days from now, federal agents would seize on this detail. The coincidence of the girl and his connection to her. Charleston was a small town, but coincidences of this nature ran against the paranoid instincts of the intelligence crowd. Since 9/11, every signal in the noise was a relevant data point.

"I'm sorry," he said as he turned back to the woman across from him. "I spaced out for a second there. What did you say?"

"A penny for your thoughts."

"My mind wanders," he said by way of apology.

"I can see that," she said. "I have calls to make, if you need some time to get adjusted."

"I'm here," he said, and he took what he hoped was a flirtatious sip of coffee. "I was just thinking of an article I need to write," he lied.

"Which one?"

"A man drowned out on Folly yesterday, and there's no explanation for the circumstances."

"What was he doing out there in this weather?"

"Exactly. It happens on occasion: riptides, accidents from people drinking too much, poor swimmers. If this were July, his death might not even make the paper, but who would go out into the water right now?"

"You think it was murder."

"I couldn't speculate."

"You always say that, Wyatt. You've got a better imagination than most people in the city, but you refuse to use it. At least tell me what you're thinking."

Fair request. Her name was Ashley, and they'd spent a generally pleasant night in the Francis Marion Hotel, where she was managing a corporate event. She was a former public relations source who had hung out her shingle and now enjoyed the perks of a hotel suite. The two of them had been having these occasional hookups for several years now. At one point he thought it might lead to something serious, yet he'd been relieved when she'd told him she had no interest in family life. Like Wyatt, she'd had a kill shot of love in her younger years and kept everyone at a distance. Now, although she offered him the crutch of companionship without commitment, it was not a relationship in which he could unburden himself.

"I was just thinking about ghosts," he said. "I don't know how many dead bodies I've reported on. I've been doing this —fifteen years?—and I've literally lost count. So here I'm adding another one to the heap and was just thinking about what it might mean for me to be cataloging so many dead."

"Well, it means you're recording their stories. That's important."

"I know."

"Seriously, Wyatt. You're summoning up lives, and saying, 'This person lived. They mattered.' I hope someone as sensitive as you writes my obituary."

"You're saying I won't be around to write it?"

"You are older than I am."

"Thanks," he said, and he stopped himself from adding anything further. What could he say? That he was getting weary of the way death always crept in? That he could feel himself hinging into middle age, his life a vessel with nothing to fill it?

"Something else is going on," she said.

"I had to write an obituary yesterday, for an old friend's father. He passed away this week."

"Oh, I'm sorry. Were you close to him?"

How to answer that? Harry Cope had been a South Carolina legend. He'd worked his way into Charleston society via New Haven, mysterious connections from his wife's family, a murky legal business that landed him a judgeship in his later years. Wyatt's write-up for the Metro section had been flattering, but he knew a darker side of the story.

"It's okay. I hadn't seen him—or my friend—in years, so it was a blast from the past to see his name pop up in an editorial meeting."

"Are you going to the funeral?"

"I don't know," he said, embarrassed to admit it had not occurred to him and he hadn't looked up the arrangements.

"You should. Funerals have a way of bringing people together. Maybe you'll reconnect with your friend. Was it a girlfriend?"

"You got there fast," he said.

"Intuition."

"Yeah," he said, "a girlfriend from college." More than a girlfriend, but no reason to bring up that ancient history. *Tempus fugit*, he thought.

"Do you think she'd want to see you?" Ashley asked.

Wyatt thought for a moment about how to respond. There was so much to say about Mary Grace, but opening that door would mean revealing a lifetime of secrets and sin, his entanglement with a family of power brokers living in the shadow of the Cold War. Love and betrayal. Murder and theft. No,

6

she would not be at the funeral because she had died in a car accident nearly twenty years ago. Now that her father was gone, the only one left would be her mother, Lillian Archer, a woman he would not be able to face.

He shook his head. "I don't think so," he said.

She must have intuited she'd hit a buzz saw, because she tapped her mouth with her napkin and said, "Speaking of, I should get on. You mind waiting for the bill? You can charge it to the room. My client's paying."

He agreed, and he hardly noticed her leaving as the rain lashed outside and his mind corkscrewed into the past.

"Tell us again, when did you decide to go to the funeral?" the man in front of him asked ten days later, when all the secrets had come out and Wyatt could no longer deny his role in what he might politely soften to less-than-patriotic activity. A dead Spanish lawyer, half a million dollars, and half a lifetime of keeping it secret.

The man in front of him did not look like a spy. He looked like an accountant: mid-fifties, reddish thinning hair, portly, a little thick in the neck, small ears, round glasses, and a way of squinting his eyes while wrinkling his nose as though examining the details of a funky W2. *Just a clarification, Wyatt. You filed one exemption, but your employer is taking out taxes for two exemptions.*

His partner—a young woman with large brown glasses, freckled skin, a flannel shirt, and cowboy boots—was inscrutable. She hadn't said a word since hello, and while she was a couple of years too old to be the office intern taking notes, she may as well have been for all she registered with Wyatt.

"I can't tell you," Wyatt said.

"Well, you just told us it didn't occur to you to go to the funeral until your friend—Ashley?"

"Ashley."

"Mentioned it over breakfast."

"That's right."

"Seems a bit odd, is all. A man you know dies. You hadn't seen him in years. You say you weren't close with him. An old girlfriend's father. You write a quick blurb about him after your editorial meeting and put him behind you. Yet the next day, your girlfriend"—the man raised his hands to stop Wyatt's objection—"whatever she is, she suggests the funeral, and suddenly you're taking off work, driving across the state, to what? Re-connect with this woman's family?"

"What's your point?"

"When was the last time you saw the girlfriend? Or her family?"

"Twenty years ago? We were in college."

"Long time ago."

"I don't know why I went to the funeral," Wyatt lied. "I only met Harry a few times, but—we went to their beach house on Kiawah one summer, back before it was what Kiawah is today. He and I went running together. You bond with someone if you work out with them."

"Did you know about Mary Grace's car accident?"

"I heard about it a few years ago, through a friend on Facebook."

"You didn't contact her family then?"

"Like I said, when we'd split, we'd split. I moved on with my life." Another lie. "I didn't see the point in calling Harry up years after the fact."

"But you went to his funeral."

"Maybe I felt guilty for missing hers. I couldn't say."

"Couldn't say. Well. Then I guess I still have the same question."

"Which is?"

"Why now?" the man asked, a bit too smugly. "If you weren't hoping to reconnect with your old flame's family, and you hadn't seen them in twenty years, I'm trying to understand why now. Why choose this day, this event, to change your life?"

Wyatt stared at the wall behind the man. They were in a historic home tucked away on King Street just south of Broad. The building had been converted to a suite of office buildings with a plaque labeling it the John C. Calhoun Professional Center. Nondescript from the street but huge once you got into it, with a central stairwell and old creaky wood floors, silent as a library of yesteryear. They'd set up in a windowless conference room with a six-person table, a TV on a roller in the corner like the kind his old grade-school teachers would bring in when they wanted to show Bill Nye the Science Guy rather than teach a lesson. There was a tent card on the table with detailed instructions about how to access the Wi-Fi, and not much else to look at. The office had a musky smell as though gases trapped during the building's nineteenth-century construction were still slowly being released. The HVAC rattled in the ceiling. Wyatt pictured big pipes lined with black plastic, metal quivering against the current of air. The equipment sounded tired.

Bert and Penelope. That couldn't be their real names. Who has such names?

As far as Wyatt knew, he was still here of his own volition and was not a suspect in a crime, not under arrest or even privy to the people who would be arrested. He'd come in voluntarily when Bert and Penelope came to his house and said the U.S. government had a few questions about his recent activity and would he mind making a statement. The same way he'd known the request had not been optional, he knew he could not simply put his hands on the table, slide his chair back, say it was nice to meet them, and go on with his life.

Too much had happened for him to shut it all down.

Chapter Two

A<small>FTER LEAVING</small> Ashley and the Swamp Fox, Wyatt arrived at the office too late for the morning editorial meeting, which was fine because he had his assignments for the coming week and made it a habit to stay out of the fray of office politics. These days the newspaper business was all about *digital-first* and *transformation*, which made the newsroom a game of musical chairs with buyouts and layoffs in a quarterly rotation. Wyatt had come into a good bit of money when he was in college. Thanks to the miracle of compound interest over twenty years, he had a parachute ready any time and could focus on the business of reporting stories.

When you had no ambitions in your work, and nothing much at stake in your home life—no wife, no kids, no expensive hobbies, an easy mortgage—you were free to come and go as you liked. Wyatt didn't care whether his beach corpse article made it onto A1, or even made it into the paper at all. He'd had his name on enough by-lines that as long as his direct deposits continued every other week, he was content to do the work for its own sake.

The newsroom had mostly cleared when he arrived, a few journalists at their desks pounding away on the keyboards on deadline. A couple of fresh-faced copy editors and his friend Fitz were leaning on a counter by the coffee pot and debating what effect another looming board takeover would have on the newsroom.

Fitz was a reporter of the old school. Shaved his head when he hit fifty and drove a twenty-year-old pickup as if to say to the world he had no use for its consumerist charms, he was happy and self-sufficient, thank you very much. Sinewy like a weightlifter on a cut, gravel voice like a man who knew his whiskey, Fitz was one of those guys who made you feel like a screwup no matter how good you were at your job. He smoked Camel cigarettes and didn't apologize for it.

"You know we'll just keep riding this horse into the sunset," he was saying. "Not like we're going to find a way to suddenly find ourselves in a different business."

"You don't think the new reader API is going to give us some new revenue?" asked one of the young copy editors, a scenester named Dylan sporting a mustache without irony.

Wyatt suspected Fitz and Dylan would be out of a job after the next investor call, Fitz with his pension intact and the copy editor with a letter of recommendation and a useless skillset. He'd seen enough layoffs that he had an instinct for who was next on the chopping block.

"What do you think, Brewer?" Fitz asked. "You think turning our website into a social media app is going to be the innovation they've been looking for all your career?"

"We got to wait for the new building for that," Wyatt said. It was an old joke in the newsroom. The *Charleston Daily Dispatch* had moved into this office building in the mid-2000s advertising its convenient location, the parking garage, and the modern amenities. The building was a long time in coming, promised for a decade, so throughout the nineties the reporters had joked about how the new building would fix all the managerial issues. Fifteen years later, they were still waiting—with nearly everyone in the community, from politicians to businesses to their own readers, trying hard to take over management's efforts to push them out of business. He added, "Maybe if we sync the app to Instagram, we'll have a daily long enough for you to retire."

"You think?"

"I don't think we're going anywhere that fast," Wyatt said, mostly for the benefit of the copy editor. The future was an abstraction, but most days he felt like the proverbial frog in a boiling pot, the temperature rising so gradually that the poor creatures didn't notice until it was too late. These years felt like an inflection point in world history, but there was nothing to do but remember the past and keep moving forward.

Bemused, Fitz took a sip of coffee and asked, "How do you think we're going to be writing stories once Chat GPT copy floods the internet? There won't be any ad dollars left to fund a Piggly Wiggly circular."

"People still need to know what's going on," Dylan said. He leaned into the conversation with the swagger only a twenty-something could muster. High energy and low vision, he would do well in the new world order.

"People have social media for that," Fitz scoffed. "Look at the school redistricting. They just announced the project, and there's already an activist group ready to stage a protest if the board tries to move little Jaden to a different middle school. They're organizing on Facebook, so they don't need us."

"When did you become such a cynic?" Wyatt asked.

"That's what growing up in the seventies will do to you." Fitz took another gulp of coffee. "Anyway, we missed you at the morning editorial. Where were you? Hot date last night?"

"I wish," Wyatt said, though he wished he'd not come into the office after all. Fitz may play dumb, but something about the way the old reporter looked at you and narrowed his eyes, Wyatt felt like the man had his number, like he could smell Ashley on his lips. "Hey, is Bonnie around?"

"She should be here somewhere. She made the meeting,

though I don't think she'll be taking Reece's job any time soon." Reece, their editor-in-chief, was rumored to be retiring soon, which meant an open position at the top and a cascade of other managerial slots. Bonnie was the production manager, but, more importantly, she'd referred Wyatt to AA and been his sponsor in joining the Catholic Church a few years ago, when he was thirty-five and thought he could make the second half of his three-score-and-ten mean something. AA had taken, until last night, but the church had not. Before he could take his first communion, he'd fled as if spooked. Today he felt the overwhelming urge to confess all he'd shied away from in reconciliation: Mary Grace, the money in Spain, the life he'd wasted for twenty years. Maybe Bonnie could absolve him with a quick pep talk and a few Hail Marys.

"Thanks, Fitz."

"Hey, were you wearing that shirt yesterday?"

Wyatt flipped him off as he headed down the hall toward Bonnie's office.

"Don't be so uptight, Brewer," Fitz called. "We all need a little companionship from time to time."

Wyatt knocked on Bonnie's door and asked, "Got a sec?"

"Wyatt! I thought you said you were out on the Folly Beach piece."

"I should be, but I'm waiting on a few callbacks." He took a furtive glance down the hall and then, seeing no one, shut the door. "I fell off the wagon last night."

Bonnie looked up from her computer and blinked a few times as if trying to assess the damage. He wasn't bloodshot and stinking like a man who'd passed the night in a back alley, but as anyone in recovery knew, backslides weren't always so dramatic. A couple drinks could fool you into thinking you could control it, but the challenge came the day after, or the day after that. He knew this, yet there was always a *but* lurking in front of him. *I know I'm not in control, but…*

"Take a seat," she said. "You want to talk about it?"

"Not really. Not much to say. I split a bottle of wine at dinner."

"You were out on a date."

He nodded. Bonnie had his number.

"You going to a meeting tonight?"

"I don't know if I can make it."

"It takes a lot of work," Bonnie said. "You don't have to go it alone."

"I've actually been thinking I need to go back to talk to Father Jim."

He'd never told her about what happened, why he'd quit going to Mass. She said once or twice, back then, "I've missed you at church," to which he'd replied, "I've been a little disorganized." She'd had the tact not to press him, though Father Jim had emailed him once to ask if everything was all right. What could he say? That he'd confessed his sins in the abstract, pointed to greed and envy and gluttony and pride, always pride, but never the brass tacks of what he'd done. He'd performed the act of contrition for his thoughts but not his deeds.

"I'm sure he'd love to see you." She studied him thoughtfully, and then asked, "What's really going on?"

"I should have told you last week, but remember the write-up I did on Harry Cope?"

"The old judge?"

"Yeah. I sort of knew him, years ago."

"Why didn't you tell me the other day?"

"I didn't expect being reminded of him would dredge up so much."

"This has something to do with why you quit the church?"

"I don't know. Maybe. But this morning I thought I saw someone else from years ago, and it feels like—what's the thing where when you experience something once, you see it everywhere?"

"The frequency illusion. Baader-Meinhof."

"That's it," he said. "It feels like a confluence of things are coming together, and I don't think I should ignore it. I might drive up for the judge's funeral."

"You should," she said. "When is it?"

"It's in the upcountry tomorrow."

"Come to a meeting tonight. Better yet, why don't we go to lunch now? We can talk more out of the office."

"Maybe when I get back."

"No, no, no. Get your coat."

She rose from her desk wearing well-cut black leather pants that seemed made for her curves and a general I-know-I'm-a-badass attitude that would have turned him on in different circumstances, but she'd been a mentor to him in so many capacities—the newspaper, the church, AA—they'd crossed a threshold in their relationship. She comported herself with a decidedly firm, Mom-command aura that compelled Wyatt to listen to her advice—and he usually took it.

She led the way out of her office, but his phone buzzed while they were in the hall.

"Hang on, I need to take this," he said. An automated voice reminded him of a dental appointment next week. He held up one finger and said, "Uh-huh, uh-huh, tell me where you are and I can meet you."

Bonne leaned against someone's nearby cube and struck up a conversation, glancing back at Wyatt every few moments in a way that said it wouldn't work to slither out of lunch even for a source. He could hear her castigating him: *The trouble with you, Wyatt, is you never know when to sit down and reflect. You're a beautiful reporter, but you spend too much time chasing other people's stories and never pause to take care of yourself.*

She'd been clean forever now, after what sounded like booze-fueled teenage years and bad behavior in her early twenties that resulted both in a son and in living homeless for a short while. Whatever the cause, a switch had gone off in her brain when she was twenty-five—perhaps the same switch that had flipped in him at thirty-five—and she stumbled into AA, Jesus Christ, and, after some basic job training and a GED, a job in the newspaper's pagination department.

The last time Wyatt had gotten black-out drunk at an office happy hour, Bonnie had driven him home and put him to bed. The next day, while he was fighting off a blistering hangover and swearing off alcohol, she quietly told him what had worked for her and to let her know if she could help. He believed she'd seen something special in him, plucked him out of the masses, and the pressure of living up to that real or imagined expectation had served him well.

Until now.

Now, he knew she would tell him that backslides happen, that he could rebuild, one day at a time and all that, but he wasn't prepared for the weight of failure. He said "uh-huh, uh-huh" into a dead line on his cell and waited for her attention to be diverted.

When she was distracted, he ducked down the hallway and bolted for the stairwell.

Chapter Three

TEN DAYS LATER, in the interview room on King Street south of Broad, Penelope Lowe could tell Bert was dissatisfied with Wyatt's account of his movements. He liked to let silence fill the room as a way to encourage others to talk. Props were his tell that an interrogation was not going well.

After Wyatt explained his journey from the Francis Marion Hotel to the Swamp Fox restaurant to the *Daily Dispatch* offices, Bert pulled out a document, an eight-page, single-spaced witness statement Wyatt had written before the meeting. The subject had sketched out a timeline of his movements.

Bert turned to the middle of the document and set it in front of Wyatt. He pointed to a middle paragraph and then, showing off a little, he read the passage upside down.

"'When I left the breakfast with Ashley, I headed into the office, thinking about my article about the body on the beach, and also maybe that my relationship with Ashley had run its course. Harry wasn't on my mind.' Now, that's not quite true, is it?"

Bert leaned back. His eyes rolled up to a corner of the room, and he put his tongue out on his lips.

"The problem I have with your account, Wyatt, is that your actions over the next few hours don't substantiate what you're saying. If you were worried about your article, why'd you run out on your editor? If I'm reading this correctly, you never went back to the office. Instead, you took the next day off and drove up to Harry Cope's funeral, where you had at least one clandestine meeting with a potential enemy of the state. I don't understand how you can sit there and tell me you were just feeling a little nostalgic for an old fling. Instead, what I see is a guy methodically trying to cover his tracks. What would you think if you were me?"

Wyatt said nothing, and Penelope found him unreadable. He was slim, still looked young for forty, a guy who would be okay to sit beside at a corporate luncheon. He dressed like a suburban dad, sneakers and a wrinkled button-down. The file said he was sitting on more than a million dollars, yet he was still a beat writer making sixty grand. He ran a half-marathon every fall. He drove a ten-year-old midsize pickup. Did he really have this hidden life of intrigue?

Bert scrunched his face. "Maybe we take a few minutes. You want a soda? Bathroom break?"

"I'd like to get this wrapped up," Wyatt said.

"I can't do anything about that. You got somewhere to be?"

"I'm expected back at the office in the morning."

"We've talked to your editor. She understands."

"You did what?"

"Relax, Wyatt. We have a relationship, so I told her I'm just borrowing you until we get this whole story ironed out."

"What kind of relationship?"

Bert ignored him and turned to Penelope. "Penny, could we huddle for a moment?"

She followed him to the kitchen, where he shut the door, rested his hands on the counter, and stared out the window at the decaying palmetto leaning against the house.

"What do you think?" he asked.

"What am I supposed to be looking for?"

He turned to her. "There's not much there, is there? We know there's more to it around Harry Cope, and he flinched when I brought up the money, but I don't see him trying to cover for anyone. There's some ghost in his past that's eating at him, but what does that have to do with the here and now?"

Penelope waited for Bert to finish, but he shook his head.

"Keep taking notes. If you see any tells, let me know before you put anything in a report for Diane. I don't want her zeroing in on anything until we know what we're dealing with."

Diane Neubecker was Bert's supervisor and oversaw their unit from Northern Virginia. Penelope had only met her once, when she'd first transferred in. Diane had smiled from behind a desk and said, *It'll be great to have some fresh energy on the team. Bert can be a little grouchy, but you'll learn a lot from him. And I know he's excited, because you're the first person he's requested in years.*

No one had ever explained to Penelope why she'd been requested, or what Bert wanted another staffer for.

"Does she want to read anything about this interview?" Penelope asked.

He thought a moment. "Maybe not. You'll get to know her. She's—unpredictable. Listen, how about you ask Mr. Brewer a few questions? I don't think I'm getting anywhere with him. It's too stuffy in here for me."

When they returned to the front room, Wyatt was still where they'd left him, but he'd folded his hands over on the table and appeared to be praying. Only when Bert and Penelope sat down did he acknowledge them.

Bert clicked a pen and took a few loud breaths through his nose. Like the building's HVAC system, he seemed worn out and over-used, but working steady. There was some heat left in him, she knew, stuffy room or not.

When he'd hired her two years ago, Penelope hadn't

understood that he'd been shunted into a Southeast outpost far from the action of Washington, D.C. They were a small team in the Infrastructure Surveillance Division, or ISD—investigations into money laundering via government contracts or insider trading from intelligence reports. It wasn't the most glamorous way to ride out a career that began with such a moral imperative, but it allowed Bert to leverage the old methods of intelligence gathering. Slow, methodical, patient work to draw a noose around someone so discreetly that by the time they were under investigation, it was too late to escape. Most of the peers she'd come in with had higher profile lives, in the tony D.C. suburbs or stationed abroad, but Bert reminded her of her father and had a seemingly endless well of war stories that made the work fun if somewhat pedestrian.

They'd first met at a cybersecurity conference at the Washington Convention Center. She'd been a few years out of law school, jobless, heartbroken, looking to start over in life. Raised in Richmond, she'd moved in with her older brother in Bethesda after a nasty breakup, took up powerlifting, and discovered she had reserves of courage and self-discipline she'd never tapped into.

She'd always suspected spies were on every corner of D.C. You could just feel it, walking around the city in autumn, as the light dimmed early and the shadows covered the concrete and the marble, as the tourists bustled by and the street hustlers watched the city goings-on with side-eye. The tone of the city was one of duplicity and insinuations. How much access did you have? What kind of strings could you pull? Who did you know well enough to text? Everyone had a story about themselves, and offered a knowing grin or a mysterious shrug to imply a hidden story.

Yet it wasn't until she was in the back of a conference breakout room, listening to some yoyo shuffle through slides as he tried to pitch his company's nebulous cybersecurity offering that she met a spy in the flesh.

More precisely, ten minutes into the yo-yo's presentation, Bert Wilson, sitting beside Penelope, got up and walked out. She quickly followed so she wouldn't have to open the exit door a second time. In the lobby, Bert neither said anything nor acknowledged Penelope's presence, but when she followed him out the front door to the sidewalk, he offered her a cigarette from a pack that came out of nowhere.

"They didn't tell me this was going to be a conference of sales pitches," he grumbled. "I feel like I was having a stroke in there with all that jargon. Could you tell what he was actually pitching?"

She accepted a light and shook her head.

"Me neither. I think he was offering to come in and give your employees a seminar about phishing scams, even though phishing scams have been with us for fifteen years and are the easiest cybersecurity threat to ward off."

He puffed angrily for a few moments.

"I'm convinced all these cybersecurity firms are running the biggest con job in all of American business. They're preying on what people don't know and charging them out the wazoo for very basic stuff they could do themselves. Did you go to the threat analysis panel this morning?"

"I missed that one."

"Some *goo-roo* was talking about a special report that could analyze your business and assign a grade to your *threat readiness*. I don't know what your line of business is, but a threat readiness report is about the biggest waste of money I can think of. All they do is give you a survey and use a software program to spit out a three-page report. The software costs a thousand bucks, and they're off charging businesses ten, twenty thousand dollars. Total scam."

He took another long drag on his cigarette, and then it must have dawned on him that he didn't know anything about this young woman standing next to him, because he said, "You're not working for one of those firms, are you?"

"Not right now, but I came here to find a job."

"Ha! You're not a regular smoker, are you?"

"How could you tell?"

"You're holding the cigarette like it's a joint. It's okay. It's a bad habit, and I officially quit a few years ago when I was transferred to Charleston. Only smoke when I'm back in D.C." He exhaled a cloud of smoke. "So you got bored with Mr. Phishing Scam's presentation, saw I got bored, and followed me out here thinking I might be a good lead for you in your job search."

She wouldn't have put it like that, but once he'd said it, she understood two things: one, he was right about her. Two, he was sharp and cagey. She liked his style.

"Let me ask you this. Honest opinion. What do you make of me? What do you see when you look at me?"

She gave him a once-over. He was wearing un-ironed khakis that were looking a little threadbare at the ankles, and had been washed so many times that they were a little short on him. A frumpy checkered shirt and a blue tweed blazer. A conference ID hung from a lanyard and read "Bert W." and identified his company as "Government Bureaucrat." Again, she liked his style and decided to take him at his word when he asked for an honest assessment.

"I see a guy who clearly doesn't want to be here. You said you'd come back to D.C., so I'd guess you've spent a long time working here. The way you're talking about the presenters reminds me of my father when he gets a letter from the IRS. He'll complain for two days about the idiots that can't figure out how to move his paperwork from box A to box B. A smart guy working in a system that works against you. I assume your field has something to do with cybersecurity, and you obviously know enough to see through the con men. It also sounds like you've got solid ethics, if you're this upset about a guy

22

ripping off businesses. I don't know. Have you run into a ceiling? Maybe you moved to South Carolina to get away from the D.C. politics? I imagine it's nice to be out of the fray, but maybe there's not a lot of opportunity for you to move up. But the way you phrased your job title makes me think you don't want to move up. I see you're married. Um, you're not worried about making an impression with your clothes. What?" she finally asked.

Bert was grinning and smacking his pack of Camels against his palm. "No, this is great. I should hire you as my therapist. No one ever tells me what they really think."

"Was I close?"

"In places. I'm amused that you think I'm stuck in my career, especially if you're looking for a lead of your own."

"Just because you're stuck doesn't mean it's not interesting work. Besides, I like the humor of 'Government Bureaucrat.' At least you're honest."

"Well." He squinted at her name tag. "Penelope L., Law Professional. What if I told you I wasn't trying to be funny? Maybe I work for an agency without a name, and this is all one big disguise. Maybe I'm extremely conscious of my, um, sartorial choices. Maybe this whole thing"—he waved his hand up and down his body—"is a show."

"To what end?" When he didn't answer her, she said, "I mean, you might be putting on a show, but I refuse to believe you have a closet full of Armani suits at home and smoke Benson & Hedges. Maybe you're not who you say you are, but you're not James Bond in disguise either."

"Benson & Hedges. There's an obscure reference."

"I knew a lot of advertising people in college. Mine is the generation of self-promotion, so we know our brands."

"And what is your brand?"

"I have a closet full of Ann Taylor Loft and do the rest of my shopping at Target. I'm a straight shooter and don't suffer charlatans."

"Well, Penelope L., Law Professional, here's a card with my contact information. I'm in town another two days if you want to set up a formal interview. Maybe tomorrow morning, if you're free. I'd love to talk more when we're not standing in the street."

She went through six weeks of training on everything from how to spot surveillance to how to hack a target, legally, to how a shoot a gun. As a researcher, she'd not been issued a firearm, but the company had bought her a plane ticket home to Richmond—only to have a trio of military dudes pick her up in the airport parking garage, stuff her in the truck, and spend two days mock-interrogating her in a box in Shockoe Bottom.

Her patriotic indoctrination had come, ironically, from a British MI6 officer named Winston Shields, who was somehow connected to Bert's unit. A curious man-without-a-past type who populated much of the agency, Winston started as a liaison of sorts from MI6 doing transportation analytics on a contract basis. Back in the nineties, he'd led a number of operations around Latin America, but after 9/11, with an underlying charge in all diplomatic relations, the British had been the agency's closest international partners. Shields allegedly had a line to 10 Downing Street, which she discovered when Bert had her compile a dossier on him. Her new boss mistrusted MI6 for reasons beyond her.

"Operations aren't about having God on your side or liberating people," Winston had told her class of eighteen candidates. "What we do is about national interest. The media and the politicians get all ginned up about freedom and rah-rah, but take it from my country, ideals will only get you so far. Our job should have been making sure the sun never set on our empire."

From the back of the room, one guy laughed and said, "Your country hasn't had an empire in seventy years."

"But we're still standing here," Winston said. "Strong as

ever. That's all it was ever about. It's a game, my friend. All the world's a stage."

Game. Stage. These were the correct words. As part of the next generation of officers, Penelope's experience was that the agency was desperately in search of a mission. Tarnished by scandals from the wars in the Middle East and branded the "Deep State" by a hostile U.S. president, the intelligence services were as fractured as the rest of America, and you never quite knew who was saving the country and who was shuffling paperwork in the long march toward a comfy retirement.

Now, Penelope's stage involved a target in a box, South of Broad in Charleston. When Wyatt crossed their radar—first writing about the dead Estonian and then attending Harry Cope's funeral in the Carolina upcountry—Bert put her on point to learn everything about him. His finances, his friendships, his fitness abilities. In Wyatt Brewer, she encountered a man living a double life, carrying the past like a cross. After a week of tailing him, they pulled him into their King Street office and watched him flush as warm air from an overhead vent blasted down on him.

"So you bolted out of the newsroom and left your editor bewildered as to where you'd gone," she said. "One minute Bonnie is standing there waiting on you so she could take you to lunch and maybe swing you over to an AA meeting. Meanwhile, you're there faking a conversation on your phone—then, bam! You're out of there."

"That's right," Wyatt said.

"Did she try to follow you?"

"Not that I know of. Maybe. She probably would have looked around for me, maybe poked her head in the stairwell."

"And where'd you go?"

He held up his hands in supplication. "To the beach. I had a story to write about the dead man."

"What time was this?"

"Maybe eleven, eleven-thirty."

"Which puts us a few hours in."

"Into what?" Wyatt asked.

Penelope consulted her notes on the legal pad. "I'm sorry?"

"A few hours into what?" Wyatt repeated.

"We're trying to build a timeline for how you got here, in front of us. Presumably, ten days ago you were Mr. Innocent Reporter, writing up biographies of the Lowcountry dead, and now here you are, looking at charges for conspiring with money launderers, and"—she glanced at Bert, and then into Wyatt's eyes—"potentially treason."

It was the first time anyone had said anything about charges. Penelope paused to let it sink in, to see what he might volunteer.

When he said nothing, she went on, "We're marking that day at the Francis Marion as day one because, in your written statement, you said that's when you decided to go to Judge Cope's funeral. Is there a better time for us to start?"

Chapter Four

Where to begin? As a reporter, Wyatt's job was to tell a story, and a story had a coherent beginning and ending. The difference between storytelling and life was that in life, you could always go back to an earlier beginning: the moment he accepted to split the wine with Ashley. The day he quit drinking or the first Sunday he missed going to Mass after his conversion. The breakup with Mary Grace. Meeting her in the first place. His childhood, his birth, his parents, all the generations that led to this moment, sweating in the house South of Broad.

As a southerner born in the media age, he'd never been burdened by the weight of history. Maybe his grandparents had opinions about the Lost Cause and reflected on Pickett's Charge for an afternoon every July, but Wyatt's was a childhood of action movies, grunge music, and video games. In middle age he lamented the outsized role dialogue from *Die Hard with a Vengeance* still held in his brain, but TV had been his outlet until he was old enough to drink. Some people needed to zonk out, and he apparently was one of them.

What had he been zonking out from? His father, a dreamy academic, had left the family to take a teaching job in

Tuscaloosa when Wyatt was in second grade. His mother had moved back in with her parents in the village of Gaffney, South Carolina, home of the giant peach water tower off Interstate 85. His childhood was a blur of years— *The Legend of Zelda*, *Terminator 2*, Nirvana; then *Sonic the Hedgehog*, *Billy Madison*, Bush; then *Resident Evil*, *Armageddon*, Foo Fighters. Then he surprised everyone by doing well enough on the SAT to get a scholarship to Wofford. His mother said she was proud of him. She was dating a guy who installed cable lines, a man named Mitch who gave him a hundred dollars and a pocket knife. His grandmother baked him a cake. His grandfather had passed on.

Three things happened at Wofford. First, to fit in with the sea of preppy Pi Kappa Alpha types with big bellies and big sunglasses and big red ties under blue blazers, Wyatt learned to drink.

Second, surrounded by these WASPY good old boys, he realized he'd been in a pop culture matrix his entire life, and he found himself studying history to try to figure out who he was and how he came to be here.

Third, he met Mary Grace Cope at a mixer with some Converse College girls. Two years in college, he was still out of place among the debutante daughters of textile executives, lawyers, politicians, and doctors.

Mary Grace came from such a family, yet she was cut from a different cloth. Wyatt could tell that just by looking at her, the way she carried herself. He wasn't the most intuitive man on campus, but he recognized someone pretending to fit in. There were introductions. She laughed at something he said. She caught his eye on her way out of the mixer. His chest clenched.

About love: You're lucky when it happens, because it reframes your entire existence, and you're unlucky if it ends. Wyatt's luck and un-luck began not at the mixer but the next week, at a deli where he went once a month for a barbeque

Cuban sandwich. Spartanburg was an old mill town, grown up enough to be termed a city by Carolina standards and a virtual metropolis compared to the backwater where he'd grown up. Because he could, he walked everywhere, and his walking took him to the edges of Converse's campus where by chance he ran across Mary Grace.

"Hey!" he yelled, sober now but feeling the courage of drink from when they'd met.

"Hey yourself."

"Where are you off to?"

"I have a class." She stopped. She carried a large brown bag slung over her shoulder. Black leggings and a large white shirt. Hair highlights and a nose stud. "History of the British novel." When she rolled her eyes, he knew he was living in a moment of fate.

He said, "You should skip it and come with me to get a sandwich."

It took her a moment to size him up. He was generally a shabby dresser, jeans and an ill-fitting flannel shirt, perhaps, and he wore his hair long and had a scraggly effort at a beard. It was a wonder the Wofford administration hadn't excommunicated him, for while South Carolinian men did get caught up in the sixties fervor (albeit during the seventies when it no longer counted), business prep style had reasserted itself by the time Wyatt hit young adulthood. Investment, real estate, family life, and Southern Baptists owned the culture. If you were a college male, you better play ball or plan to get out of dodge.

She followed him to the deli, where they fell in love over a long afternoon. It turns out that Mary Grace, too, was a South Carolina insider-outsider, raised by a family with money in the Lowcountry, a father who could have sent her to any university in the country but who for some reason unknown to her insisted she stay close to home. When she'd mentioned receiving some marketing literature from Converse, he'd looked up from his reading, narrowed his eyes, and surprised her by saying, "That would be a good choice." Charlestonians believed the upcountry scruffy and libertarian, a working-class kind of place, which would suit her fine for the effect she believed it would have on her father. But Harry came from upcountry stock. She knew he was from Castle County, of course, and had visited extended family there on occasion, but she also sensed he was embarrassed by his roots and had ambitions to keep her away from the mill hill culture of South Carolina's backcountry.

What she failed to appreciate were the dynamics of upcountry social class. Harry grew up in a cotton mill town, the son of a farmer turned mill worker. He went to school with town kids—the children of mill owners, lawyers, bankers, doctors, girls bound for finishing school and boys with bright horizons—and these children looked right past him all through grade school. Were he to go to a class reunion, they wouldn't remember him, but he would remember them, and he enjoyed the idea of sending his daughter to the same finishing college as the daughters of the mill boss. Fifty years old at the time, and he'd not gotten over the scars of his childhood. Converse was where the daughters of mill owners went, so it would please Harry to have his progeny join their ranks.

So there she went, an all-girls school sometimes referred to as "The Convent." The other men she'd met from Wofford, or around town, were pleasant enough idiots who could talk about NASDAQ or the ACC but who also felt entitled to the American dream. Work hard, make some money, and live life like their fathers before them. She would sooner hang herself than spend an evening alone with that lot. Wyatt was disheveled in a way that most women overlooked, but over Cuban sandwiches he spoke about Zbigniew Herbert's *Report from the Besieged City* the way most men spoke of football draft picks.

"When he was fifteen," Wyatt said, "he wrote a poem

about bombs dropping over Poland while this couple made love. I love that mingling of the personal set against the public stage."

She got the sense part of him wished he lived under an oppressive regime so he would have something to rage against. Instead, all Wyatt and Mary Grace could rage against was American consumerism and the old conservative values that held on in the new millennium. After he and Mary Grace made love for the first time, lying beside her in the dark and unable to sleep himself, he thought about Herbert's poem. *When it got very bad they leapt into each other's eyes and shut them firmly.* He was convinced whatever he was set on earth for had something to do with this woman he'd met and what life they might build for each other.

Then he met her father.

Chapter Five

WYATT AND MARY GRACE started dating in November of their sophomore year. He met her parents when they came up for a long weekend in January, over a lunch in which they had little to say to him—or Mary Grace. Her mother chattered about old neighbors that Mary Grace might remember. "And the Carters? Their oldest son is leaving for a job in Zurich. Something to do with the foreign service, I can't keep it straight. And how are you dear?"

Her father made a few comments about the latest from Mayor Joe and his urban revitalization efforts. "Charleston's still a rough and tumble place in a lot of districts. I never did feel comfortable when you and your friends went out on the town after dark. I sleep better knowing you're here."

"In the Convent, he didn't add," Mary Grace told Wyatt later. "I mean, what does he want from me? To marry some beau I meet in college—no offense—and just start having babies? What am I saying? Of course that's what he wants. I can't believe it's taken me all these years to realize he wasn't trying to raise a smart, independent thinker. He was just trying to keep me in a box until I was no longer his problem. What's your problem?"

They were sitting in a bar downtown in Spartanburg, nursing cheap beers and deconstructing the evening. She had brunch scheduled with her parents the next day, a brunch Wyatt was not invited to. Not that he was eager for a replay of the evening.

"Hey, what is it?" she pressed.

"I don't know," he said. "I guess I just—I don't know why I was there tonight."

"You were there to meet my parents and see what I come from. Did you think they were there to get to know you?" She grinned and took a long draw of her beer. "Did you notice how they never addressed anything to you? It was all, how are *you* and what are *you* doing. Don't feel bad. You were there to see who they were, and that's them in a nutshell. They've never taken an interest in my life outside of how it fits in their little world."

"So am I not the beau you were supposed to meet in college?"

"Who knows." She looked away. "You know what it is, I don't think it's occurred to either of them that I'm an adult making her own decisions. When she was my age, my mother moved by herself to South Carolina while her fiancé was in the Navy. He ended up getting killed in a training exercise, so she married his older brother. Yeah. I still don't think I have the full story on that one. My dad's younger brother was in naval intelligence and had a whirlwind romance with my mother, proposed to her and sent her South to meet his family and wait for his next leave when they could get married. Why she left Connecticut, what she must have thought about rural South Carolina, and how you fall in love with the brother of your dead fiancé—she's always been cagey about all that. What I do know is that when she was twenty-two, she'd been engaged to one man, married another, and had me on the way. And I'm here in an all-girls school—excuse me, a *woman's college*—supposed to do what? Get an education that will help

33

me make conversation with my ambitious, successful husband while I raise his babies and make a nice Southern home for us."

"You know I don't have any ambition, so that life won't work if you were thinking of marrying me."

"I know, dear, and that's why I love you."

She took his hand, and like that their relationship shifted.

The second time he met her parents was at the end of the school year when they came to move her out and back to Charleston for the summer. He arrived at her dorm in late afternoon and found her father sitting on a couch in the lobby with his feet propped up and reading the local newspaper, sweaty and cross, Mary Grace and her mother nowhere in sight. "Hey, Wyatt," he said. "They're going to be late for dinner. They're still upstairs cleaning."

Wyatt sat across from him and picked up the sports section.

"I don't know how she deals with the heat in here," Harry said. "Maybe I've been in the Lowcountry too long, but I've gotten used to central air. These dorm rooms are like ovens. It's as bad as the mills where I grew up. You ever been in a cotton mill?"

"I have not," Wyatt said. "I grew up all around them, but…" He threw up his hands as though trying to explain why he'd not played football in high school, why he chose history as his field of study, why his parents' marriage failed.

"It's okay," Harry said. "I wouldn't have ever set foot in one if I could have avoided it. People will make you feel bad about the opportunities you took in life, but what you ought to feel bad about is the opportunities you didn't take, for whatever reason." He finished reading the last paragraph of an article from the paper, and then he folded the section and set it on the coffee table between them. "I can't understand why

Mary Grace waited until this weekend to start getting her stuff together. She knew we were coming to move her out. I just can't figure what she's thinking."

Perhaps because Wyatt and Harry had bonded in the dorm lobby, or perhaps because someone had given him a talking to, or perhaps because it was summer and his business was booming and he had a clear head, Harry engaged with Wyatt over dinner at a quiet steakhouse at the edge of town. He seemed interested to learn Wyatt had picked up a Spanish minor.

"I took it in high school and just kept going with it," Wyatt said. "I came in with so many credits from my AP class that it's not hard to pick up another minor."

"That'll help you if you ever go into business."

"You speak Spanish?"

"Not a lick, but I've already made my career. If I were a young man—you never know what will come in handy."

After a lull, in which Harry sipped his wine and appeared to have something on his mind, a thought that wouldn't quite lodge in place, he blinked a few times and asked about Wyatt's parents, life in Gaffney, a few friends of friends they shared.

"I always wondered what became of Lou Batson. We called him Pound Batson back then, 'cause his initials were L.B., and if you'd asked me at the time, I would have said he'd never become more than a fry cook at the Huddle House, or maybe an insurance salesman if he could find a good woman to make him a home. You're telling me he owns a *bank*?"

"Gaffney Town and Teller."

"My word, America really is the land of plenty."

Harry wore a suit although it was eighty-five degrees. Because Mary Grace had warned him, Wyatt had tucked a polo shirt into jeans but nonetheless felt like a small-town rube. He drank plentifully and, fortunately enough, Harry was letting his small-town rube roots shine through.

"You know, Castle was such a small town back then,

Pound and I used to drive up toward Charlotte about once a month to do our carousing around. In high school, we worked a shift in the mill after school, and then from six to noon on Saturdays. Sundays were for God and family but that left a long stretch of Saturday that we had on our own. There used to be a honky-tonk called the State Line—not far from where you're from—and my word we'd have ourselves a good time. Was a wonder we made it home some Saturday nights, but I think the threat of not being in church Sunday morning helped at least one of us sober up enough to navigate the car home."

"Daddy! I never heard about this," Mary Grace said from across the table.

"You never asked."

"Did you know about it?" she asked her mother.

"I don't know that I did," Lillian said. "Your father was clean-cut and in business when we met, so I never knew him as anything but."

"I can't believe this. I'm having another drink," Mary Grace said, daring her parents to deny her even though she was still underage. "You want one, Wyatt?"

"Sure."

She flagged the waiter over and said to her father, "You never worried about drunk driving?"

"Oh yeah, we worried about it, but it wasn't really a thing back then. You didn't worry about seat belts, you didn't take off work when you had the sniffles, and you piloted your car home so you'd be in the pew for church. They were different times, though I have to imagine Castle hasn't changed all that much."

"I don't get down to Castle, but Gaffney's not all that different from what you're describing," Wyatt said. "I think I heard my grandfather talk about that old State Line bar. We get a lot of folks down from North Carolina at our mini markets even now."

"Yeah you do. People gone do what they gone do."

What Wyatt didn't realize until later was just how rare of form Harry was in that night. "I learned more about him by eavesdropping on your ten-minute conversation with him than I learned in eighteen years under his roof," Mary Grace told him on the phone from Charleston, where she was spending her summer vacation. "How'd you do that?"

"Do what?"

"Draw all that out of him?"

"Maybe we just bonded over our mill town roots, I don't know. I think he was drunk."

"Yeah, he was drunk, and that's another thing I've never seen."

"You get any more stories out of him since you've been home?"

"Nope. He works all the time, so I only see him at dinner. He's got some kind of hush-hush thing going on with his work. Maybe it's a trial coming up or something, but he'll listen to my mom or me chatter about nothing and then disappear into his office for the night. I did run into him late the other night, when I was coming home."

"Carousing around the seedy streets of Charleston?"

"Exactly. No, seriously, I went to a bar in Mount Pleasant. My high school does kind of an informal reunion night out once a summer. I had a friend drive me home and tried to sneak in, but he was sitting in the living room with a notebook and a glass of bourbon.

"'Oh, hey,' I told him, trying to be smooth, but he knew right away I was in bad shape. He covered whatever he was working on, and if my head weren't filled with sludge, I might have asked him flat-out what it was.

"Instead, I tried to fumble through it and said my friend Kelly drove me home, I was responsible, all that. If I'd been quicker witted I might have said something about how he and —what was his name? Pound?—how he and Pound used to

37

do the same thing and I was just following in his footsteps, but he just looked at me and said, 'That's good, honey. You have to be careful out there.'

"And that was it. I don't think he ever told my mom, because God forbid her daughter ever had more than one drink for style. She would freak, but so far she hasn't said a thing. It makes me a little worried about him. Maybe—oh, I haven't brought this up. We're going to Kiawah Island for a week in August, and they said I could invite you. Want to come? We'll have to sleep in separate bedrooms, and you'll have to put up with my weird family, but…"

"I'd love to," he said.

"You think you can get off work for the whole week?"

"That's no problem," he said. He was working at a coffee house where almost no one tipped. If they didn't want him taking off for the week, he'd just quit. He'd be out of there when school started back anyway. With his new-found gift for drawing stories out of people, he would get a job with the campus newspaper, a career he'd never considered until Mary Grace had pointed out what he was good at.

"Great," she said. "Well, while we're out there, maybe you can talk to him. See if you can get anything else out of him."

"Like what?"

"I don't know, Wyatt. Be creative. Is he just stressed at work? Are my parents about to break up? Are they bankrupt? Does he have cancer? Something's going on, and I'd like to know what it is."

"All right, how about this. When we're down there, you distract them, and I'll sneak into their room, dig out this mysterious notebook, and take photos of every page."

"I don't think that's necessary," she said, less convincing than she might have liked.

"It'll be real James Bond. You can be my Bond girl."

"I was thinking conversation. Maybe you and he could

bond over the grill or something. Maybe get him drunk again."

"Just be sure to destroy the negatives," he said.

Chapter Six

A REPORTER'S work in the twenty-first century wasn't as glamorous as it once was, even during Wyatt's college years when he took his first fledgling steps toward becoming a journalist for the campus newspaper. Now there were no crowded newsrooms with agitated writers banging away at typewriters, smoking and yelling across the room in a mad rush to get the paper set by deadline. In fact, for a small daily like Charleston's *Dispatch*, most of the content was aggregated from the wire or one of a dozen advertising sources they subscribed to. With the exception of sporting events and the occasional late-evening drama, most of the daily paper was finished, proofed, and submitted for printing before the traditional close of business. Reporters—the few who remained—worked on quiet laptops and only came down to the wire out of procrastination. Most would grumble about how many inane press releases they had to sift through, and how frequently corporate assigned staff meetings. It was typical office life. In other words, routine.

Wyatt was therefore inappropriately excited by the dead body on Folly Beach, the most peculiar case he'd encountered in recent memory. A man wearing camo cargo shorts and a black t-shirt washed up a mile south of the pier, in a largely residential district far from the surfers and beachcombers that populated the beach half the year. If anyone had seen or heard anything on the beach that night, they were keeping it under their hats. A jogger found the body in the morning, bobbing in the surf and blue as a newborn fresh out of the womb. The guy had no ID, was too old to be a student, and too clean-cut to be a vagrant or surfer. One of the investigating officers was an old friend of Wyatt's, and told him off-hand and off the record that the guy had the cut of someone ex-military. The officer hadn't elaborated, but Wyatt pictured pecs and some kind of tattoo on his biceps, an anchor or sword or firearm.

He'd written a quick blurb for Metro last night, before his date with Ashley, but his assignment now was to follow the police investigation, report the ID of the man when they figured it out, and sniff around for anything that might sell a few papers. The initial report said the man drowned, but no one could explain why. The night had been clear but bitterly cold, no weather for a man in a t-shirt and shorts. A storm system was on the way but the water should have been as calm as it ever was. Did the man wander into the sea? Drunkenly fall off a fishing boat? Or something more sinister? Wyatt's friend had promised to text him if and when anything noteworthy came up in the police investigation, and Wyatt had been doing this long enough to know the police investigation would take months. He had a message out with a contact in the Coast Guard to see if any empty boats had been recovered, but there was nothing newsworthy in his notes so far. To keep his editor happy, his next stop would be the neighborhood to see if anyone had heard or seen anything suspicious. An argument, screaming, headlights. A citizen talking about a late-night altercation might get the story onto A1, which would ensure the paper covered the story until it resolved.

After barging out of the *Dispatch*'s office, leaving Bonnie bewildered and concerned for his well-being, he drove out to the end of Folly Beach. The rain was still lashing the coast, and temperatures had fallen since this morning. It would be sleet before it was all over. Outside the town crossroads, the houses were mostly scruffy rentals. A lot of students who thought they were getting the deal of their lifetime, not realizing how miserable the beach is during the winter. A bleak apocalyptic landscape. The sea was a turbulent gun-metal gray and melded with the sky so that the coastline appeared to be the very end of the earth.

He parked on Ashley Avenue where the trees and houses fell away. A square of police tape secured to road barrels blocked off part of the beach. No police, no one at all nearby. A *Dispatch* photographer had come out here yesterday and shot the dramatic blue lights pulsing in the evening, but Wyatt didn't need astonishing visuals to make a newsworthy article. He needed information. The death had occurred in such a quiet strip of beach that he doubted he would get much, but he slipped on a raincoat, grabbed his messenger bag, and sloshed over to the closest house, a poorly constructed, vinyl-siding number on stilts. He rapped on the door and jammed his hands in his coat pockets.

He was about to knock again when a young woman answered the door in her pajamas, a cup of coffee in hand and a pen behind her ear. "Yes?"

"Hi there," Wyatt said, and he identified himself as a reporter with the newspaper. "I'm working on a follow-up about the death, um, over there." He nodded his head back toward the police tape.

"Well, I didn't do it," the girl said.

"I know." He smiled, privately noting that she'd leaped to murder. "I was hoping I could ask you a few questions about the past few days. Have you noticed anything odd? Hear any arguments? That sort of thing."

"Do you have any ID?"

"Um, yeah. Hang on." He dug through his messenger bag —two notebooks, Kleenex, a stack of business cards, a pair of earplugs from visiting a box manufacturer last year—and pulled out his office badge, a hologram of the Trident Media logo shimmering in the corner. "I have a business card as well."

"It's okay," the girl said. "You can come in. We've had a lot of people stopping by this week, and it's starting to weird out some of my roommates."

It never failed to surprise him when a potential source opened the door and let him inside. The South had a reputation for friendliness, and today's college students seemed dumber than they were twenty years ago— which was saying a lot, given how dumb he'd been in college—but still. They could have talked on the landing, in public view.

"You mean cops?" he asked.

"Yeah, there were some cops, but then there were some other guys, I don't know who they worked for. The FBI or the Navy or someone."

"Huh."

"That going into your article?"

"I don't know that it means anything just yet," he said as she led him into the living room. She had a large window overlooking the ocean—a view he was sure justified a high rent when the girl had signed her lease in September. "How many roommates do you have?"

"There's three of us here. CofC students. But the other girls are in class. I only have a few minutes."

"Of course." Following her lead, he sat on a wicker chair and pulled out one of his notebooks and a pen. She had a chemistry textbook open on a side table. Graph paper with equations. Big handwriting. "Maybe we could start with your name? You said you're a student?"

"Amy Southerland. Yeah, a junior."

"You from South Carolina?"

43

"I grew up in Mathews. It's a little crossroads between here and Columbia."

"I've seen the signs for it off 26."

"Everyone has. So, what can I do for you, Wyatt Brewer?"

"Well, I really just wanted to get a sense of what some of the neighbors might have seen. I don't know much more than we reported in the paper."

"I don't read the paper," she said. "Sorry."

He smiled. "Not many people your age do. It's okay. What I know is a man was found on the beach the other morning, and it appeared he'd drowned. But it wasn't clear whether he was on the beach and waded in, or if he was out on a boat and just washed up. I thought maybe someone might have heard something."

"You mean, someone shouting, 'Oh no, don't shoot,' and a gunshot?" She laughed and shook her head. "Nothing like that, I'm afraid, but I can tell you there was a group of guys partying out on the beach the night before."

"Really? In this weather?"

"This was before the rain came. It was cold as hell, so I didn't go out there, but we all saw them. They'd built a small fire and were drinking around it half the night."

"Could you tell how many?"

"Three or four? They were drinking and shooting fire-works, and then they settled down and just sat out there. Every once in a while, we'd hear one of them scream and then they'd all laugh. It was obnoxious more than anything."

"Did you tell the police all that?"

"Of course I did. They must have found all the empty beer cans and the remnants of the fire."

"Hmm."

"I don't know if the guy they found was one of them, or if it was just a coincidence, but they were definitely out there. I also told the police, we get people out there every few weeks. Most people that want to party on the beach go out by the pier, but some folks insist on coming way out here to the end of the island."

"Do you know what time they packed it in?"

"I don't. We all fell asleep before they did, but it was past midnight, I can tell you that."

"Did the cops—or any other investigators—say anything about who they were, or who they found on the beach?"

"Don't you have a source in the police to fill you in on this?"

"I do, but they're not always the most forthcoming."

"Well, sorry, I can't help you. They wrote down what I told them, same as you're doing, but they didn't tell me anything."

"You're not curious?"

"Of course I'm curious. A dead body shows up a hundred yards away, I want to know who did it and why."

"Assuming it's murder," he said.

"Yes, assuming it's murder. If there's a killer on the loose, I want him locked up."

"Assuming it's a he," he said.

She rolled her eyes and stood up.

"If there's anything else, that's my cell on the card. Call, email, text," he muttered as he packed up his things.

He tried a few other neighbors, but no one else answered the door. Then, although it was still raining heavily, he followed the police tape around the edges of the crime scene. Water saturated the sand and seeped into his shoes while he looked for evidence of a fire, empty beer cans, anything that would substantiate what the girl Amy Southerland had told him. Whole lot of nothing. An empty stretch of beach with a few rivulets in the sand that could have been a body uncovered or could have been the natural formation from ancient wind patterns. The sea air tossed his hair and shook his jacket. His socks were growing wet. He watched Amy Southerland walk out and, without looking his way, get into a blue Jetta and head toward the main highway.

In his truck, after quickly reviewing his handwritten notes and embellishing a few lines while the interview was still fresh in his head, he took a final look out to the beach and still saw nothing. Down Ashley Avenue, however, he saw a man sitting in the driver's seat of a long dark sedan parked in front of a line of scrub. Wyatt squinted to see the man more clearly, but he was too far off. The man appeared to be talking on a cell phone and ignoring the world around him, but after a quick glance Wyatt's way, the man started his car, pulled onto the road, and drove off toward civilization.

Chapter Seven

THE NIGHT the body had landed on Folly Beach, Penelope and Bert had gotten a tip from one of Wyatt's colleagues that the dead man was Estonian. Suicide, accident, or murder: when someone from the old Soviet bloc died of anything but old age, it was of interest to the agency. Bert had called her in late evening and said, "We need to go check this out."

At ten o'clock Wednesday, while Wyatt had been sipping his first glass of wine in a decade with the PR lady in the bar of the Francis Marion Hotel, Bert and Penelope cruised east along Ashley Avenue, past the pier and hotel and restaurants huddled around the center of Folly, out beyond the public beach accesses, to the strip of lonely houses buffering Charleston from the Atlantic.

They parked on the roadside fifty yards from the web of flashing blue and red lights. Police. An ambulance. A body on the beach.

Rain spit on the windshield and a chill took over the car after Bert killed the ignition. He sat still for a few moments and chewed on his lower lip. They watched as a white forensics van passed them and parked by the scene. They watched as investigators set up lights and road cones and police tape.

There was a knock on Bert's window, which made Penelope jump.

Bert pulled a badge out of his coat pocket and then turned the key to electrical so he could lower the window.

A detective shined a light on them and said, "What are you all doing here?"

"We're federal agents assigned to Charleston," Bert said, handing over the badge. "I got a call from a local colleague that you may have a dead foreign national out here?"

The officer examined the badge. "This doesn't say who you work for. What's the Bureau of Special Services? Is that FBI?"

"We're under the Department of Homeland Security. A small group, kind of like the TSA only we don't do anything with airports." Bert smiled. "Do you know your victim?"

"I can't disclose anything."

"Well, if it's just some local, that doesn't concern us and we'll get out of your hair."

"Again, you're going to have to talk to my captain."

"That won't be a problem, but I don't want to waste anyone's time."

The detective handed back the badge. "Do you need a number?"

"I've got all I need."

"I'm going to have to ask you to leave until I get authorization. From my department."

"Understood, detective."

Bert turned on the car and rolled up the window. The officer stepped aside so he could do a three-point turn, and they cruised away from the scene.

Penelope gave him a few miles, until they reached the highway back to the mainland, before asking, "What was that about? You want me to call his captain?"

Bert shook his head. "I don't want the locals looking into

us. That's going to open up too many questions. Besides, he gave us confirmation that whoever died isn't local."

"He did?"

"He would have told us we were wasting our time."

"Do you know who it is? Out there?"

"I've got a pretty good idea," Bert said, but he wouldn't elaborate.

"Privet?" she asked, referencing the code name for one of the team's agents in the field.

Without rolling down the window, he lit a cigarette. "We need to get Jarman on this. It's his agent."

"Where is he now?"

"Trip to D.C. Diane has been asking for more reports lately, and I don't have the patience to sit through her twenty questions. Jarman has a soothing effect on her, but it's a bad time for him to be away."

Bert puffed a few times, and then asked her, "Ready?"

"Sure."

Penelope had been working with him for more than two years, and she'd reassessed him several times over since their first meeting at the D.C. security conference. She'd come to learn that although she got a few things right in her initial assessment—he was stymied here in Charleston, he did have ethics, and he was smarter than most people—he was also something of a cipher, capable of being what he needed to be in a given situation. She trusted him, but she wasn't sure he trusted her.

For decades now, he had been chasing a cipher of his own, an attorney named Harry Cope who, Bert believed, was a kind of broker for corruption within their agency. The story, as best Penelope could follow, went back to Bert's early career under Reagan. His job had been to draft white papers about the security of U.S. infrastructure overseas. Airbases, oil tankers. Did the U.S. need to worry about dirty bombs, pirates, tainted water? Bert, being a thorough and nosy analyst, stumbled onto a scheme in which an old agency operative, Everett Archer, had been making money in the financial markets from global instability. With the inside scoop from intelligence reports, he shorted currencies, sold bonds, and the like. He made a small fortune on the side passing tips to Wall Street and his old chums from Yale or Phillips Exeter. He took a bath on occasion—no one saw the Shah being overthrown—but even fast-moving events seemed to have their own inevitability.

The question that interested Bert was: Could you orchestrate seemingly random events? What if you falsified an intelligence report to flick the first domino and then swooped in to profit from the ensuing calamity? Was it possible, and did it happen?

By the time Bert began wading through ancient agency history in the mid-nineties, Archer was in an assisted living facility near Tampa and most of his colleagues were dead or retired. The only loose end, the thread Bert couldn't help but tug at, was Everett's niece, Lillian, and Lillian's husband, Harry Cope. You needed someone on the outside to act as the broker, and a nondescript southern lawyer appeared to be just the man you might want. But no sooner had he started digging into the obscure South Carolina attorney than he'd gotten shipped to a tiny office in Arlington, where everything from the beat-up office chair to the cigarette-stained desk to the cloudy strip mall windows suggested there would be no more promotions. He'd blundered into the No Man's Land of agency corruption, and his Arlington post was a quick punch from the powers that be. Lay off or your career is wrecked. Archer, long retired, must still have had friends on the inside.

Fast forward to the War on Terror, and Bert was summoned to the agency HQ for a meeting.

"Bert, how are you?" said the woman who would become his boss and protector in the agency. "Diane Neubecker. Thank you for coming."

"Not a problem," he said.

Penelope pictured his initial meeting with Diane being much like hers, brief and unclear. A brash, silver-haired New Yorker, Diane was part of an obscure function that laddered up to the Chief Compliance Officer. Bert surely must have believed himself out of a job when Diane fiddled with her glasses and said, "You're on our agency's listserv. Do you read the newsletters that go out?"

"On occasion. Most of my work doesn't really require email, so."

"We see that in our established officers," she said. "Another vulnerable communications medium."

"Old habits," he said.

"No, you're right to be worried. I don't know what they're going to do in twenty years when we're all retired and they're left with Millennials who don't see anything wrong with email. Anyway, if you see the newsletters, you know the mantra these days is all mission, mission, mission, so the powers that be are so excited we have a good old-fashioned war going where we can connect mission to mission."

He wasn't tracking with her, and she must have seen it.

"My point is that, I feel—and this is just one woman's opinion—we've gone away from our original mission of service while we chase after the new mission of I-don't-know-what. I sometimes come to work thinking our agency exists simply because it always has. We were created for a specific purpose, in the opening of the Cold War, and now we're fumbling around trying to figure out the role of intelligence gathering in a world of hot conflicts."

"That I get," Bert said.

"I imagine it's frustrating for you as a senior officer, to be sidelined out in Arlington while other people are out making money off our core service."

So she did have some insight into what he was up to.

"I've read through your data request forms over the past

51

few years." Here she pulled out a folder, opened it, and set a spreadsheet in front of him. "Why were you investigating Everett Archer?"

"Do you know anything about him?"

"Plenty, but I want to hear your version."

"If you've read up on him, you know he died several years ago, but before that he spent his career placing illegal bets on insider knowledge. Things he knew based on agency data."

"Sure."

"Have you ever been out to the Arlington field office?"

She shook her head.

"On one side I have a parking garage. On another a Cajun restaurant advertising juicy thighs. *Bird legs are the best legs.* Their menu sucks, so I pack my lunch every day, which means I have all the time in the world."

"Time to run a secret investigation on the man who sent you out there."

"Is that official confirmation Everett was behind it?" he asked.

She smiled and looked at him over her glasses. "I presume you looked me up in the agency directory before you came in today? Saw my title and thought you were about to be fired?"

"Crossed my mind."

"No, Bert. I'm here to offer you a job. Make your sideline investigation your main line of work. The twenty-first century's going to be a much different place than the twentieth. We're witnessing a wholesale shift in intelligence gathering, away from agents and toward data. With this kind of seismic shift, there are going to be political alliances, and brick walls, and people who cut corners. I know about Everett Archer. I know what kind of man he was, and in my book, he was the worst type of public servant, serving himself rather than his country. It's too late to do anything about him, but whoever knew about him is still among us. I want you to dig into his racket, document it, and see what else you can find out."

"Build files on our colleagues in the agency?"

"Think of it as record keeping."

"To what end?"

"We're going to have to trust that the end will be there for us when we arrive somewhere," she said. "If it's not, we're all in trouble."

The two of them cooked up the U.S. field offices for the Infrastructure Surveillance Division (ISD), a collection of secret offices technically falling under the purview of Homeland Security but with dotted-line reporting to the Pentagon. Ostensibly, ISD's role was to connect the dots as the American empire expanded due to the War on Terror. Bert continued to crank out white papers about security in overseas operations, everything from Iraqi battlefields to black sites in Eastern Europe. But ISD—codenamed Project Gravy—also began building files on American intelligence officers, contractors, and associates, including Harry Cope.

When Bert had hired Penelope, he'd told her *some* of what they were tasked with doing, and it all revolved around finding the link between Cope and someone inside the agency. Now with the old judge dead, it felt as though things were accelerating. Something was coming together just outside Penelope's view.

In the box with Wyatt Brewer, partly to see what the reporter knew and partly to try to draw out Bert's angle for the future of Project Gravy, Penelope asked, "So you got all these witness statements, you went home, and you started writing up your piece. Did you know yet who the dead man was?"

Bert shifted, just slightly but enough for Penelope to recognize she had his attention.

"No," Wyatt said. "As far as the police were letting on, the man had no ID. That's partly what made it news. They wanted to get the word out to see if someone would call in a missing person."

"Did you know anything about his nationality? Was he a citizen?"

Wyatt looked at her curiously for a moment. "You know, I asked the lead detective that, and he kind of tripped up. He said they were still trying to figure out who this man was, but he added, 'or if he's even local.' I asked him to elaborate because it was one of those things where I could tell he was giving out more information than he was supposed to, but all he said was, 'We don't know if he came off the beach or fell off a boat.'"

"That was it?"

"I let it go for the time. I was on a deadline, and then I went up to the funeral."

"When did you make that decision?" Bert interjected.

"To go to the funeral? I don't know. I suppose I'd been thinking about it all day since Ashley suggested it. Maybe I'd been thinking about it since I found out Harry died."

"Even though you hadn't seen him in"—Bert flipped through his notes—"twenty years?"

"I thought it might give me some closure."

"I can relate to that," Bert conceded. "What I'm struggling with is the massive series of coincidences you're presenting us with. First, Harry—who it turns out is your benefactor, which I want to talk more about—dies. Then you fall off the wagon, encounter Molly Keagan on King Street, and get assigned this Folly Beach story. According to your statements, all of this is coincidence. Then you decide, for closure, to go to Harry's funeral, meet up with Molly, and get roped into an international scandal. When did you know you were conspiring with Estonian gangsters?"

Bert paused, but Wyatt had nothing to say.

"When does the role of chance stop and the role of Wyatt Brewer begin? That's what we're trying to understand."

"Perhaps now is a good time to tell us about your relationship with Harry," Penelope suggested.

She hoped her instincts were solid here, with Bert playing the heavy and her playing the naïve young officer just trying to figure out what's what. It was an easy role to play because she only knew what Bert told her, which is that there were no coincidences. Wyatt's past meant he might be the missing connection between old Judge Cope and the foreign operatives at work in the agency today. The only way to know would be to step with Wyatt into the past.

Chapter Eight

WYATT's third meeting with Harry took place at the family
beach house on Kiawah, a bungalow nestled in a jungle that
would stop for no developer. Tropical vines slithered over the
roofing and buffeted against the windows. Trees canopied the
yard. Snakes and palmetto bugs lurked in the woody scrub
and grasses. The house itself was a model of elegance: granite
before granite was hip, sun-drenched living spaces, a gas cook-
top, a range hood, a built-in wine rack, wainscoting in the
dining room. A smattering of shells and other seaside bric-a-
brac reminded you that hey, you were at the beach after all.

Harry gave him a hearty handshake and said he needed
help with a manly task out back, some shingles had come
loose in a recent storm and could Wyatt help him out?

"Well sure," Wyatt said, and he gave Mary Grace a look as
he followed her father into the house. She smiled, shrugged,
and offered a thumbs up, which he couldn't quite read.

"You ever nail shingles down?" Harry asked.

"I supervised my grandfather once."

"It's easy enough, but easier if you have another pair of
hands. You mind helping me ferry a few things up the
ladder?"

On the roof, Harry—who was wearing a pair of khaki shorts and a golf shirt—stripped away a few old shingles that had been damaged from a tree limb. "Hand me that hammer if you will. How's the Spanish coming?"

"Bueno."

"You have any classes lined up this fall?"

"A special topics in the Spanish Civil War."

"I read *For Whom the Bell Tolls* in high school," Harry said. "Not a great book but sounded like a nasty war."

Wyatt humored him with a smile.

"You ever been to a Spanish-speaking country?" Harry asked.

"No, but I'd like to. Wofford's got some study abroad programs, but I'm not sure about the expense."

"Uh-huh."

Wyatt felt like he'd uttered a faux pas, bringing up money, but matters of the wallet mattered more than a future journalist cared to admit. His scholarship covered his tuition, but his mother could offer nothing but a little walking-around money. A ticket to and from Spain or even Mexico would require some economic Ju-Jitsu.

Solving Wyatt's financial quandary didn't seem to be part of Harry's game, because he asked him to get another packet of nails, and when Wyatt returned to the roof, Harry was standing on the slope with one foot higher than the other, hands on his hips like a man conquering a mountain. Indeed, there was something mythic about the way the sun cast his body into shadow so that all Wyatt could see was Harry's broad shape and wide angles, like someone carved out of stone rather than tissue and bone. He said nothing on Wyatt's return, stood staring into the woods like a bird of prey hunting its next meal, patiently waiting for the mouse or snake to emerge from its cover in the forest. For a moment Wyatt himself felt like he was among the prey, and it occurred to him he should not underestimate this man whose daughter he was

—what? Courting? In love with? Wyatt felt a moment of dislocation, as though everything around him was dissolving, flesh to bones, forest to shapes, the earth itself to geometric space, Wyatt and Harry mere algorithms.

Then everything snapped back together, lines to the grid, the house on the island, the meat on the bones. As Harry turned to him, the light shifted, and he became a man once more, an attorney on vacation wearing shorts and a golf shirt, casually repairing the roof of his rental house on the South Carolina coastline.

Wyatt couldn't return to terra firma fast enough.

Harry's game continued over dinner, when Wyatt and Mary Grace had unpacked, made out in her bedroom for a while, and returned to the kitchen where her father had laid out filets of salmon to grill and her mother was snapping green beans.

"We thought we'd take a walk down to the beach after we eat," Mary Grace said.

"Be my guest," Lillian replied. "It should be a lovely evening, but the bugs are too much for me."

"Surely you're not going to stay indoors the whole week?" Mary Grace said.

"Oh no, I've got plans to put your father to work while I join you at the beach tomorrow."

"Mary Grace tells me you're a runner," Harry said as he dried the salmon with a paper towel.

"Me? Yes," Wyatt said.

"There's a solid path through the woods—you'll take it tonight to the beach—and then out to a lookout point. It ends up being about a 5K. I usually run it in the mornings. You're welcome to join me if you want."

"Harry, they're on vacation. The boy may just want to relax."

"No, I brought my shoes," Wyatt said. "I don't like to take too much time off."

"See? The boy knows. You just set the pace," Harry said, which Wyatt thought presumptuous. He wasn't the fastest runner, but he doubted Harry naturally kept a faster pace—with thirty years and thirty pounds on Wyatt.

"Look at you and Harry," Mary Grace said while her father was out tending to the grill.

"I guess he likes me."

"Mm. Don't get too comfortable with him." She gave him an appraising look he couldn't decipher. "What's going on with him lately?" she asked her mother.

"Your father's all right," Lillian said. "He promised me he's off all week, and he's already more relaxed than I've seen him in months."

"Maybe it's because I don't see him all the time, he seems awfully wound up."

"He's got several business deals in the air right now."

"I thought he was winding down his practice? Wasn't he up for some judgeship? Something he could use to coast into retirement?"

"There's never a sure bet with those kinds of things," Lillian said vaguely.

"So what's he doing with himself?" Mary Grace asked.

"You'll have to ask him."

"Ask me what?" Harry said, coming in with an empty plate and a pair of dirty tongs that he put in the sink.

"Mom was just filling me in on your work situation. I thought you were supposed to get nominated to be a judge or something. Slowing down at the firm?"

"Oh, there's some political talk, but that's…well. I've let the right people know I'm interested, but they still have to run it up the legislative ladder which, I'm learning, moves slow as a molasses. I should have put my name in the hat right out of law school."

Lillian put a hand on his arm and said, "You had other responsibilities then."

She kissed her husband on the cheek, and Wyatt thought he saw Harry lower his eyes. He glanced at Mary Grace, but she'd missed the exchange.

The next morning, Wyatt got up early and found himself on a jog with Harry, who waited until they were on the beach before casually mentioning a business opportunity in Madrid.

"One of my clients here in Charleston has contracted with a kind of engineering firm in Spain," Harry said, hardly breathing heavy despite the quick pace of the jog. "They manage capital projects, things like parking lots. My client recently won a contract to help build a radio station in Saudi Arabia, and has hired this Spanish firm for the civil engineering."

True to his word, Harry had let Wyatt set the pace, and Wyatt had started like a rabbit and was too embarrassed to slow down. He couldn't respond, merely huffed an approximation of, "Uh-huh."

"Anyway, my firm has handled the contract between our Charleston client and the Spanish firm, but the owner in Madrid is a little mercurial. He likes things to be handled in person. Since he insists on working with me or someone from my office, the bottom line is I have to pick up a design proposal from him so my client can run it through the bureaucracy of the U.S. Navy."

Wyatt had no idea what the man was talking about, so he said nothing. Focused on his feet plodding the sand and the soreness that had crept into one of his ankles on the unstable ground.

Harry grew irritated with him. "My point is that I don't have the time or interest in going to Madrid. I don't speak Spanish, and I've done enough travel in Europe to suit me for the rest of my life. I could send a paralegal, but I thought, with your interest in Spain, you might want to go on my behalf."

"To Madrid?"

"To pick up some blueprints, yeah. It'll take you an hour once you're there. The pay won't be more than your airfare and hotel, but the job is easy. Stop by a Spanish lawyer's office to drop off a contract and then go to the engineer's office and pick up a parcel. Should just be a binder. You could do it over Labor Day weekend, and enjoy a few extra days in Madrid, if you can take the time away from your classes. Bring Mary Grace if you want, though I'd ask you to keep the business confidential. My client requests NDAs from anyone I contract with, and he might raise an eyebrow if I had my daughter sign one. What do you think?"

"Have you talked about it with Mary Grace?" Wyatt asked.

"I think it's best if I stay out of it with her. You heard her last night, she's not all that excited by how active I still am in my legal work. Besides, you can present it like a surprise. A romantic getaway."

"Paid for how?"

"I don't know, Wyatt, make something up. Here's our turn-around. I'd like to jump in the water real quick to cool off."

Shoes and shirt and all, Harry waded in and dived under a wave. He broke through the surface farther out than Wyatt would have thought. Rolled to his back and kicked around in the surf. Wyatt knelt in the wet sand by the shore and splashed water on his face and hair. When he stood, he had gritty sand on his knees and hands, which he then tried to rinse off without getting his shoes wet. He made more of a mess of himself and would need to shower when they returned to the house.

That evening, nuzzling up to Mary Grace on a sand dune during their postprandial stroll, he thought about her father's proposition. A free trip to Madrid, a simple transaction. He should have been more excited about it, or more skeptical, but as he took in his girlfriend's warmth and the soapy scent of her skin, all he could think was that the man who raised her could not be a bad man. The job would be fine.

Still, he felt a stone in his gut at the prospect of broaching the trip with Mary Grace.

Chapter Nine

Wyatt was a small-town South Carolina boy used to clean air, pine trees, peach orchards, two-lane highways, and two-story skylines. Madrid was big, dusty, smoggy, noisy, hot—but arriving with Mary Grace on his arm made him feel like James Bond. Perhaps it was her floral green dress, the way her cool hand tucked neatly into his, or the unknown of his mission for Harry, but his abiding impression of their arrival was one of experiencing manhood for perhaps the first time in his life.

Of course, he might have been drunk off cognac. They arrived at nine in the morning after a redeye out of Atlanta and a short hop from Paris. Determined to have the most fun out of this surprise trip—and believing fully Wyatt's story that he'd picked up several extra shifts all summer, lonesome without her and now flush with cash—Mary Grace had ordered a drink as soon as the Air France flight had taken off, savoring the freedom of being of age in Europe. She'd woken him somewhere over northern Spain, proffered a glass of amber liquid he took to be a Coke, and said, "We're landing in a minute. Finish this for me."

When he slugged it down and widened his eyes, she went

into hysterics. He coughed a few times, cursed, and said, "That was awful."

"But didn't it taste so right?"

He looked at her and thought a few moments, felt the alcohol course into his system. Too late to undo it, he took a few breaths and watched the scrubby Spanish ground rise to meet the plane. Flat land, the haze of mountains in the distance. "Looks like earth to me," he muttered while they taxied in.

"Of course it does. What were you expecting?"

They picked up their bags, went down an escalator, and arrived at the front of the airport, where a line of taxis and buses waited.

If there were customs to go through or a gate to get their passport stamped, they'd somehow bypassed them. The whole airport was more like an American truck stop, a pass-through.

On the bus from the airport to the hotel on Gran Vía, he couldn't get over how flat the land was. Like the American southwest, the sky loomed over a smattering of dark green scrub over dusty clay hills. Squat buildings. Graffiti on the roadside barriers. Cypress trees jutting out of the land like sentries. In the twenty-minute trip, they drove into ominous scud clouds and the day darkened as they got into the city proper. Tall buildings and concrete. Everything looked like everything else.

He took Mary Grace's hand and leaned against the window, listened to the vibrations, and tried to tamp down his nausea. He had a crick in his neck from the overnight flight, and it hurt to hold his head up. The bus let them out in the rain, and the first thing Mary Grace suggested was hitting up a bar. "I saw a place across the street. We can start there," she said. "I want to get the full Spanish experience."

"We got to drop off our stuff first."

"Yeah, I know. Just let's don't get too comfortable. I think if I sat down I'd sleep until we had to pack up and leave."

He wondered if that was a veiled reference to the length of the trip. When he'd suggested it, he'd fed her the story her father cooked up: After a summer of hard work, he wanted to visit Spain. Romantic weekend. All that. "Why don't we go over Christmas break? Stay a couple of weeks rather than a few days?" she'd asked. "You don't go to Europe all that often. It would be nice to enjoy it."

"I don't want to go in the winter," he'd said. "I found a deal on a flight, and thought it would be fun before I get too deep into my Spanish novel class."

"I'll have to miss a few classes."

"How often do you get a chance to go to Europe?" he'd thrown back at her, and she'd not brought it up again.

His plan for tomorrow afternoon was to suggest she take a nap while he went for a walk. Harry had given him the address of the lawyer's office and written out directions for how to get there. The job shouldn't take more than an hour, but he'd decided that if she didn't want a nap and wanted to stay with him, he would tell her the truth. It was one job, so how bad would it be if she found out?

The first thing they discovered on checking in was that Spaniards did not operate on the same temporal wavelength as Americans. There was a snag with the room, so the desk clerk invited them to wait in the lobby, where an episode of *The Simpsons* was playing on the TV, Homer and Bart's voices dubbed over in Spanish, the son's mischievousness and the father's outrage a universal language. The second thing they discovered about Madrid was that for such a large city, space was at a premium. When they finally received their room assignment, the elevator barely held the two of them and their luggage, and then the room itself was a shoebox, with two single beds rammed together rather than a double. The beds were low to the ground and were covered in two ratty blankets.

"I asked for a double," he said stupidly.

"Uh-huh. Did you make the reservation in your Spanish or English?"

"It was through a travel agent."

They looked at the bed, and then at each other, and she burst out laughing. "How are we supposed to have sex on this thing? You should have asked for a queen bed. *Una reina.*"

"You're married to an idiot," he said.

She giggled and kissed him lightly. "We're not married."

The rain had quit when they got back to the street, so they wandered off to find what she called a more *authentic* bar, the nearest being too touristy, too Americanized, too businesslike. They headed down a few streets off Gran Vía and finally found a warm tavern with dark wood furniture and a short and stubby smiling man behind the bar.

The cognac from the plane had all but worn off, and his head was starting to ache. He ordered a rum and coke, and she asked for a mojito, which came with so many crushed-up mint leaves she couldn't drink it. She slid it over to Wyatt and ordered a glass of red wine. He drained his rum and coke, put in a fair effort at the mojito, and finished the second half of her glass of wine. When Eric Clapton came on the radio, Wyatt followed her to another bar, and another, chasing after —what? Flamenco sounds and low-cut blouses?—and losing all concept of where he was or what he was doing. At one point they had a deep conversation about Carl Sagan. At another, he thought she was yelling at him. At another, she dragged him into the street and confessed she had no idea where they were. She leaned back in his arms and nearly pulled him over.

"You're supposed to hold me, Wyatt."

In the shadow of palms and marble architecture, woozy from booze, he gave her a passionate kiss and felt her light body fold into his arms.

"I think our hotel is over there." He pointed generally

toward a tall white concrete building. "Doesn't that look like it?"

"They all look the same. What about that one over there?"

"Hell, I don't know. I thought you were paying attention."

"This city," she yelled, laughing. "Whatever. Let's just take a cab."

The rest of the night was patchy in his memory. Dinner in the hotel, split pea soup, low lighting. Crawling into bed, attempting to make love, blacking out. Waking in the dark with a roiling stomach, a scramble to the bathroom, what felt like hours by the toilet.

As far as he could tell, Mary Grace slept through the whole episode, but he never went back to sleep. He lay on the tile floor of the bathroom and dozed, woke, dozed, and then he shakily took a shower at the first blush of dawn.

"I thought we could go to the Prado this morning," he said when he came out, putting on as brave a face as he could muster.

"You're the tour guide," she said. She gave him a once-over and smirked.

"It's supposed to be the best museum in the city."

"I need some coffee."

He got directions from the front desk, a walking route that took them through some lovely gardens he couldn't enjoy due to his hangover. He bought a bottle of pineapple juice from a nearby tienda, but when the entrance to the museum was in sight, his stomach churned again and he leaned over and threw up in an arrangement of flowers by a fountain.

"Doing all right?" she asked from somewhere behind him, and she lay a hand on his back.

"I don't know what's wrong with me," he said. He worried how he was going to make it to the law office that afternoon. One job, and he was about to muck it up. "I'm never drinking again," he said.

"Sure, Wyatt," she said.

She knew him well, because that night over dinner, he ordered twice the drinks he'd had the day before. But with good reason: what he would see in the afternoon would drive anyone to drink.

He somehow made it through the wide halls of the Prado and began to feel better over a tapas lunch in which he ate an assortment of seafood he'd never encountered before and a glass of tempranillo.

Back at the hotel she said she needed a long siesta. When he took a glance at his watch, she said, "Where do we have to be? I read up for this trip. All the locals are resting for a late dinner."

"I'm not all that tired," he lied. "I might take a walk."

She was closing the curtains. "Make sure you have the energy to take me dancing tonight. You don't want me running away with some dark-haired Spaniard."

"I'll be fine," he said. "We'll have *un buen tiempo*."

"After last night, you might need a rest more than I do." She slid into bed and gave him big watery eyes. "You sure you don't want to just relax? No? Well, at least write down the address of our hotel in case you get lost. And don't drink anything without me."

"Don't worry about that," he said as he casually dug through his suitcase. She was facing away from him toward the wall, so he slipped out a yellow envelope, folded it, and discreetly tucked it under his arm. He thought he heard her roll over on his way out, but he didn't look back to see if she'd spotted the envelope. "I'll be back in a few," he said from the door, shutting it softly behind him.

He took a breath. Although he had plenty of time to get to the lawyer, he checked his watch repeatedly while waiting for the interminable elevator. They were on the ninth floor, but it must have been quicker just to walk down to the lobby. Thirty seconds. Forty-five. A minute fifteen.

He punched the button for the lobby, and it took another thirty to get to the ground floor. It was just after two and he wasn't expected until two-thirty. The lawyer was a ten-minute cab ride away. He still had time.

The lawyer's office was in an office building on Calle de Villanueva that had the look of a NYC brownstone, but with every window a siesta balcony. The cab lacked air conditioning, so he was damp with sweat when the driver dropped him on a narrow street and wished him a *buen día*.

Wyatt shuffled his way into the lobby.

"Excuse me? May I help you?" the man at the reception desk asked. Was it so obvious Wyatt was an American? He wore slacks and a short-sleeved button-down, and although he wasn't dark enough to be local, he felt like he could have passed for any number of northern European countries.

"I have an appointment with Luis del Estal."

"Ah." The man was already back to his computer screen. "Take the elevator to the third floor. Someone there will direct you."

Another narrow elevator, another reception desk. A woman with a narrow, V-shaped face and big hair greeted him in Spanish.

"*Buenos días. Tengo una cita con Luis del Estal,*" he said in his faltering Spanish.

"*Bueno. Su nombre?*"

He told her his name, and she told him *momentito*, and he sat down in one of the three chairs to wait for Sr. del Estal, who kept him waiting twenty minutes before showing up as a study in the new business casual: a sport coat but no tie, dark jeans, loafers, the friendly grin of a man who got more than enough sleep last night.

"Mr. Brewer. Welcome."

He guided Wyatt to a modern conference room with a long wooden table and a view of the Calle de Villanueva below.

"Did you have a nice flight?"

"We did. A little turbulence coming in from Paris, but nothing too bad."

"First time in Madrid?"

"First time in Europe."

"Ah. Welcome. Spain is a great place to start, but if you have the time, it would be worth traveling out of Madrid. Are you here alone?"

"I brought my girlfriend."

"Pretty girl?"

"I think so."

"Good man. There's more than enough entertainment in Madrid for a young couple. So."

The man waited, his repertoire of small talk apparently exhausted. Wyatt pulled out the envelope he'd brought from Spartanburg. Sr. del Estal reviewed the documents quickly, nodding, pen in hand. Then he looked up at Wyatt, gave a wide smile, and said, "Everything looks to be in order." He took another look at the fine print and said, "We appreciate your firm's indulgence. Sr. Oliva likes to do business the old-fashioned way. Not like our generation"—charitably including Wyatt in the generation of grown-ups conducting business rather than the overgrown child he still felt like.

"Of course," Wyatt said.

"Well. Everything seems in order," he said again, and he set a briefcase on the table. "Your firm wired us this payment this morning. I believe Sr. Cope mentioned this to you?"

"Um."

"A deposit for the first leg of work. If you will, please bring it to Sr. Oliva. I believe your plan was to pick up a folder from him?"

"Yeah, I'm heading there next."

"Where is there?"

"To his office? In Centro?"

"Ah, but I'm afraid Sr. Oliva is home today. He was planning to meet us here to save you a trip to his office, but he phoned yesterday with a, how do you say, migraine? If you don't mind, you'll please bring this to him and pick up your folder from his flat."

"You don't want to hold it for him?"

"As I said, he's old-fashioned. He likes to see his security. Likes to shake hands with the people he does business with." Sr. del Estal threw up his hands as if to say you can't do anything with a grandfatherly man of yesteryear. "When you meet him, you'll understand. He's very, um, formal. Wears a tie even if he's not planning to leave the house. Probably dressed up so he could stay at home with his headache."

"I see. Well, I can bring it. Would you call me a taxi?"

"Of course."

While he waited at the curb, Wyatt checked his watch and saw he'd been gone for more than an hour already. Mary Grace was likely already awake, and certainly would be when he finally made it to her. He would have to tell her he got lost again. He just hoped she would wait for him in the hotel rather than wandering off.

He leaned against the building and watched the traffic crawl by at a glacial pace. Down the way, he saw a couple across the street making out against a wall. The man had his hand down the woman's skirt, and when the woman grabbed the man in return, Wyatt looked away, thinking that for such a Catholic country, the Spaniards sure were frisky. There was still a measure of innocence to him, even then, aged twenty and no stranger to bad behavior. The difference being that as a South Carolina boy raised Presbyterian but no longer believing, he maintained a secret life. He kept his thoughts and actions behind closed doors.

Repressed, he would later think. As a journalist, he would learn you had to meet people where they were if you wanted them to trust you with their story. Wyatt would soon change, quickly and irrevocably, but this afternoon he was still a clean and unbroken little egg.

The first thing that went wrong in his evolving plan was that Sr. Oliva lived across the city, and it took half an hour for the cab to get him there. "Would you mind waiting for me?" he asked the driver. "I have to drop this off, but it shouldn't take more than ten minutes."

"I have to charge you for it," the driver said.

"That's fine." Wyatt gave him the money for the lift so far, and he hoped he had enough euros to cover the ride back. He had another two hundred in the hotel but hadn't brought it all with him.

Sr. Oliva's flat was on the top floor—a slow elevator ride, more time—and as Wyatt calculated the time down, he hoped Sr. Oliva would be faster than Luis del Estal. The flat was at the end of the hall, and he took a moment to compose himself before knocking.

No answer.

He waited a few moments, knocked again, and then tried to peer through the peephole. After no answer again, he tried the knob and discovered it unlocked.

"Hello?" he called as he cracked open the door and poked his head in. "Anyone home? *Buenos días*."

He looked back into the hallway, and then at his watch, and then—an action he would replay continually in his mind, but would never confess to another—he opened the door and let himself into Sr. Oliva's flat. It was much like an American apartment, a kitchen to the left, a living space to the right. White carpeted floors, a modernist painting on the wall, a TV in the corner, a hallway toward the bed and bathrooms.

"Hello?" he called again. He closed the door and eased toward the bedroom. "Sr. Oliva? I heard you might be ill. I have a package from Randall & Cope, in the United States? Are you back here?"

He stopped on the threshold of the bedroom. Sr. Oliva—or what he presumed was Sr. Oliva—was on the bed, on his back, his chest and bed ripped up by what appeared to be a shotgun blast. Blood was spattered on the wall and pooled around Sr. Oliva's body, his eyes open and vacant.

The bed had posts but no canopy. This was the detail that would stick with him the most vividly. Why would a man own such a bed? Did all Spaniards have such furnishings? Was it inherited?

The next detail that burned into his mind's eye was the way Sr. Oliva's knee was bent and propped against one of the bedposts, as though he'd sat down for just a moment, leaned over, and used the leg to prop him in place while he grabbed something from the floor, and that was when the shot took place.

Later, Wyatt would be embarrassed that his first reaction was not one of fight-or-flight. He had no instincts for combat, no experience with danger, so he stared stupidly for several moments before realizing that (a) whoever did this could still be in the flat, and (b) the police may already be on their way. If he were caught here he might be arrested for the crime himself. He would be hard-pressed to explain to the police why he had a briefcase full of cash.

Half a million dollars, he would later discover.

He listened for a moment but heard nothing in the flat. If someone was still here, they would have heard him blundering in and announcing himself. He backed away, looked down the hall toward the door, and crept toward it, tightly holding the briefcase, making sure not to touch anything, not to put a hand on a wall or leave a scuff mark on the floor.

In the front room, he took another look around, and his

eyes alighted on a package on the kitchen counter. He didn't know what he'd been sent here to pick up, but Sr. del Estal had said it was a parcel. Harry had mentioned something about a report, and the package on the counter looked like it could hold a binder. He grabbed it quickly and scurried out. Something, habit perhaps, made him lock the door behind him.

In the elevator—for once, he was glad for a slow ride—he set the briefcase on the floor and opened it. Although he'd suspected a case full of cash, it still took his breath away to see the neat rows of hundred-dollar bills stacked together. The elevator pinged the second floor. He stuffed the parcel in with the money and shut the briefcase, standing up just in time for the doors to open on the ground floor.

The cab driver was still waiting for him, double-parked on the street.

"That was quick," the driver said.

"Just picking up a package," Wyatt said, and he asked to go back to the hotel.

He leaned down in the back of the cab and looked around the street. He didn't see anyone suspicious, or anyone following them as the cab headed down the street. But then, he wasn't trained in espionage or gangster tactics.

He wouldn't know what to look for.

The hotel room was mercifully empty when he arrived. He knew Mary Grace would ask him about the briefcase, so he pulled the bag out of the wastebasket in the bathroom and transferred the money into it. The bag was heavy but took up less space than a shoebox in his luggage. He covered it with a sport coat and packed the rest of his clothes on top.

He still had to get rid of the briefcase, find Mary Grace, and process what he'd seen this afternoon. He tried to think: who might come for him? The money seemed to have originated with Harry, as payment for the parcel. So long as Wyatt had grabbed the right parcel, he would have delivered on his job. Harry should be satisfied.

The same went for the Spanish lawyer. Sr. del Estal had given him the briefcase but hadn't expected anything in return. Presumably, Sr. Oliva had the firm on retainer, so Sr. del Estal had no stake in the money.

Wyatt's biggest concern was who killed Sr. Oliva—and would they be looking for Wyatt? Perhaps his death had nothing to do with Wyatt or Harry. If he was the type of man to request cash payments in person, he likely had business deals like this all the time. It made sense that eventually a deal would go wrong. Whoever killed him had not taken the parcel, which was in plain sight, so presumably they'd gotten what they came for. So long as no one had seen Wyatt—and he was fairly confident no one had—then no one should be coming. Sr. del Estal was the only person who knew Sr. Oliva would have a briefcase full of cash this afternoon, and Wyatt couldn't see any reason where the presence or absence of money would come up with Sr. del Estal. If it did come up, he might logically assume the killer took the money.

Panic struck Wyatt with this thought, because it dawned on him that there would soon be an investigation. Police would discover Sr. Oliva's body, start asking around, and inquire about Oliva's business dealings. Estal would inform them Wyatt had been on his way to see Oliva and therefore may have been the last person to see him alive, which would put Wyatt on the short list of suspects.

Today was Friday, and he and Mary Grace were set to fly home Monday morning. When would someone find Oliva's body? He thought about it and, remembering that he'd locked the door on his way out, he thanked whatever cosmic hand had guided him. No one would accidentally stumble onto Oliva, so assuming he wasn't expecting company, it might be Monday before he was expected back at work. It might be midday Monday before anyone went around to check on him, perhaps later before the body was discovered. Plenty of time to get out of the country.

But then what? Wyatt knew nothing about the state of extradition. Could the Spanish police track him down in South Carolina? What would happen if they did?

He drank a glass of water and then grabbed the briefcase and left the room. No one in the hallway. He considered chucking the briefcase in a trash can somewhere in the hotel, but thought better of it. He rode the elevator down and tried not to look too suspicious as he walked out with it and down Gran Vía. Down an alleyway, he found a dumpster behind a restaurant. He glanced around before pulling a bag of trash out of the dumpster. He wedged the briefcase in and put the bag back on top to hide his tracks. Then he skipped out of the alley and set out to find Mary Grace.

Chapter Ten

"And where was she?" Penelope asked. "I presume you found her again."

"I did. She was in the hotel bar with another mojito. I guess she'd been there the whole time. I tried to act casual when I walked in and sat next to her, but she asked me, 'Where the hell have you been?' Rightfully so, but instead of giving me the chance to tell her, she launched into a tirade. Where was I, what had I been doing? It was the first time we'd ever really argued."

"Did you tell her where you'd gone?"

Wyatt studied the agents across from him. He'd been with them for hours but hadn't truly taken note of Bert and Penelope as individuals. They wore bureaucratic business suits and each had a blankness to them. He doubted he would be able to pick them out in a lineup a week from now, assuming they eventually cut him loose. However, they'd settled in for the long haul and ordered a delivery of sandwiches for dinner. Penelope had taken off her jacket to eat. She had toned arms, kind eyes, a soft way of asking questions, and a comfort with silence that made it impossible for Wyatt not to keep talking, as though he were in therapy. He recognized the strategy and had employed it himself in difficult interviews. Let the other person speak first. Don't interrupt. Don't fill the silence. People will tell you more than they ever mean to if you wait them out. He knew the strategy, but he'd never been interviewed like this himself.

Penelope smiled at him and waited.

"I didn't tell her at the bar," he said. "She yelled at me and drank her mojito, and then it was like a light switched off. She suggested we might as well have dinner, and that was that."

"Just like that."

"Yep," he said, omitting that Mary Grace had needled him throughout the evening, like she'd known he'd been on the job for her father. He wondered if there had been earlier boyfriends with similar jobs, but he would never know.

"You still had two days on the trip to fill," Penelope said. "She never brought it up again?"

"We ate at a loud restaurant, so we couldn't really hear each other well to chat. I had too much to drink, again, and when we left I needed her help getting back to the hotel. I think she could tell I wasn't in shape to offer anything. She might have asked where I'd gone, but I don't remember."

In fact, Wyatt remembered the evening more clearly than he would ever admit. The stumbling walk home, leaning on Mary Grace, both of them drunk but him unable to stand. In the elevator, she shoved him against the wall and demanded to know, *Where did you go?*

When?

When do you think, Wyatt? This afternoon.

I just wanted to take a walk. Soak up Madrid.

She held his eyes with a rage she could not mask. *All afternoon?*

You know how I am. You're my compass in all this.

He reached for her, slipped his hand up her shirt, and then the elevator came to a stop. Without warning, he threw up on her and made a mess of the floor.

She spun away and stomped out, leaving him to sink to the floor of the elevator, where he'd passed out. Another couple had found him sometime in the night, and although he couldn't understand their jabbering, he understood their mix of concern for him and fear for their safety and indignation at the state of the elevator. He thought he might have heard the word *policía* and quickly skedaddled. He wandered a random floor of the hotel until he found a concrete stairwell, and then he drunkenly shuffled up to the room.

His head pounded as his body processed the night's alcohol and he began to sober. He had a mysterious ache on the side of his neck, as though he'd strained something, and by the time he let himself into the room, navigated to the bathroom to brush his teeth, and found the empty half of the bed, his neck was throbbing so that he could barely hold his head up. He lay on his back and closed his eyes. Every time he took a breath, he felt the tweak in his neck, a knotted muscle that refused to relax. It should have concerned him more, but there in the dark, everything caught up to him at once: the whirlwind schedule of classes on Wednesday, the midnight redeye, the stupor of Thursday, and the surreal events of today.

Mary Grace breathed deeply beside him, in a dreamless slumber herself from the mojitos. He'd embarked on the trip believing he might one day marry her. *We're not married*, she'd said just yesterday, but in a loving way that suggested she might have been open to the possibility. Now, he couldn't say what the state of their relationship was. She'd yelled at him, and he'd groped her in the elevator and vomited on her, and she'd left him for dead. He'd grown up quickly in the last twenty-four hours, but he was still a South Carolina rube to his core. He didn't know how to navigate the unknown waters of the human heart.

Twenty years later, he told none of this to the agents in the house on King Street. Shame was private, so he waited through Penelope's patient silence.

"So you don't know what you told her," Bert chimed in, clearly bored with the whole conversation. He wanted to know about the funeral and Molly Keagan.

"Well, I don't remember precisely, but I'm sure I didn't tell her about the money or working for her father."

"How can you be so sure?"

"Because she found out a few days after we got home."

Wyatt had to deliver the parcel to close the loop with Harry. He'd half-expected him to meet them at the Greenville-Spartanburg Airport, with news of the dead business contact and a laundry list of questions about the money. Instead, Wyatt and Mary Grace had gone through customs in Atlanta, caught the puddle jumper to GSP, and strolled right out of the airport with few words between them. She'd taken his hand somewhere in the dark over the cold and unforgiving Atlantic, so he let himself believe he'd not caused irreparable damage to their relationship with his disappearance and his drunkenness. They were both exhausted when they got home. She was glad to sleep for twelve hours before returning to class. He was glad to make it back to his apartment without Harry, the police, or some posse of Spanish gangsters confronting him. He stowed the cash in the bottom of his closet, beneath a stack of old bags, souvenirs, and other accouterments he'd acquired since moving in. It was his I-don't-know-what-to-do-with-it pile, and the cash fit right in.

The agreed-upon plan—before they left, before the murder, before the cash entered the picture—had been for Wyatt to drive the parcel down to Harry's office on Tuesday. If he'd better understood Harry, he would have known the man stuck to the plan. A lifetime of meticulous organization and careful execution had taught Harry that stability and predictability were roads to prosperity, and that deviance was the road to ruin. Therefore, even if he had known about the fate of Sr. Oliva, Harry doubtless would have waited for Wyatt to bring him the package on Tuesday. He most certainly would not have met them at the airport, for who could have known what attention Wyatt had drawn?

But Harry had not heard about Oliva Monday, didn't hear about it until Tuesday morning, shortly before Wyatt showed up at his law office with the parcel.

"Wyatt. Glad you made it back. How was your trip?" Harry said in the office lobby.

"Relaxing," Wyatt lied. "Just the right amount of time." He still had a crick in his neck from tweaking it in the elevator. He'd tried to rest Monday night and showered Tuesday morning, but sensed he looked underfed and overwrought. A man to keep away from clients.

"Come on back."

The law offices of Randall & Cope were in an older corporate office park in North Charleston, a building that looked sleek enough from the outside, with tall dark windows, red brick, and a wide expanse of parking, but which had not been renovated inside since its opening in the mid-seventies. They had dark wood furniture, heavy-duty stuff that projected a stable brand, undercut by the dated forest green carpeting that suggested frugality and antiquation, perhaps a whiff of vulnerability. Harry, however, was on his way out. Wyatt understood him to be in line for a judgeship, and if not that, then an early retirement. His founding partner was long gone to a Hilton Head golfing community, and the firm's other, younger partners were ready for changes.

Harry led him to a windowless conference room and shushed Wyatt until he'd closed the door and sat down. As a reporter, Wyatt would later experience all the ways people took control of meetings. Harry's was the boldest, but perhaps he got away with it because Wyatt, at the time, was still meek and green.

"I see you have the parcel. Did you have any trouble?"

"Not really. I wasn't expecting to have to make several stops."

"Oh?"

"Sr. Oliva wasn't feeling well, so the lawyer gave me a briefcase and sent me on to his flat."

"Hmm. That wasn't the plan. What was wrong with Oliva?"

"Migraine, he said. He seemed fine when I saw him."

"But you did see him?"

"Just for a few minutes. Enough to drop off the briefcase and pick up the parcel."

"Did you open the briefcase?"

Wyatt shook his head.

"Did Luis tell you what it was?"

Wyatt was an inexperienced liar, but he had the sharp instinct to stick to the truth as much as possible. "Yeah. He mentioned you'd wired some money, so I kind of figured what was in it."

"But you didn't open it to make sure?"

"I was in a hurry by that point. Mary Grace was napping at the hotel, so I was trying to get back to her before she noticed I was missing."

"And did she?"

"They move slower in Spain, so she was pissed when I got back. But no, I didn't tell her what I'd been up to. I didn't tell anyone."

"Good." Harry examined the parcel, fingered the tab that sealed it, and said, "I'll be right back."

While he was gone, Wyatt drummed his thumbs on the table. Yawned. The room was warm, and he'd been traveling nonstop for days. He had a long day of classes tomorrow, but he knew he would be worthless until he had a weekend to catch up. He shared an apartment with two other guys, but they both had girlfriends and spent most of their time away, which meant that unless something unusual went on, he would have the place to himself this weekend. Then he could think about what he should do with the money. Assuming Harry didn't bring it up during the rest of their meeting. He'd been gone a long time, and Wyatt's heart thrummed as he considered the possibilities. Would the police come in and arrest him here in the lawyer's office? Did Harry have connections in the underworld? Were the walls of this conference room soundproof? Would anyone hear him scream?

Harry returned sans package but with an envelope that had Wyatt's name on it. "A little bonus for you," Harry said. "It isn't much, five hundred. You handled everything this weekend perfectly, though I'm sorry to report it might have been for nothing. Oliva was found dead yesterday morning at his flat."

"Dead?"

"Yes, and unfortunate circumstances at that. Appears he was shot in a home invasion. Robbery, the police think, according to his lawyer."

Wyatt must have blanched.

"Yeah," Harry went on. That's why I wondered how he was when you saw him. If you noticed anything."

"No. I mean, I only saw him for a few minutes. Maybe he was a little under the weather, but…"

"With the migraine and all," Harry said.

"Right. But everything seemed normal on Saturday."

"Well. You did your part, and the parcel you brought has some engineering specs for our Saudi airfield. I'll have to find a new contractor, but maybe these specs will help save them a step."

Harry stood, and Wyatt followed.

Harry tapped the table. "Don't forget your check."

"Thanks."

"Okay, well, be seeing you. I think we'll come visit Mary Grace later this fall. Maybe we'll see you then."

"I hope so," Wyatt said, and he shook the man's hand.

That was the last time he saw Harry, but it wasn't the end of his Spanish journey. In the downstairs lobby of the office park, Wyatt ran into Mary Grace on her way in. She'd clearly gotten more sleep last night than he had—that, or she had a deeper well of energy, because she was showered, had her hair curled, and wore a smart blue business suit that made her look five years older.

"What are you doing here, Wyatt?" She shook her head. "How did you get to Charleston?"

"I drove down this morning. If I'd have known, we could have carpooled," he joked. "What are you doing here?"

"Having lunch with my father. You know he works here, right? Of course you do. You must have seen him."

"I did. You look great. I feel like I haven't seen you in ages."

"Even after a long weekend. That's sweet."

He was disoriented by her, and how grown up she looked here in the office. Wyatt was wearing jeans, a flannel shirt untucked, and an old field coat. The look may have suited him on a college campus in an overgrown small town, but in a corporate office park he felt like a goofus.

Mary Grace didn't seem to notice the disparity between them, and he wondered if she might overlook his reason for being there and invite him to lunch. He was trying to figure out how best to decline when she said, "So why are you here again?"

"Oh, you know."

"I actually don't. What business could you have with my father?"

She had a flirtatious note in her voice, and if he'd been quicker on his feet, he would have understood the most logical reason a young man in love goes to see the father of the woman he loves. Wyatt may have grown up on the trip to Madrid, and he may soon be set for a career of ferreting out information from the most cynical of sources, but that Tuesday morning he was tired, or rattled, or just not as smart as he liked to think of himself, for he said, "Oh, it was just a small job."

Her face darkened. "What kind of job?"

He realized his mistake. "Well, not a job, per se. More of an errand."

"Was this about our trip? Was this why you disappeared? I knew it! Of course it makes sense. I should have known you didn't have the money to take us to Spain. I just thought, with your Spanish history class—I'm so stupid."

"No," he said. "It's not—"

"It's not what I think? What is it, then?"

"He found out I had a background in Spanish, and thought we might like a romantic weekend abroad."

"Right, because he's so sensitive. What did he have you doing?"

"Just getting a package from one of his clients."

"A package. Do you know what was in it? Do you know what kind of business he's in?"

"It was, I don't know, some kind of engineering plans. I thought it might be good for us. You know, give me a leg up with your father. We kind of bonded at the beach, and I thought it might, you know, help us if your father liked me."

He almost told her he wanted to marry her, but a moment later he was glad he'd held his tongue.

"I take it back," she said. "You're the stupid one. My father's a bully and he's a *criminal*. I picked you because you weren't like him. You're kind, you care about people, and you don't fly around the world picking up mysterious packages. If I'd wanted to date a future business bro, I would have picked one out. I thought you were different."

She spun on her heels and huffed out of the office, apparently deciding to forego lunch with her father. He watched her speed off and then walked to his own car. He looked up at the building and saw the shadow of her father, or what he imagined was her father, staring down from a third-floor window.

That had been the end of the Spanish fiasco. At least until Harry's obituary popped up on the wire in the newsroom twenty years later.

"But that wasn't the end of it," Bert said, engaged again and leaning across the table. The sun had gone down outside, they'd finished catered cold cuts and were grinding into the night.

"Well, I never saw Harry again. When I got back to Spartanburg, Mary Grace wouldn't return my calls. I finally caught her after one of her classes, walking back into her dorm. She told me she just couldn't see me after that. That I'd betrayed her and proven myself something other than what I pretended. That if she couldn't trust me, she couldn't be with me. Best to cut our ties."

"When did you hear she died?"

"Not right away. She never joined Facebook, so——" He paused, realizing how much a person's digital life became their actual life. He seldom saw anyone from high school or college, so if they were not online it was like they didn't exist. Like Mary Grace had never existed. "Anyway, I googled her one night and found her obituary. I hadn't seen her in a few years then, but I wish I'd known. I wish someone had reached out."

"It was a car wreck?" Penelope asked.

"Yeah. I tracked down one of her old roommates and sent her an email, a long apologetic thing I'm embarrassed by now, and she sent me a few lines back to say Mary Grace had a nice service."

"What do you think she meant when she told you her father was a criminal?"

"At the time? Nothing. It took me a few hours to process why she was angry. It was a long drive home, and somewhere in the empty stretch above Columbia, I decided she was being dramatic. That she had some issues with her father, but they were your average girl-trying-to-grow-up kind of issues."

"We have to reject our fathers to find our place in the world?" Penelope asked.

"I was twenty. I didn't know what I didn't know. She complained about her father, about both her parents, plenty, but nothing more than your usual generational discomfit."

"Ha. Discomfit. You still believe that?" Bert asked.

"I don't know. You replay these things, and gain some new insights, but who's to say we know any more now than we did then? It's like defining noise."

Bert pinched his nose. "You know what I think? I think you're a very smart guy, but I also think you're full of it. I asked you a simple question: Do you still believe Mary Grace's relationship with her father was just one of an angst-filled college student, or was there something else to it? What do you think she meant when she called her father a bully?"

"I think he was a brute of a man who was emotionally cold to her if not physically abusive. And I think that's one reason she dumped me. She didn't want to see someone in business with him."

Wyatt stared at the agent until Bert grinned. "Now we're getting somewhere. Truth. That's what we're after. What did you do with the money, Wyatt?"

The question seemed to come out of nowhere, but Wyatt knew there was a calculation behind Bert's thick glasses and his squinty eyes.

"I don't mean to be insensitive to your personal issues," the agent continued, "but the money is still in your bank account, isn't it? You can talk about the Spanish fiasco being over, but the money's been accumulating interest for, gosh, twenty years. Did anyone ever come knocking?"

How could Wyatt convey the magnitude of his paranoia? He'd been waiting every day for twenty years for someone to knock on his door and had told himself every night that he was in the clear, that Oliva's death had been deemed a robbery, so if anyone had known about the money, they would have assumed the robbers got away with it. Yet he'd also woken every night in a cold sweat, listening for the slide of a key into the lock in his door, footsteps on the floorboards, a gloved hand at his throat.

"I waited and eventually put it in the bank," he said.

"Just like that?"

"Well, no, not just like that. You've got a file on me. You must know where the money is."

"Humor us."

He'd left the money on the floor of his closet for the rest of the semester. A former roommate was a business major, and one night over drinks he cautiously picked his friend's brain about how to launder money. He'd gleaned enough to find an attorney who specialized in unique financial situations, and for a tidy fee the man had advised him of a bank in Miami where he could deposit large sums of cash, no questions asked, and, against federal regulations, without reporting the deposit to the IRS.

"Ha! So you drove half a million dollars to Miami to put it in a bank run by cocaine cowboys," Bert said. "Whatever you paid that lawyer, you didn't pay him enough. We've got a fat file on you, Wyatt, and we know how much money you have in the bank, how much it's grown over the years, that you've diligently paid taxes on the dividends, and that you now have a cool million-five in an investment account managed by a South Florida private equity group. What we didn't know until today, what's not in your file, is where the money came from. It just materialized one day, and while we've been able to put a lot of the pieces together, it helps to see the big picture."

Wyatt remained silent. He'd not been issued any Miranda warning, and since no one else knew where the money came from, he'd said nothing that could be used against him in court. Mary Grace was dead, so while these agents—what agency *did* they work for, precisely?—could verify he went to Spain at the start of his junior year in college, and could verify Oliva's death, there was nothing to link him to that money except hearsay and speculation.

Still, he waited to see where these agents would lead him as evening bled into the night in the office on King, South of Broad, Charleston. He was not concerned about the money or the origins of his finances. What concerned him was the sequence of events that had transpired between the day at the beach, when he was working on a simple news article about a mysterious death on Folly, and this morning, when these agents had shown up in front of his house.

Wyatt, may we have a word?

Bert had sounded so friendly and looked so innocuous. Wyatt had been waiting for a knock on his door for twenty years, and he'd known when Bert opened the back door of his black Sonata: he was hearing the knock of fate.

Part Two

Chapter Eleven

THE WYATT BREWER DOSSIER landed on Penelope Lowe's desk on Thursday, two days after the Estonian agent wound up dead on Folly Beach and the same morning Brewer woke up in the Francis Marion Hotel room. Day Zero, in the intelligence log. One of Penelope's colleagues in ISD—the southeast field agents operating below the radar within U.S. borders—photographed the reporter nosing around the beach and interviewing neighbors. The agent, Jarman Nzuve, had been tracing the police investigation (1) to capture any information local law enforcement might stumble onto about the Estonian national and the money laundering, and (2) to make sure ISD's Project Gravy was not tied to anything law enforcement uncovered.

It was routine. Jarman had been running the source for six months and hadn't gotten close enough to give anything serious away. Besides, Jarman was an experienced professional, trained by Bert Wilson, and Bert Wilson was the best. Everyone in ISD was upset to be losing six months, but cleanup was a formality, one of Bert's many procedures. Bert gave you a lot of latitude, but one thing you didn't do was question procedure. None of them questioned it. ISD was a small cog in a big system, but everyone here felt lucky to be part of it. It was a nice sandbox, the type of unit that attracted methodical, procedure-minded agents who didn't feel at home in the rest of the system. Jarman's cleanup was nearly complete. The Estonian had no identification, and law enforcement seemed to think he was a late-night reveler who died on the beach, rather than a man dumped in the ocean. Simple forensics should show the man had washed ashore but it had been a bad year for murders in Charleston. The priority seemed to be drug crimes. A body no one could identify— with no one asking about it and no leads as to means or motive—was a good one to leave on the unsolved docket.

Then the frumpy reporter showed up in his sad sack pickup, and Jarman could tell by looking at him that he had the time and imagination to dedicate to the Estonian. You work in the field long enough, you develop instincts. Some people felt electric, got your antenna tingling. Jarman captured Brewer's license plate, snapped a few photos of him nosing around on the beach, and made a note to talk to Amy Southerland again to see what the college girl had talked about with him.

Jarman filed his report, uploaded the photos to the unit's SharePoint, and called Penelope to let her know to look for it.

"I sent a text to Bert," he said. "I know this thing is about closed out, but."

"You've got good instincts," Penelope said. A Google search and a background check had yielded fruit already. "He wrote the first news article about Privet"—code name for the Estonian asset. "Actually," she went on, "he seems to be the only reporter who's taken an interest. None of the TV stations have covered it. If the city paper ran a blurb, they didn't put it online. Let's see: Brewer's been with the *Dispatch* eighteen years, currently on the Metro beat, a long list of press association awards, Wofford graduate. Now this is interesting. His tax returns show he had nearly a hundred grand in investment returns last year."

Jarman whistled. "Where'd he get that kind of money? Trust fund?"

"I don't see it. He's been diligent about reporting and paying taxes, consistent returns year to year. I can't find where the money came from or where he's stashing all this cash." She tapped a pencil on her desk and continued scrolling through information. "Mother and father both still living... Dad's a professor in Tuscaloosa...Mom works for a land-scaping company...neither of them makes much at all." She sat back and put the pencil in her hair and stared at the screen for a few moments. "I don't know, Jarman. Unless he had a lucky run in Vegas when he was in college, I don't see how he has this kind of money."

"How about that. I'll keep nosing around here. You in the office tomorrow?"

"No, I've got to go up for Buttercup's funeral."

"Bert's got you following him to the very end, huh?"

"This is his white whale. We're all here because of him."

"Got to love these old spies. By the time Bert is satisfied, everyone involved with Buttercup is going to be dead or retired. I guess we still have Nazi hunters dragging ninety-year-olds out of the Brazilian forests, but I'm trying to picture what leads you're going to find in a little country church."

"It's his life's work," she said, referring to Bert.

"At least he's got a purpose."

"You're not a believer, Jarman?"

"You know me. I'm as patriotic as the next guy, but if I were reliant on the agency for my life's meaning? I'd have hung myself a long time ago."

"It can't be that bad."

"You wait, girlie. As soon as you start to care about some-thing, they'll use it to break you open. The only thing you can do is enjoy the day-to-day and get your therapy in the paycheck."

"Have a good night, Jarman. Good luck closing everything out."

After hanging up, she did the same thing they always did with new personas in their system. Bert was paranoid, so they kept spreadsheets on offline computers—laptops with their wireless cards removed so they could neither connect nor be connected to. The only truly safe connection was no connection.

She felt a pang of concern for Bert. Harry Cope had indeed been his life's work. He'd filled her in on the story in her first week, how the only reason ISD existed in the first place was because Cope had been involved in something with an old dead agent named Everett Archer. Archer was gone, so Cope was Bert's last lead to uncover whatever there was to uncover. Although she'd not voiced it to Jarman—who was a brilliant field officer but not the most strategic of thinkers— she wondered if there would be an Infrastructure Surveillance Division this time next week.

And where was Bert anyway? He'd said something about a lead with the Navy, but he'd not been in the office all day.

She logged Brewer's information, meticulously cataloging the information they had, how they came about it, and what their next steps would be. In this case, nothing was in line for Wyatt Brewer—at least until she ran into him at Harry Cope's funeral.

Then began the great unraveling.

Chapter Twelve

WHILE PENELOPE DUG into Wyatt Brewer, Bert was having dinner with a retired captain in the U.S. Navy at a little sea shack on Shem Creek. White linens on a screened-in deck and food served on paper plates, a restaurant impossible to find unless you knew to look for it, which meant they could talk relatively freely about the good old days without some bumbling tourist or drunken college student jostling their table. Whereas Bert's good old days involved tracking targets in London, Berlin, Prague, the Navy captain, by the name of Allen, had run a guided missile cruiser, the *USS Oswego*, through the eighties and nineties. The U.S. ostensibly had been at peace, but there had been a number of skirmishes in the Middle East and the Scandinavian seas.

"I don't have to tell you, we were constantly flirting with war even when there wasn't always an enemy," Captain Allen said.

The captain had a grandfatherly persona and a Mississippi twang to his speech that Bert knew would mean they were going to be here for a while. Fine by Bert. He'd known Allen long enough that he knew the captain would throw him any nugget of truth rattling around in the back of his brain.

"I remember patrolling off the coast of Libya, we had some guys start firing on us from the coast. I had gunners tearing up the shore with cannons for half an afternoon. Things like that never made the news back home, but it happened all the time, and it's a wonder we haven't found ourselves in a full-on World War Three by now. What they don't tell you is we've been fighting a hot war with them for half a century. I'm not talking proxy wars, but hot wars in the ocean. I don't know how the Russian government deals with it, but as long as we're not losing sailors—or can explain away deaths as training exercises—everyone's having a grand time out there playing pirates."

"Hey, it was the same in the agencies back then," Bert said. "If I could tell you how many times we had agents caught over would-be enemy lines. The only thing between us and an international scandal is they were doing it too."

"As long as neither side wants to admit what they're doing, we can all pretend like nothing's happening."

"The emperor's new clothes all over again."

The captain ordered another drink while they waited for their food. "So what are you up to these days, Bert? Thinking about retirement?"

"Me? No, I've got another few years before I can start drawing benefits. I may just stick it out to the end. Don't know what I'd do if I retired."

"Join me in the private sector. More pay, less work. Plus you can talk about what you do, to some extent. I imagine you've never been free to tell people what you really do."

"That's true. My wife thinks I work for the Department of Agriculture."

Allen laughed. "Does she really? Be honest, does she suspect?"

"Oh, she definitely knows it's not true. Agriculture's been a low-stakes affair in South Carolina since about the forties, when they ran a campaign about iodine in the soil. I guess it was worthwhile when everyone was worried about nuclear war, but since then there's no reason for an Ag worker to be working overtime like I do. Besides, I think the Department of Agriculture is blown cover anymore."

"You should have told her you were in logistics. When I told my wife I wanted to go into a partnership with E & J Enterprises, she asked what I'd be doing. I made it through about three minutes before she changed the subject. Hasn't asked about it since. Throw in a few talking points about invoices and continuous process improvement, and you've made it as real as your wife would need it. Might actually believe you were as dull as you sounded, though I must say the work will earn you a bloody fortune."

Allen's logistics company was a supplier for public-private partnerships, such as between the Navy and the energy companies. Private equity loved this business model, so Allen had levered up considerably in retirement.

"I did want to talk to you about that," Bert said.

The captain took a swig of beer and swished it around in his mouth. "I had a feeling you didn't invite me out for a night to reminisce. Figured you either wanted a job or information."

"You know me. I hear your firm might have a stake in a new airfield in Estonia."

"Where'd you hear that? Jesus, Bert, the government truly is a leaking ship, isn't it? Last I heard, the Navy was still trying to write a statement of purpose."

"My group ladders up to Homeland Security these days, so we get a lot of requests to write white papers on security concerns. Nothing popped up about this airfield, but when I'm in the database, I like to check on what my cohorts are doing."

"So, yeah, you know about the airfield. *Potential* airfield. I'm skeptical it'll happen, given the diplomatic situation over there. Those Eastern European countries never did forgive us when Obama dropped the plans for missile defense. They only trust us as far as our dollars flow into the region, and with the Ukraine money drying up..."

"The U.S. doesn't have allies, only interests," Bert said.

"Exactly. I don't know what you've read, but you know the Baltic is the nexus for energy in Europe. Oil, gas—it's all there. Exxon Mobil and BP need a secure place to operate, which means they need American defense."

"But you have to get around Russia."

"But we have to get around Russia," Allen agreed. "On paper, they don't want us anywhere near the region."

"But in practice?"

"Everything's for sale, Bert."

"Buy off some Russian oligarchs, you mean, and they turn a blind eye to a U.S. airfield a stone's throw from St. Petersburg."

"Look, the old model of national governments working in their own self-interest is being upended right before us. I know you're a patriot, but what actually makes America—or Russia —a country anymore? It's all economic opportunity zones, and having energy companies in the Baltics is lucrative for everyone."

"Yeah, but the U.S. still has to worry about diplomacy."

"An airfield in Estonia is about optics," Allen said. "Every foreign service worker—ours and theirs—knows distance is an illusion. The U.S. military can get anywhere in the world in a matter of hours. We can't be effective without some more lead time, but we can rain scud missiles over you and—pffffffftt— no problem. The problem is the illusion. The U.S. wants a presence in the Baltics to maintain the illusion that these companies are still beholden to America. They're assets of our empire, but you know they would sell out to Russia if the price were right."

"Are you in negotiations with the Russians?"

"Me? No. No, I've got all the business I can handle without getting into bed with those gangsters. I'll leave that mess to our government. I presume someone in your shop has a line on your counterparts in Moscow?"

"I should hope not," Bert said. "Negotiations like that, on behalf of private industry—"

"Wouldn't look too good, you're right. But we've been around the block a few times. We both know how this works."

"I'm looking for a name, Jim. I had a contact with a local Estonian until two days ago, but he's dropped off the radar."

Found dead on Folly Beach, more like it, but he wouldn't give that card away. He'd known Captain Allen a long time, but the one thing he'd learned about life in his career was that it was a long life. People reinvented themselves with new alliances and allegiances.

"I don't have anyone for you," Allen said.

"Would you tell me if you did?"

"I don't know."

Bert believed him. He could see Allen still trusted him enough to level with him on the limits. The waiter brought their food, which gave them a merciful respite, like a boxer returning to the corner of the ring between rounds. Bert had saved his real questions for the next round, knowing Allen wouldn't give him a name or admit to more about the airfield than he already had. What Bert wanted to know was how the project might be changing now that Harry was out of the picture. An airfield didn't just happen. You needed *stakeholder engagement*, a.k.a. support from the intelligence community. Had the old lawyer been a major player, or had he handed the reins over to someone else?

Bert never stopped asking *who*. Who's getting paid, and by whom, and to what end? Those were the three questions to answer to ferret out any corruption, and he'd been asking *who* for nearly twenty years.

While they ate, the captain regaled him with stories of life on the *Oswego*, ports of call in Istanbul and Marseille, rowdy men away from home. After the deployment to the Mediterranean, they moved north to the Norwegian Sea and crossed the Arctic Circle on the way home. Although it had been twenty years, the slow journey through the icy northern waters obviously had made an impression on Allen. Bert could imagine him standing on the bow of the ship in the Arctic's perennial dawn, the icy spray hitting his face and chapping his cheeks, the American flag whipping on its post, rings creaking and the ship groaning as it cut through the bleak waters of the Northern Sea. Endless ocean in all directions, the abyss below them, and always with them, the knowledge that if something happened, they were on their own. It was true that the U.S. still had a strong and able infrastructure, but sending a scud missile into some forgotten corner of the earth was one thing. Rescuing sailors from a wrecked ship was another. The oil companies were smart to lobby for an airfield in the Baltic, and even smarter to ask the military to fund it.

"Before we go," Bert said as they were on their last rounds of drinks and their plates had been cleared.

"Here we go," Allen said.

"I know you don't have a name. I'd like a name, but I respect our friendship too much to press for it. Two last questions. First"—and Bert was careful to make this sound like the throwaway question—"does Capital PAC mean anything to you?"

"I don't think so. Like backpack?"

"No, like P-A-C. Basically an organization that might be officially funding your project."

"What's their deal?"

"Pro-capitalist agenda, I don't know. So far they haven't made any donations to any candidates, so there's limited information available, but there's a rumor it was the slush fund for your airfield."

"First I've heard of it," Allen said. "I assumed the Navy was funding us. At least, they're who I'm contracting with."

"Fair enough."

"And the second question?"

Bert leaned in, his real question already answered. He could see Allen had never heard of Capital PAC, and if he hadn't been in touch with the financing, Allen wasn't the man to give him real information. Still, he might be able to help with the question of Harry's successor. "Can you tell me this: has anything changed about your project recently? Is the airfield still a go?"

"You mean since your Estonian contact 'disappeared'?"

Bert waited.

"Look, Bert, everything I do is above board. Are there dirty operatives in the system? You bet, but by the time someone pulls funding together and issues the first purchase order, the machine is up and running. I don't know who your Estonian was or what he had to say about my airfield, but they weren't running the show."

"Who's running it?"

"My contacts are all in procurement. The Navy has issued a request-for-proposal, and we won a bid. If you're looking for someone in charge, look to your own agency. Or the Pentagon. Or I don't know."

"That's all I needed to know," Bert said.

Even though Harry Cope was dead, whatever role he served continued. Bert felt like nailing down corruption in the agency was like identifying a black hole. You knew it by the stars getting sucked into its orbit, but he didn't yet have the necessary equipment to see the corruption in itself. Someone in the agency had set up Capital PAC, ostensibly to promote American interests but with the hidden agenda of promoting the transnational interests of the oil companies. The PAC was funding the airfield, and someone in his agency was getting kickbacks to jumpstart the project. It was a far cry from old Everett Archer's financial wheeling and dealing, shorting currency when he had a tip that the CIA was about to orchestrate a coup, but it was the same principle: shady dealing, two sets of financial books, private profit at the expense of public policy.

He still needed a name, two names actually: whoever inherited the mantle from Everett Archer, and whoever inherited Harry Cope's side of the business. The accountant and the lawyer, the spy and the heavy.

Bert paid the tab and stood in the sandy parking lot of the seafood restaurant. He watched Captain Allen give a wave and stumble off to his Miata. When the captain had driven off, Bert was still leaning against his car, listening to the silence along the water. From here, where Shem Creek joined the Cooper River at Victory Point, he could see the lights of Charleston's market and battery. The spires of churches along the peninsula. Somewhere in the Holy City, there lived a shadow. Bert had been chasing this shadow half his career, and now, for the first time, he felt like he'd seen the shift in light out of the corner of his eye. He may not have the names, but the airfield project confirmed the names existed. If he were going to catch the shadow, the airfield project was his last best hope.

Chapter Thirteen

FRIDAY MORNING, after Jarman filed his report on Wyatt Brewer, Penelope got up early and went to the gym with the other ambitious five a.m. exercise enthusiasts. Three years into her new life as a powerlifter, she was still single but was ready for two plates on her back squat. While everyone else at the gym tortured themselves on the treadmill or haphazardly worked the isolation machines, she began warming up in the power rack. Today she was trying a heavy single squat and felt a knot in her gut over the milestone weight. Upward of a thousand squats, a tweaked neck and more than enough bruises and strains that she shouldn't feel nervous, she nevertheless felt about a barbell the way she felt about firearms. You either hit your target or you didn't. You either lifted the weight or you didn't. You could cheat on the margins, but on a heavy squat to parallel, you either stood back up and racked the weight, or you dropped it on the safeties. That was what she loved about it: the clarity of the endeavor. In a world of fog and nuance, equivocation and deception, the barbell told you the truth.

When she'd first joined her brother's gym, she got a lot of unsolicited advice—about the width of her stance, about her knees, about the need to mix in some cardio, about how it just wasn't functional to lift big weights. Personal trainers were the worst. Maybe they were concerned about liability, or maybe they were just weak themselves, but they never failed to stop by and tell her to be careful with those big plates. They were almost always men, and she could almost always hear a *little lady* implied at the end of their mansplaining. Well. She'd stuck with it, and in her first few months at the gym in Charleston, she'd heard more of the same well-intentioned advice, packaged with a Lowcountry lilt. Then something happened. She graduated from one plate to two on her dead-lift, so now the bros in the free weight area left her alone.

This morning she finished her warm-up sets in a hurry and felt great as she loaded the final thirty pounds on the bar. She had a dance mix streaming through her phone, and she adjusted the earbuds and clicked forward to find a good track. There weren't many people here today. A couple treadmills buzzing, one skinny dude doing curls, a steady thrum of whirring, and music from a spin class in the other room. She gripped the bar and held her head down between her shoulders, as if in prayer, and then she slid under the bar and wedged it into her back. The weight was fine when she stood up with it and walked out, and the weight was fine when she took a few breaths to steady herself before taking a deep belly-breath. She squatted below parallel, hit her bounce, and was just starting to grind back up when her music abruptly shut off and her ringer buzzed in her ears.

The distraction was enough to break her concentration, and after a moment of quivering mid-squat, she slammed the bar on the safety rails. She cursed as she stood up and shook out her shoulders. Then the skinny dude and one of the staffers were by her side asking if she was all right. Her phone was still ringing through her earbuds, and the blood pounding in her head gave her a dizzy deafness.

"What?" she asked as she pulled out an earbud.

"Are you all right?" the staffer asked, holding up his hand as if trying to decide whether to steady her.

"I'm fine," she said. She pulled her phone out of her back pocket and rejected Bert's call.

"You shouldn't have your cell phone on the floor."

"I wasn't taking a call," she growled.

"That's a lot of weight," the staffer said. "You should be careful. Looked like you were grinding pretty hard there. You don't want to hurt yourself."

"Thank you, Captain Obvious," she wanted to say, but she smiled with her lips pursed. She flexed her shoulders and could tell she hadn't tweaked anything, so after she called Bert, she'd have to come back and set the weight up all over again. She hoped the staffer and Mr. Skinny were gone by then, and she hoped the staffer wouldn't try to talk to her or, heaven forbid, come over to spot her. She might have to find a new gym.

She did a few squats with the bar to loosen up and then started adding weight again. An old Kesha hit streaming through her earbuds, she gripped the bar and ducked under it and wedged her shoulders into it. You didn't have to be a spy to sense when people were staring at you. As a woman in yoga pants in a weight room, she knew when eyes were on her, lust and skepticism and envy over the weight. Screw 'em. They could stick with their ellipticals and functional training. *Don't stop, make it pop, DJ, blow my speakers up.* She had a long day on the road ahead of her, to be followed by weeks of uncertainty as they figured out what ISD would be without Harry Cope. She needed a strenuous workout to carry her through, so she took a breath and stood up with the weight and walked it out. Still sensing the eyes on her, she squatted it once. Twice. And grinded out a third rep. Yelled to get to lockout.

She was crying with relief when she set the barbell back in the rack. Lower back tight, shoulders scraped, but she'd done it. Whatever else was in front of her, they couldn't take that away from her. Without looking around at the shadows watching her in the gym, she re-racked the plates, picked up her water bottle and her keys, and walked to the locker room to shower before she hit the road for the funeral.

"Hey, Bert," she said from the parking lot when he answered her call back. "What's going on?"

"I'm sorry to call you so early, but I thought you might already be up and on the road."

"I'm heading out in about an hour. Was just trying to work out."

"Good. Well, I wanted to get your take on Jarman's report last night. He said he briefed you on this reporter who was nosing around out at Folly yesterday."

"Right. Yeah."

"You find anything else on him?"

Her gym was in a strip mall in West Ashley next to a FedEx office and a Starbucks on one side and a Sprint store and a vitamin shop on the other side. In the parking lot, a woman had gotten out of a minivan with a walker and an oxygen tank, and she appeared to be struggling to load a package onto her walker. "Just what I filled Jarman in on," Penelope said.

"Well. Okay. The thing is, his name showed up in my database of Harry Cope's contacts."

"Oh yeah?"

"Yeah, just one reference, more of a footnote than anything. You remember how we had him audited a while back? Got a list of his firm's clients going back twenty years? Well, a few of those clients looked more promising than others for our purposes. Investment firms, construction contractors, anything military."

"Sure."

"I had a temp on rotation in the agency a few summers

ago and had him do some research into those firms, just to catalog what they did and who they worked with. Sometimes those second-order suppliers can be useful—either for information, or the group getting the payoff."

In the parking lot, the woman was still struggling with her package, so Penelope went over, pinned her phone with her shoulder, and picked up the box for the woman, who gave a self-deprecating laugh and said, "Thank you, dear." She started to say more but saw Penelope was on the phone. "Uh huh," Penelope said to Bert as she carried the woman's package into FedEx for her. "I'm not sure I'm following."

"You know a business is bigger than just the company, that thousands of contractors and suppliers help fill in the gaps. Say I'm a paper company working with your procurement department, I'm a first-order supplier. But if I hire someone to manufacture the paper for me, that person's the second-order supplier. It's how companies get past labor laws and evade taxes. Get deep enough into the supply chain, and you lose the trail. Shell companies within shell companies, and pretty soon you have just a guy doing a job off the books."

"I'm with you," Penelope said, back in the silence of her car.

"Well, Cope's audit revealed an investment advisory called Opal Developments was a major client. Now, Opal Developments handles primarily government contracts, to build bases overseas, so they've been under scrutiny. Have to file all kinds of paperwork. My temp combed through the Army procurement archives and pulled out all the reports on Opal Developments. Sure enough, Cope's firm is listed as a legal consultant, kept on retainer. But the real punch line is that buried in the paperwork, Opal at one point submitted a list of contractors —second-order suppliers—and our reporter has a line item under Cope's firm."

"I'm sorry, what?"

"Seems Mr. Brewer did a job for Cope's law firm when he

was in college, and the nature of that job was somehow related to Opal Developments. Because it was overseas, he fell into some type of government reporting net so his name was in the file."

"Overseas. What was the job?"

"I don't know if it was listed, but my temp just pulled the list of suppliers and the dates of service. I'm sending Jarman back to the Defense Department archives to see if there's anything else to it."

Penelope took a breath. She knew Bert well enough to know he didn't believe in coincidence. Charleston was a small town, so there were countless possibilities. Brewer had a summer internship with Harry's firm. Or Harry partnered with the college for some kind of work-study program. One of Harry's partners might have hired him. Or it could be a different Wyatt Brewer altogether.

As if anticipating her objections, Bert said, "It could be anything, of course, but I've seen major operations hinge on less. Every terrorist incident we've ever had has been anticipated by a paper trail of footnotes. What really troubles me isn't that Brewer showed up in a footnote. It's that he has such a large sum of investment accounts, dating back to his college years. That's the kind of financing we look for in our world."

"So we're adding him to our list of people to watch?"

"I think for the next couple of weeks, to see what he does. Who he contacts."

Penelope smiled. Bert was nothing if not consistent. He was always seeing the shadow in the alley. He saw traces of the prey where no one else did. She sometimes felt as though they were chasing Bigfoot. Where anyone else saw a cut in the mud or a broken tree branch, Bert saw evidence of a phantom. With Harry Cope dead, Penelope thought they might close the case and call it unsolved—or take it off the books altogether, a collection of evidence for a crime that never existed.

Bert, however, was certain the corruption that began with

the old officer, Everett Archer, continued within the agency. Bribes, currency shorts, payoffs, money laundering. Every day was a new theory, and until a few days ago, all roads had led to the officer's son-in-law, Judge Harry Cope, a.k.a., Buttercup. Now that he'd passed, their list of potential suspects had narrowed: Harry's wife, his remaining law firm partners, and the mystery reporter in Charleston.

Chapter Fourteen

THE DAY after reaching a number of dead-ends about the man on Folly Beach, Wyatt drove to the Carolina upcountry in search of other answers to other questions. Perhaps it was seeing Harry's obituary, or the girl in the street that had so resembled a young Mary Grace, or the mountain of cash he had quietly accruing interest in a South Florida investment account, but he felt the need to attend the old man's funeral. He arrived at the country church in Castle, South Carolina, on an auspiciously sunny Friday afternoon, a humble exit for a man of such accomplishments. Harry Cope may have died a well-regarded judge in Charleston, but he was born the son of a country mill worker. You never escaped where you came from in this life, try as you might.

At one time, Wyatt had known this area well. It was only a short jaunt up to Spartanburg or Gaffney, and all these mill towns had the same history: a big-money cotton operation, Depression-era labor, the hard-scrabble push for a life better than eking anything out of a drought-stricken mountain farm. Driving in, it was clear how much Harry had hit the lottery when he'd married the gal from Connecticut and hoofed it down to Charleston, using Lillian's inheritance and good sense to make his fortune in business.

Coming off the interstate, Wyatt passed piney woods and cow pastures, and then he crossed the old bypass, which was still nothing more than a two-lane highway littered with fast food joints and a general store. Past the mill hill, the houses jammed together like tobacco plants dried up and cut down to stalks for the winter. The mill was long gone, torn down for safety, but a lone brick smokestack still towered over the mill hill, a reminder to the poor who lived there that they came from trash and were trash still. The best they could hope for was to work for the man. As a Gaffney boy himself, Wyatt picked up these signals of a small town, and although he'd been gone for half a life, the region still had a pull on him.

Then he crossed the river and the railroad tracks, and he was in town proper. The courthouse with its giant black and white clock tower. The main street shops with the mock-Roman columns, as if trying to suggest some connection to ancient power. The proprietors likely were still freemasons, with their rituals and signs and rah-rah ceremonies. Wyatt's grandfather had been one of them. He'd never had the interest himself, but was unable to tune it out. At the town square, a star of roads converged, a Confederate obelisk and cannon standing in proud defiance of the lost cause.

The First Baptist Church was a simple brick building nearly indistinguishable from the crumbling businesses beside it. He parked in a lot across the street next to a couple of stringy middle-aged ladies smoking Virginia Slims, who eyed him as though he were a cousin they couldn't place. He nodded and walked across the cracked gray pavement to the church itself, into a yellowed interior anteroom that smelled of mildew and reminded him of church potluck dinners from his childhood. Always a dusty old building, always a smell reminiscent of old people. Why couldn't you ever keep a church clean? Make it smell nice and you might recruit more members.

A receiving line to the right, people milling around to the left, and a doorway in the center to the sanctuary. A man with big glasses and a long face gave him a program and a pen to sign the guestbook. "I'm sorry for your loss," the man said, and only then did Wyatt realize he worked for the funeral company or the church and was not part of the family. Of course, given how small a town Castle was, the man doubtless knew Harry, by name if not in person.

"Thank you," Wyatt said, looking around.

The receiving line had two old guys (a beanpole and freemason), and an elderly woman, and it took him a moment to realize she was Lillian, Harry's widow, transformed mightily since he'd seen her last. Twenty years ago, she'd had crow's feet and cropped hair but otherwise was a vibrant middle age. Now she was stooped over, with scars on her cheeks and iron veins running through hair quickly fading to the color of pavement. Beside her was a young woman—*the* young woman from King Street yesterday—and he suddenly understood why he was here. Mary Grace had always been the one he loved. Whoever this young girl was, she was clearly related, and the sight of her took him right back to those crazy, frantic, carefree, love-sick months at twenty years old when his life hit pause. A romance on a sun-drenched college campus, and everything after was a funnel leading him here.

When she saw him, Lillian narrowed her eyes and held his gaze for a moment as if to place him. "Wyatt," she said finally. She gave a half-smile, half-laugh, and said, "What are you— you're here."

"Hey, Lillian. I heard the news."

"You write the news."

"I do, and everyone in my newsroom knew about Judge Cope. I hope it's okay that I came."

"It's perfect." She let him lean in to kiss her cheek, and she said, "He always thought fondly of you. Years later he would still reference 'that nice Wofford boy.' Thank you for coming." She held his hand a moment longer than she should have, and then she introduced him to the girl, "This is my granddaughter, Molly Keagan. Though she's a Cope through and through."

"I'm sorry for your loss," Wyatt stuttered.

Molly Keagan gave him an unnerving stare with precocious green eyes but said nothing. Her long hair made her look young, but her curves suggested womanhood. Her gaze told him nothing about what was happening behind her eyes.

And then he was shunted onward in the receiving line, where he shook the beanpole and the freemason's hands, whoever they were, and fled to a pew in the sanctuary.

The casket was open by the altar, but he had no business viewing the body. The sanctuary had been renovated—dark wood and a modern look with exposed beams in the ceiling, fresh white walls, and windows set in bright blues and greens. The image of St. Francis with his animals, Mary and her son, Jesus and his flock, one of the apostles on a boat on the water. Wyatt sat near the back and admired the stained glass while he waited for the organ to start and for the family to be ushered in. He'd grown up in a church like this, conservative Presbyterians with a choir up front and a preacher's severe sermons about how difficult it was to get into heaven. Before Covid, he'd started RCIA to become a Catholic, and he preferred the sacrament of reconciliation to the doctrine of the elect. The instructions were clear, even if he'd been unable to clear his conscience. He still had work to do on his soul, that much was certain.

The organ started up and the family proceeded in and took their seats up front. The beanpole accompanied Lillian to the front of the church, kept putting a hand on her back while they walked. He may have been trying to comfort her, but he came off like a gangly teenager who didn't know how to act naturally.

An old woman beside him was saying something.

"I'm sorry?"

"I said it's going to be a mason's funeral."

"What does that mean?"

"They'll do a little ceremony after the ceremony. Heavy on pomp and circumstances. I reckon Earl there will deliver the eulogy."

"Uh-huh."

"I used to date Harry's brother, Tommy," she continued, apparently unconcerned by the non-sequitur. "He had a mason's funeral too. I guess they were all members, though my husband was never part of all that. He was a decent man, but he didn't go in for all the ceremony. More of a lone wolf, you might say. Like yourself?"

Wyatt said nothing.

"You from around here?"

"I grew up in Gaffney."

"And how did you know Harry?"

"Oh, I did some work with him, many years ago."

"Oh, that's nice. He was so successful in business. One of the more successful from his generation, I'd say. You know, I never would have pegged a Cope for amounting to much. Back in the Depression, they came out of nowhere and started buying up property in parcels west of town. My daddy never could figure it, how country folks could come in under hard times and just make a life for themselves, but people found all kinds of ways back then. That before Harry's time anyway."

"Uh-huh. Hey, I'm trying to figure out the story of his granddaughter up there. I'm not sure I knew he had any grandchildren."

"Oh yes, that was from his daughter, God rest her soul."

He must have looked perplexed, because the old woman's

eyes lit up, glad to be able to deliver some juicy gossip. "His daughter died when she was out of college, don't you know. Raised her in Charleston and sent her back to the upcountry to a finishing school up in Spartanburg, where she promptly got pregnant."

His heart clenched. "She had the baby in college?"

"Oh, I can't remember the exact year, but right about the time she finished at Converse."

"Was she involved with the father?"

The woman pursed her lips and rolled her eyes. "I don't believe the family ever knew the father, but since they were down state, I couldn't say. One day she was up at school, the next she had a baby, the next she was in a car accident. Harry and Lillian raised the granddaughter, but they sent her up to Yale where she promptly changed her name and forgot where she came from. Learned their lesson with finishing schools, I reckon, though it remains to be seen how she'll turn out. Plus, Lillian's got some Connecticut family, don't you know."

"I don't think I did." He wanted to ask more about the baby but was too shocked to think straight.

"Oh yes, can trace her mother's family all the way back to the Mayflower, I believe. If I understand correctly, her mother made good when she met a Yale man, and then her daughter fled south. What those Yankees must have thought. Well, it was nice to talk to you, Mr. ..."

"Wyatt."

"Mr. Wyatt. I'm glad I got to see you today."

At the start of the service, the preacher barreled through Harry's biography, embellished details for his audience, about hard work and the man coming from salt-of-the-earth Christians. Maybe some of it was true, but the man Wyatt knew was not the kind of gentle soul you'd read about in *Reader's Digest*. With the wisdom of twenty years, Wyatt had come to know Harry as a cold and manipulative businessman, who would use his daughter's naïve boyfriend to run a nefarious errand. Although Mary Grace died in an accident, Wyatt couldn't help but feel her father was somehow to blame. The whole of religion may not have stuck with him, but the story of original sin rang as true as anything he'd ever read.

"Now, Harry was a successful man," the preacher said. "A family man and a judge down in Charleston, but to get where he was he faced trials and tribulations, which are inevitable in this life. Trials and tribulations. He had a brother who died in service to his country, he had two loving parents who went to be with the Lord when their time came, a daughter who died too young. But through it all Harry endured. As it says in Lamentations, *Because of the Lord's great love we are not consumed, for His compassions never fail. They are new every morning; great is your faithfulness.* Harry was faithful. He raised a family, a beautiful granddaughter Molly, he served his country as a judge in charge of mercy and justice."

The preacher went on in that vein, sharing more details about the old man, details he could have gleaned from Wyatt's newspaper article as easily as anywhere else. It was clear that Harry hadn't set foot in this church in decades and had never met this preacher, but it was all a show for the widow—and the granddaughter, if she was a believer. Something told Wyatt she was not. Lillian and Molly sat up front—the girl's blonde hair so big her head looked like it might topple. The girl held her grandmother's hand and stared placidly up at the preacher, perhaps a little bored, Wyatt thought.

Beside her, Lillian, the beanpole, and the freemason looked appropriately somber. She had a trace of red under her eyes as though she'd cried late into the night, but her eyes were dry today. Now that he took her in, in her dotage, he was startled to see the transformation was not as dramatic as he'd first thought. Beyond the surface markers of aging, he could see the same woman from twenty years ago, when she would have been not much older than he was now. He was struck with the thought that the next twenty years would go equally fast, and he would be there, waiting for his turn to shuffle off this mortal coil.

With the instinct people have when someone is watching them, Lillian glanced back and caught his eye. He pursed his lips and nodded to her, and then looked away.

The preacher wrapped up with a metaphor about rest at the end of a long day. "Death isn't a period. It's a comma that marks the end of the long day and the beginning of the evening when you go home to Jesus. As it says in First Corinthians, *Listen, I tell you a mystery: We will not all sleep, but we will be changed—in a flash, in the twinkling of an eye, at the last trumpet.*"

When he finished, everyone sang a few hymns—"Victory in Jesus," "It Is Well Within my Soul," "That Old Rugged Cross"—and then it was over, the mystery of the end thoroughly gone over, hope given to the hopeless, comfort doled out to the faithful. Wyatt was neither hopeless nor faithful, but rather was in the fog of his midlife malaise. Been there, done that, bought the t-shirt for most things in life, and he was feeling okay about the inevitable *last trumpet* himself.

Wyatt ducked out a side door rather than try to speak to Lillian again. Although it would have been best to drive straight home to Charleston, stop drinking, quit his casual flings, go back to church, confess his sins, and try to get his life into some sort of shape, he instead pulled into the Hardee's on the bypass and placed a call to his mother.

Chapter Fifteen

VISITING Castle County for Harry's funeral, Penelope discovered small towns still existed in pockets of America. She'd grown up in suburban Virginia, which could feel like a small town when you saw someone you recognized at Kroger, but which ultimately was an anonymous non-place. Castle, meanwhile, was still a town of less than five thousand, and a meaningful percentage were at the funeral. Everyone appeared to know each other, which made it easy for her to spot the only other outsider.

Whatever Bert had been hoping to find out at the funeral, having the Charleston reporter show up surely would be at the top of the list. Penelope had little sensibility for God and fate, but seeing Wyatt Brewer here a day after the man's file landed on her desk, she felt like a player in drama already written. It was an eerie feeling and one she didn't care to interrogate.

Wyatt shoved his hands in his pockets and shuffled with a stoop through the receiving line, studying the room just as she was studying him. She caught his eyes once but quickly turned away to flip through the program. If he was here to meet someone for a business deal, he was doing a remarkably nimble job of playing the part of a respectful visitor.

He stood a head taller than Lillian Cope, and as he leaned over to greet her, Penelope thought she saw a flash of something in the widow's face—more than recognition. Almost titillation. Here was someone she knew, from some time ago, disrupting what would otherwise have been a scripted funeral. He shook hands quickly with a pretty young blonde standing next to Lillian, and then he took a seat a few rows in front of Penelope and busied himself with the program.

Penelope couldn't remember from Brewer's file the exact town where he was from, but he looked at ease here among the country folk. He was trim, slightly disheveled, ill at ease in a suit. There was something jovial in his carriage, like he wore bright white sneakers or Converse All Stars on the weekends and was not above enjoying a lollipop.

After the service, she scuttled out to her car and pretended to fiddle with her phone as she furtively watched the other attendees mill about. The sun was already beginning to set, the shadows long and the light burnished with that somber hue that signified the end of things, yet no one seemed in a hurry to go to the graveside. A few people looked downright happy to be out, as though the funeral were the most excitement they'd had all week.

She was about to get out to search for Wyatt when he emerged from the church, his fly unzipped, his hands in his back pockets. He watched Lillian and the pretty blonde get into the black Town Car at the front of the procession, and then got into his own vehicle—a green Chevy Colorado with an extended cab—and drove in the opposite direction.

She followed at a distance to a nearby CVS, where he pulled in and studied his phone for several minutes. He placed a call and got out to pace around his truck a few times. Then he returned to the pine-lined highway north.

On the Bluetooth, she gave Bert a call. His rumbling *hello* came through her car speakers like a drive-thru intercom.

"You'll never guess who showed up at the funeral."

"No," he said.

"Yes," she said, surprised but not surprised that Bert's mind already went there. That supported the possibility of Brewer as a real threat, and a chill passed down her spine. "Everything else about the service was in place and as you'd expect it, but he showed up solo, greeted the widow, and skipped the graveside service. I'm tailing him northwest on Highway 9, in a little town called Lockhart right now."

"Has he made you?"

"I don't think so. If he has, he's better than I'll ever be at this job."

"Well, keep your distance until we know what we're dealing with."

"Any idea where he might be going? Jarman had me build a file on him, but I wasn't expecting to see him."

"Gaffney," Bert said without missing a beat. "His mother still lives there."

"You've really zeroed in on this guy."

"You know I don't believe in coincidences. When I found out he was on Harry's payroll, I figured he might show up in our orbit."

She was trailing a hundred yards behind the Colorado, and plugged Gaffney into her GPS.

"You got an address for his mother? Might be good if I turned off here and caught back up with him there. I hate to lose him, but."

"Great idea. I can't get Jarman up there this evening, so it's worth the risk to keep you off his radar. Let me call you back."

"Hang on. One more thing. There was a young blonde woman at the funeral, in the receiving line next to the widow."

"Twenty years old, about five-nine? Long flowing hair and expensive taste in clothes?"

"You know her."

"I'll fill you in when you get back. Anything make you suspicious?"

"Just that she was there."

"I wouldn't worry about her right now. Jarman's compiled a file on her already."

Penelope slowed and allowed Wyatt to pull ahead, and then she turned onto the next state highway. A moment later Bert texted her an address, and she took the roundabout path to get there.

Wyatt's mother lived in what would be a million-dollar mansion if it were located in Charleston. A Queen Anne on a corner with an enormous weeping willow shading the front lawn. Magnolias created a fence between her and the neighbors. Penelope thought she remembered from the file last night that Wyatt was raised by a single mom, father unknown. Perhaps he used his income from Harry to set his mother up in a house above their station.

She made one pass by the house to spot Wyatt's truck tucked in the driveway and then cruised around the block. She parked on what looked to be a main row of homes, far enough from Wyatt's mother that he would have to be looking for her to see the car, and would likely have to come out to see the car was occupied. She hoped none of the other neighbors would be concerned enough about a strange vehicle to call the police. It looked like that sort of town.

Like the funeral in Castle, everyone saw the aberration.

After a while, Wyatt and his mother came out and headed off. Rather than follow them, Penelope took a chance and walked up to the house. It appeared dark, but she rang the bell to be certain.

The house was in shadows here at day's end, the sun nothing but a bleed in the west. The block was empty, so she checked a few windows and then went around back. There was an open window to the master bedroom, so she jimmied off the screen and climbed into the house, reattaching the screen behind her. It took a few moments for her eyes to adjust. The house smelled of laundry detergent and cigarette smoke. It reminded her of an aunt's house, a woman fastidious in the order she kept in her home but out of control in her vices.

Careful not to touch anything, Penelope crept through the downstairs, inspected the wastebasket—a newspaper, some plastic wrapping, an orange peel—but saw nothing that indicated *crime syndicate* or *money laundering*.

In one of the upstairs bedrooms, Brewer's suitcase lay open on the floor by the bed. A change of clothes, his laptop, a paperback copy of an old James Lee Burke novel. She opened the laptop, but she didn't have time to try a guessing game with the password. If Brewer was anyone of consequence, he likely had a random combination of letters and numbers, and maybe the security set so that he would get an alert if someone tried to log in without the right password.

She folded it back and returned it to the suitcase, and then she nosed around the bathroom. She risked turning on the bathroom light but found nothing. She clicked off the light and sat on the bed in the dark and thought for a few moments. The simple—innocent—explanation was that he read about Harry's death, and feeling a pang of nostalgia he decided to attend the funeral. Bert may have no use for coincidences, but he grew up in a different era, one where order and reason were the guideposts of the day. Penelope, raised in the age of reality TV and the internet, school shootings and the War on Terror, felt more comfortable with uncertainty, chaos, and chance. For her, life was the proverbial random walk, nothing but a coin toss separating truth from fiction.

Still. Bert had locked his sights on Wyatt Brewer, and Bert's instincts were better than Jarman's. If Jarman could pick out the signal in the noise, Bert, without hearing anything, could tell you a signal existed and send you off to find it.

The house was deadbolted from the inside, so she scuttled out the same window she'd come in, replacing the screen for the second time. She barely made it back to her car when Wyatt's truck returned. She considered phoning Bert again but had nothing to report. She would wait until the lights went out in the house and then see if she could find a motel. Over the next hour, she watched Wyatt drinking a few glasses of wine on the porch. Their file said he was a recovering alcoholic, but he didn't appear to be drinking out of a mania, or anxiety, or anything that would suggest he was in a downward spiral. He seemed genuinely bored out there, smoking and scrolling through his phone and rocking steadily.

Penelope was about to call it a night when a black VW hatchback pulled up and the girl from the funeral got out. Penelope noted the girl's license plate and shot a quick text to Bert and Jarman. Her phone buzzed repeatedly, but she was too busy squinting at the porch and debating whether to try to creep up to eavesdrop.

After a short conversation, Wyatt pulled out his phone and appeared to be taking the girl's contact information, and then she left him alone again on the porch. He'd poured the final glass of wine, so he went in and got another bottle and drank most of it, smoked one cigarette after another, and then he swayed into the house and shut off the light.

Penelope scrolled through the messages on her phone and stopped on the main message from Bert.

Pack it in now.

Come back to Charleston.

More soon.

Chapter Sixteen

WYATT'S GRANDPARENTS were long gone, but his mother, Carla, still lived in the old family homestead a short ways from downtown Gaffney. The town had long since commercialized, now known as an interstate pit stop and for its outlet malls, but if you got away from the I-85 sprawl, you could still find traces of a quaint southern community, a two-story brick town surrounded by peach orchards. His grandfather had managed the service department for the local Chevy dealer, and Wyatt remembered spending much of his childhood there among the smell of oil and tires, burnt coffee.

His mother had never figured out what she excelled at. Bagged groceries for a while, sold clothes at the Gap outlet. Now she worked as an office manager for a landscape firm whose owner she went to church with. Wyatt had no idea if she was capable at her work or found any fulfillment from it, but she'd been with the company going on ten years and was close to cashing out at sixty-two. Thanks to his grandfather, her house was paid off, so he wasn't worried about her security. Although he had the money to support her if it came to it, and would without question, he'd never breathed a word of the money in the bank to anyone but an attorney and his accountant.

She was on the front porch when he drove up, looking largely the same as always. She dyed her hair dark and still smoked Virginia Slims, a habit he knew she'd never quit. She dropped a butt into a clay pot by the rocker and came down to give him a hug on the sidewalk.

"So you're still thinking about your old college girlfriend," she said when he told her why he was in town. "That's why you never got married?"

"It's not like that," he said, "and who says I won't get married one day?"

She squeezed his elbow, and he could see the wheels turning in her eyes. She could be witty when she wanted, but today she coughed into her hand and said, "Well, come on in. I've got your bedroom made up for you."

"I appreciate it. I could have gone on back to Charleston."

"No, no. I'm glad you stopped by. We'll have to go out to eat, though. I don't keep much on hand."

"That'll be fine."

He followed her through the house and up the stairs to his old bedroom. She'd moved into the master a few months after his grandmother passed, but Wyatt had never been upgraded from the smallest bedroom. It was odd that she still called it *his* bedroom, but he supposed it always would be, that you never fully grew up in the eyes of your parents. Or your parent, as the case may be.

"Well. I'll let you get settled, if you need to."

"I'll just drop off my bag," he said. "I can meet you back on the porch."

"I wanted to enjoy the weather while we've got it," she said.

"I don't blame you."

When he went out and sat next to her a few minutes later, she was smoking another cigarette. "You want one?"

"I'm all right."

"I guess you're old enough, if you change your mind."

"So, how are you?"

"About the same over here. I'm still working for Bobby Henderson. They've got more work than they know what to do with, I don't know how he's going to manage it all when I finally retire. He needs to upgrade his bookkeeping software, but they don't listen to me. I'm just the secretary. What's the news out of Castle? Everyone in town come out for Harry's funeral?"

"Just about. The church had a sign saying last week's Sunday school attendance was nine. The week before it was six, so they're on an upward trajectory. Had about a hundred people there today."

"They take care of their own. I never appreciated that about a small town when I was young and looking to get out, but it has its charms. Though I guess you've found your own charms down in the Holy City."

"Charleston's a small town at heart."

She nodded like she understood the words he was saying, but had access to higher wisdom. That was the maddening thing about one's parents. No matter how much things changed, or how worldly you became, they always had a leg up when it came to the sheer volume of life experience.

Why he expected more from his mother at this point in their lives, he couldn't say. Perhaps no man ever lets go of the first woman in his life, and forever believes she who protected him in the womb and nursed him into being had reserves of wisdom to dole out over the course of his life. Deep down he knew Carla Brewer would have no answers for him. He was old enough to know the only true answer would be, "Oh, grow up. Be a man. Take your lumps and be glad you live in America. As a white man at that." If he wanted an honest answer from his mother, he suspected she harbored a deep rage when she looked at him and saw the incarnation of her ex-husband, another oblivious man looking for purpose without having to work too hard. What did Wyatt Brewer know about struggle and sacrifice, Carla might ask. If he only *knew* what it was like to be a woman in this world, his list of existential questions would go—poof! How did he get to forty years old without the wet blanket of reality smacking him across the head? My word, son, you don't know a thing.

This was the conversation Wyatt and Carla did not have, which meant they spent the evening skirting the surface of today's unseasonable warmth ("It was sleeting in Charleston yesterday," "Oh, here too"), the new real estate boom ("Bobby swears he's going to hire somebody to help me, but he's afraid it won't last"), and Brewer's work ("We're lucky to have a daily paper anymore, management's doing everything they can to kill it").

At nine o'clock, Carla announced she was going to bed to read for a while. "Good to see you, Wyatt. Help yourself to anything in the kitchen."

"Night, Mom."

When she was gone, he pilfered a couple of cigarettes from her pack on the counter and put them in his shirt pocket. Then he rifled through the fridge for something to drink when his eyes alighted on an open bottle of wine on the counter. He licked his upper lip and thought about placing a call to Bonnie, who would forgive him for leaving her, he knew. He also knew his mother hadn't left the wine out intentionally. Surely she'd just opened it last night and forgot about it when Brewer called.

He poured a glass and brought the bottle with him to the front porch.

Sleet in Charleston yesterday, sixty degrees in Gaffney this evening: South Carolina winter in a nutshell.

On his phone, he searched for Molly Keagan. The woman at the funeral said she was a blogger, but all he could find were her social media profiles. Facebook set to private, Twitter a bunch of links to her Instagram, Instagram a bunch of artsy photos of concrete at night. Typical twenty-year-old vanity until he found her Substack and saw a host of commentary about corporate denial-of-service attacks, social engineering, wedding dress resale scams, and the like. The little firecracker had a brash voice and talked a big game about late-stage consumer capitalism, and he smiled at the energy of her prose. Her copy would never fly in a newsroom—too much reliance on innuendo, too many ad hominem attacks and red herrings, too many unsubstantiated claims about shadowy entities and the dark net—but he appreciated her enthusiasm.

He refilled his glass of wine and smoked the second cigarette he'd swiped from his mother, and he put his phone away. It was quiet out here in the country. There was a lot to love about Charleston—the food culture, the arts, the history, the relative anonymity—but quiet it was not, at least where he chose to live. Even on James Island, you could hear the constant hum of cars on the main highway, and there was always a neighbor making a ruckus.

He debated whether to finish the bottle of wine when someone rolled up in a black VW Golf and cut the lights in the drive. He watched the shadow of the young woman emerge from the darkness. As he'd felt at the Swamp Fox restaurant yesterday morning, he was caught between today and twenty years ago, the girl here and Mary Grace there.

"I was just googling you," he said to Molly Keagan when she walked up to the front porch. "I found your Substack."

"What do you think?"

"You've got a lot of energy, but your commentary's a little under-baked."

"That's all for show." She paused with one foot on the steps, as though waiting for permission to join him. "You have to have a brand if you want to get ahead."

"And your brand is what? Anarcho-capitalist? Neo-Marxist?"

"Young people are getting organized. I like to keep up with what's going on."

"So you can join in?"

"So I can use it to my advantage."

He poured the rest of the wine into the glass and said, "You're welcome to join me but I just killed the bottle. If you're even old enough to drink."

"I seldom drink," she said, and she sat on the other rocker.

"Lucky you. So what can I do for you, Molly Keagan?"

"Why were you at my grandfather's funeral today?"

"That's the question of the day." He raised the bottle in a mock toast. "I'm afraid I don't have an answer for you. I knew your mother, once upon a time."

"I know."

"Do you?"

"I think I know more about you than you know about me, at this point," she said. "I heard the story about your adventure in Madrid. My grandfather always thought highly of you, which I guess is why he never told you he knew about the money."

"What money?"

She smiled. "The money you were supposed to deliver to a man in Madrid, but instead kept when you found the man dead."

Wyatt took a gulp of wine. "That's quite a story. Your grandfather told you that?"

"My grandmother. This afternoon."

"If something like that happened, I think your grandfather would have come after me himself. I haven't heard from him in almost twenty years."

"Yet you came to the funeral."

"You'll understand when you're older. Maybe it's a guy thing, but in middle age you start thinking about the doors you didn't walk through."

She pulled out a vape pen and took a few practiced puffs.

Then she said, "You're lucky no one ever came after you for that money."

"Your grandmother tell you that, too?"

"I deduced it. See, if you stole half a million dollars from my grandfather, he wouldn't have let you get away with it. Since he didn't come after you, either you didn't steal it or it was someone else's money. My grandmother says you took it, therefore you dodged a bullet."

"That's pretty far-fetched. Do I look like I've been sitting on that kind of cash?"

She smiled. "Who knows? She didn't tell me everything."

"Yet here you are, with half a story and making an accusation your grandfather never did."

She took another puff from the vape, which had a synthetic mint smell. "You don't have to worry," she said. "I'm not here trying to hit you up. I'm here because I need some help with a job of my own."

"And you think I'll help you because I once did a job for your grandfather?"

"I think you'll help me because I'm your daughter."

Chapter Seventeen

DRIVING BACK from the upcountry Friday night, Penelope got drowsy south of Columbia, when the interstate miles became endless and the land was flat and barren. She stopped for coffee and snacks at a travel plaza and was about to pull back onto the highway when she got a call from an unknown number.

She thought it might have been Bert, but was surprised by the sound of humming when she answered. A woman's voice said, "Hi, Penelope, it's Diane Neubecker."

"Oh hey."

"I take it you're back home? Did I wake you?"

"No, I'm heading back to Charleston now."

"From Harry Cope's funeral?"

"Yeah, how did you know?"

"Bert already filed his status report, and I saw you were on the road today. Any news?"

"Eh, I've got a few loose ends, but I'm not sure what I'm looking for at the moment," she said, uncertain how much she should reveal about Wyatt, Molly, and their meet-up. She wanted to give Bert an update first before she went around him to his boss.

"Bert said you were looking at a reporter?"

"That's right. He's working on an article about a dead man on the beach. Did Bert fill you in on that?"

"Only that it was a person of interest. Do you think the reporter is connected to something deeper?"

"I don't know."

She must have betrayed hesitation, because Diane said, "You don't have to worry about what you tell me. Bert should be putting all of this in his reports. How has it been working with him lately, by the way?"

"Bert? Great."

"How's he doing now that Harry Cope has passed? I know he's been chasing after him a long time, perhaps longer than he should have."

"I guess he's doing all right. I know he desperately wants to find a connection between Cope and someone else, and this feels like our last chance before the trail runs cold."

"And the reporter might be your guy?"

Penelope was still parked in the gas station lot, and she strained to hear over the hissing of a semi driving by. "I don't think so," she said finally. "He might know more than your average civilian, but he doesn't strike me as an operative."

"Why not?"

"The way he carries himself." She wasn't sure how to explain it other than to say Wyatt Brewer sort of schlepped. He wasn't a man you would trust to lead an operation. A kindly middle manager, perhaps.

"But he was at the funeral," Diane said.

"He was."

"Did he meet with anyone?"

"Actually, he did. We think he might have known Harry, or his daughter, years ago. The granddaughter met him afterward."

"Do you know why?"

"No. My best guess is she knew he knew her mother. Her

mother died a while ago, so maybe she was looking for a connection."

"How long was their meeting?"

"Less than an hour. They talked on his mother's porch and then the girl took off. He didn't place any calls or go anywhere afterward. I waited until he went in and turned a light out, and now I'm on the road home."

"Good work, Penelope. Listen. Do me a favor, and keep an eye on Bert."

Penelope opened a bottle of Bai and took a slow sip before asking, "How do you mean?"

"See how he's doing. I'm a little worried about him. As you said, this might be his last chance to catch somebody before the trail runs cold, so I don't want him making any mistakes out of desperation."

"He's been on point so far this week."

"I'm sure he has. I'm sure he's told you the concern is someone working on behalf of old Everett Archer. Things have been a little unsteady here in NOVA, so if he was going to root around the Company, he might want to tread carefully."

Penelope waited for Diane to elaborate. She was never good at the political game. Although she occasionally felt a twinge of regret knowing some of the fellow officers she came in with, who were more adept at the human game, were stationed in plum locales, she nevertheless felt insulated in Charleston. Nobody much cared what went on in their little unit, which gave them plenty of leeway.

Diane continued, "I hate to ask, but has Bert said or done anything to give you pause about him?"

"Like what?"

"Oh, I don't know. Has he ever brushed off something you thought was an interesting lead, or run any operations without keeping his team informed? Disappeared for a while? Things like that."

"No, not that I've noticed."

"You're a strong officer Penelope. I think you would notice if anything was awry, so I'm probably just feeling sensitive about all of the changes in our office. It's important I know what's going on with my team, so if you would, check in with me on occasion, maybe every few weeks, to let me know how Bert is getting on."

"Will do," Penelope said, wondering if she would mention this call at all to Bert. Maybe Jarman could help her make sense of what was going on. She'd not heard anything about staff shakeups or restructuring—not that she would.

After Diane hung up, Penelope got back on the interstate and counted reflectors in the long stretch of dark road into Charleston. As the evening lengthened into the blurry hours past midnight, she fretted. She'd never had cause to worry over Bert or company politics, but now it felt as if the little world she inhabited was about to unravel. The barbarians were at the gates. The wind shook her Civic as she rode in silence the rest of the way home.

Chapter Eighteen

"I THINK you'll help me because I'm your daughter," the girl had said.

Wyatt was already thinking about the unopened bottle of wine on his mother's counter, the remaining cigarettes in the pack, another lost evening before him. Few moments in life had the power to reshape how you viewed everything, and Wyatt recognized he was living in one of those moments tonight.

Of course the girl was his daughter. There hadn't been enough time between his breakup with Mary Grace and her death for her to meet someone else. He should have realized it at the funeral when Lillian had introduced him to Molly Keagan, but you could forgive him for not jumping to the obvious conclusion.

The name: where had the name come from?

"My given name was Molly Cope," she explained, rocking beside him on the porch, "but how depressing is that? You *cope* with suffering. *Cope* is a mechanism for dealing with that which you don't want. Molly, I liked. That means *warrior*, but Cope? When I was fifteen, I found out we had some Irish ancestry. The Copes fled during the potato famine and landed in the Carolina mountains because they thought the mountains were like their homeland. They set up a successful life as farmers, and it would have been a beautiful story if the Depression hadn't sent them into the cotton mills. I wanted to reclaim my family history, so when I was eighteen I had my name legally changed before I started building my brand online."

"Why Keagan?"

"It means *fire*. Derives from an ancient Irish sun god. That's what I'm here to do: a warrior to set the world on fire."

"And how are you planning to do that?"

"Still TBD," she said. "But I have a project going that I think might be a good place to start."

"I'm sorry. I want to hear about your project, but I'm still trying to take all this in. How did you know I'm your father?"

"You dated my mother in college? Met my grandparents?"

"I did."

"Then you're my father."

"Your grandmother told you this?"

"Not in so many words. She's told me before that my father was an old boyfriend of my mother's. Her *true love*, my grandmother always said. Like something out of a movie. When you introduced yourself at the funeral, she had a look that, I don't know. You get a sense of things by watching body language. I asked her about you on the ride to the grave, and she was like, 'Oh him? He dated your mother in college.' I think she was distracted, so didn't remember she'd mentioned you quite a few times."

"It could have been another boyfriend."

"I don't think so. When you grow up without a mother—or a father—you hang onto every scrap of information out there. I've been building a picture of the two of you literally my whole life. Believe me, you're him."

"How do I match the picture you had?"

She gave him a once-over. "I can see why you made an

impression on my mother. I bet you were handsome in college."

"*Were?* Am I not still young and spry?"

"You've got a sad aura. I can see it in your eyes. Seriously, I don't think this is just me romanticizing. You look like a man who's had some grief."

"Like I lost the love of my life when I was your age, you mean?"

"You tell me."

"That was a long time ago," he said. "You never get over that first love, but it's a long life."

"And what have you been doing with yours?"

"Right now I'm wondering why Harry and Lillian never told me. They never approached me, never sent an email, never wrote a letter. You'd think they'd at least want the child support."

"I think my mother's death did a lot of damage to them. To their marriage. Honestly, I think it hurt them to have me around."

"I'm sure that's not true," he said, but perhaps she was onto something. Grief was jagged and could make you behave shamefully. Harry and Lillian no doubt thought the world of this young woman, but she was a mirror of her mother, perceptive and also possibly dangerous. "So," he said, trying to steer the conversation toward something concrete. "Here you are."

"Here I am."

"And what do you do now?"

"What do I do?"

"Yeah. You know, are you in high school, college, working, what?"

"Call it a gap year. I could give you all the Holden Caulfield details but the short version is I grew up with my grandparents in Charleston. I went to Ashley Hall—I know, I know. And I always kind of wanted to be a weather girl."

He laughed. "Now there's a career. What about your revolutionary Substack?"

"I had a teacher say *you got to dance with the one that brung ya.* It's easy to get an audience critiquing the system because nobody wants to hear their problems might be their own fault."

"Is that so?"

"It is, but I'm thinking it's time for a re-brand soon. Now that I'm maturing. Weather girls aren't just reporting the weather, you know. They give you good news to start your day. Even if it's raining, I can show you the silver lining. Sunshine on its way for the weekend."

He smiled. She had the same sly humor and uplifting cheer as her mother, and he remembered how much he enjoyed it. He said, "So you changed your name to Molly Keagan, weather girl and Irish goddess, here to set the world on fire with good news."

"Doesn't that sound like a great job?"

"It does." He thought about making a joke, *You've made your old dad proud*, but thought better of it. "So what's this job you mentioned?" he asked, thinking she might be fishing for something as simple as an internship with the newspaper.

"Well, here's the thing. I said I'm on a gap year, which isn't quite precise. At Ashley Hall, it was common for girls to get involved in some kind of cause. Several friends are in pageants, couple friends have started nonprofits. Our generation's all about doing something, you know? And I've found myself with a toe in the family business, if you will."

"And what is the family business?"

"My grandfather was in law, but as you know, he was something of a consultant for different groups, which is where I helped out. One thing I'm good at is spreading the news, so I've done a little PR work for some of his clients, helping out when they need a little social media boost, that kind of thing."

"Uh-huh." Journalists always had a skeptical relationship

with public relations folks. The dark side, they joked, doing a song and dance over here so you wouldn't look too carefully at the real thing over there.

"One of my clients needs a little boost. You wrote about a dead man on Folly Beach the other day."

"I did," he said, antenna up.

"Did you find anything in your investigation? About who he was or what he was doing out there?"

"Well, I'm still digging. The police are keeping it close to the vests."

"That's because they don't have anything either. They're just as baffled as every guy on the street."

"How do you know that?"

"I don't know how the man got there or what happened to him, but I can put you in touch with people who know who he was. They've got a story about him—a captivating story—and my favor from you is I'd like you to run it."

There it was. The shoe he'd been waiting to drop.

"I'm not looking for you to break your journalist's code," she said. "These are legitimate sources, and you can write what you like about them, but I think they have some important information to tell. I'm just here to make the introduction."

"And what information do these sources have?"

"They can tell you who the man was, and what his life was like over the last year. Chaotic. Violent. Full of intrigue. Your readers will love it."

"Mm-hmm."

"Look, just meet with them. You'll see."

"Who are they?"

"I'd rather let them tell you about themselves. I can tell you I've worked with one of the men for more than a year now. He's a respectable guy, very grandfatherly, used to be a captain or something in the Navy."

This interested him. He remembered the college girl out

on Folly yesterday telling him that she'd seen partiers on the beach shooting off fireworks. He doubted the dead man on the beach had been part of that crowd. More likely, the man had arrived on the beach alone—or possibly come in from the sea. And if he came from a boat in the ocean, a naval captain may have something interesting to tell him.

"How do I get in touch with this captain?"

"When you get back to Charleston, let's meet back up. I'll set up a date for us all. Early next week?"

He wanted to keep talking with her, to find out more about her and where she'd come from and what she was doing with her life. Eighteen, nineteen years old, and she was more put together than he was when he'd been twenty-eight, twenty-nine. It took him well into his thirties before he'd felt any measure of confidence in himself, so he was astounded by her assuredness. She was bold without being cocky. Articulate without being pretentious. Smooth without being slick.

She, however, seemed to intuit she'd won him over and that any lingering would open room for doubt. "I enjoyed meeting you today," she said. "I'm glad we finally got to connect."

"Yeah. I'm sorry to hear about your grandfather."

"Thank you. He was a good man, and I miss him already."

His mind was racing, but also fuzzy from the wine. His eyes were tired and his back hurt. He was trying to decide whether he should ask to give her a hug when she handed over a business card, stepped off the porch, and disappeared into the night with a *let's catch up in a day or two, call me*. Then she was gone, gone, gone.

He stared at the shadows in the yard and listened to the crickets, and then he went inside to open the other bottle of wine. He would wake up early, as he always did in his drinking days, and sneak out before his mother got up. He would drive home to Charleston hungover, unable to focus on anything but the blurred interstate foliage and the trucks on I-26. Was it blackmail, what she was asking of him? She knew about the old job with her grandfather, and about the money. If Harry had known about the cash but not come after him, then the money must belong to someone else, someone not to trifle with. Hadn't Wyatt known this all these years? The money was an albatross.

I have a job for you.

Perhaps there was an implicit threat about the money, but her trump card was that he was her father. What choice did he have?

Chapter Nineteen

THE MYTH of the small town in America may have died, but the dynamics of gossip and innuendo, eavesdropping and speculation, will always be with us. These forces are perhaps no more concentrated than the corporate workplace, where Human Resources established guard rails in place of old society manners, and the stink of human emotion—desire and jealousy and envy and boredom and anxiety—fermented just beneath the surface, same as in the small towns of yesteryear.

Take the *Dispatch*'s three-story offices on East Bay. The newsroom might once have been a chattering atmosphere of energetic reporters, smoking and furiously banging out copy before deadline. Some editor yelling something to the effect of, "Fitz! Where are we on A1?" while Fitz sat with a phone crooked on his ear, trying to get a last-minute quote out of the mayor's office, a stack of newspapers on the corner of his desk. A copyeditor looking over his shoulder, cigarette dangling from his mouth, as he pointed out issues with Fitz's hurried prose.

Today, the newspaper's office had a lazy and stilted corporate feel. The mission—*To be the trusted source for daily news*—in big stenciled letters on the wall at the front desk, a suite of cubicles on the first floor housing HR and IT employees decked out in business casual, stomachs rumbling while they waited for the lunch hour. News was on the second floor, and while there were still a few of the old open office plans, most of the staff had found their way to a cubicle. The photographers were the only ones who seemed to be in the offices regularly, and they didn't want to talk to anyone.

There weren't enough halogen lamp cans in the ceiling to light the floor appropriately, so everyone kind of squinted through the day, which gave them a somber and unfriendly appearance. Whether because of the lighting or the boredom or the emptiness of the floor, the newsroom was silent as a mortuary, but everyone on the second floor had the ears of a hawk and took note when Wyatt showed up Monday morning after slinking out last Thursday. Maybe not everyone had picked up on his less-than-gracious exit Thursday, but most of the newshounds understood there was some form of drama afoot. Those who saw him nodded politely when he came in, reeking of cigarettes, and furtively watched as he went into Bonnie's office and shut the door. He emerged half an hour later looking chastened and skulked to his cube, tucked in some earphones, and began work on a story.

Fitz broke the silence and brought a cup of coffee to Wyatt's cube. "What's the good word?" he asked, leaning against the soft cube wall.

The cranky photographers strained their ears to listen to the conversation.

"I don't think I've got one today," Wyatt said. "Maybe when we get the new building."

"Oh, that'll solve everything."

"What you working on?"

Wyatt's chair creaked as he leaned back and pulled out his earbuds. "Trying to follow up on the Folly Beach murder."

"So it's murder now?"

"That's an angle I'm testing. Cops are still putting me off, but I think it's clear he didn't just fill his pockets with rocks and wade into the Atlantic."

"Everyone loves a murder mystery. You talk with Bonnie today?"

"I did."

"And?"

"And what?"

"Seems like she wasn't the most pleased with you the other day. Said you stood her up for a lunch date."

"Yeah, I had a stomach bug. She understood. I met with her a few minutes ago, trying to figure out what angle to take here on the Folly guy. No-news as news. She had a good idea of trying someone in the Navy, and I found a contact who runs a shipping company."

"Oh yeah?"

"Still need to meet with him, of course. Probably head out there after lunch."

Fitz took a slow sip of coffee, aware he was performing for half the newsroom. Aware no one believed the line about the stomach bug but impressed with how confidently Wyatt gave it.

In the way of office gossip, however, as soon as it became clear there was no there-there to Wyatt's absence—not like the pair of sales reps who had been caught getting frisky in the parking garage elevator, or the previously-beloved senior executive who had been fired after a #MeToo sexual harassment allegation, or the time activist investors bought up the parent company's stock with the intention of orchestrating a takeover and insisted on touring the aging newspaper's facility for an analysis of *human capital* and *infrastructure*—the staff lost interest and remained only vaguely aware of continued murmuring between Wyatt and Fitz.

Then it was lunchtime, and the pinging of the microwave in the breakroom replaced the drone of conversation, and Wyatt slid out unnoticed. Nor did anyone take note when Fitz slipped out to the loading dock to smoke a cigarette and place a discrete phone call to let Bert Wilson know Brewer had returned to work.

In his conversation with Bonnie—during which he apologized profusely for skipping out on her, admitting that, yes, he'd done more drinking, and promised her he would be at a meeting tonight—Wyatt let her know about his new lead on the Folly story, omitting, of course, the source and the general questionability of the lead.

"The cops haven't given you any confirmation that it's a murder investigation?" she asked.

"Nothing but stonewalling."

"But your Navy guy, what's his name?"

"Don't know. I'm going to meet him over lunch."

"And he allegedly has an ID on our body?"

"That's what my source tells me."

"We'll need some kind of confirmation. Family members who say this person is missing, a plausible connection to the beach that night, and at least some kind of statement from the police, even if it's just they're looking into it."

"Won't be a problem."

"You say now. If I run this up to Reece, he may want it in the paper Sunday. That's a lot of fact-checking and sources to get straight this week. Lot of late evenings." She gave him a knowing look.

"I need a new project," he said.

"And of course you're already booked tonight."

"Right," he said.

An hour later, he was pulling out on East Bay to meet Molly and the mystery captain at a Panera Bread in North Charleston. All these magazine-worthy restaurants on the peninsula and they chose a sandwich-in-a-box spot.

The anonymous suburbs, Molly had said.

A dark brown Camry drove up behind him at a traffic light. Something tingled in his brain, a neuron that just wouldn't fire enough to carry a signal across the synapse. The car troubled him, even when he pulled onto the I-26 on-ramp and the car continued straight into the projects.

You're growing paranoid, he told himself, but he nonetheless felt eyes on him.

At the café, he bought an iced tea and scanned the dining room but didn't see Molly. He sat in a booth and sent her a quick Discord message. He didn't have her cell, just this encrypted messaging service and a Proton Mail address linked to her Substack.

He ticked through his inbox—mostly press releases from PR hacks, plus a few newsletters sharing bad news about the media industry—when Molly sat across from him and dropped a folder on the table.

"What's this?"

"Report from my Navy contact."

"He's on his way?"

She shook her head.

"I thought we were here for an interview." He raised his tape recorder as evidence.

"Everything's in the folder."

"Well, I'll need more than that."

"You haven't even read it."

"Whatever's in here, anyone could have written," he said, opening the folder anyway.

"It's notarized." She pointed to what looked like an official notary signature and stamp. "There's more than enough there for a respectable article."

"That wasn't what we discussed."

What she'd presented him with, however, was a very thorough analyst's report: public records, photographs, news clippings, maps, and a testimonial from Captain Allen, who was now the president of a logistics company out of North

Charleston. The notarized document was a first-person account, which at first glance appeared to be an explanation of how he hired a man named Stepan Boldavich, who was connected to a group of Estonian gangsters running a shipping scam. Boldavich had hoodwinked Allen, betrayed his trust as a benevolent employer, and used his computer systems to fudge import records, et cetera, et cetera.

"What am I supposed to do with this?" he asked.

"Write a story. Stepan Boldavich is your dead body on the beach. He was fronting a shipping scam, and from the circumstantial evidence, it appears he must have done something to fall out with some bad dudes. It's all very dramatic."

"I can see that. But I can't just write a story about this. Even if I wanted to, I'd need some secondary confirmation. Someone to back this up."

"Captain Allen couldn't make it today, but you can quote from his letter. Call his company, and someone there will confirm the quote."

"And Stepan Boldavich? How does he know this was the man on the beach?"

"He doesn't."

"I'm sorry?"

"Captain Allen employed Boldavich, but he didn't kill him. To my knowledge, anyway. I'm not sure he's even made the connection that an Estonian showed up dead on the beach. All the public knows is what you reported, and you didn't report anything about national origin. Yet."

"So if Allen doesn't know this is the man on the beach, who does?"

She demurred.

"How do you know Boldavich is the dead body?"

"You're a reporter. Don't you know how to do all this? Call around. Ask the police."

"The police don't have anything."

"That you know of. Call them again and ask for confirmation. Someone you trust. You'll get what you need. At least enough to ask: *Did an Estonian national show up dead on Folly Beach?* Your readers will love it."

"Who are you working for again?"

She smiled. "Does it matter?"

He felt a stab of concern toward her. To have access to this kind of information, and to have so much confidence in what appeared an outlandish tale, she was either a fantasist or working for someone with money and reach. He couldn't say which option he found more disconcerting.

He said, "If what you're giving me is real, you're working with some very connected people. I don't know what circles they run in, but you have to be careful."

"You're worried about me!"

"A little bit. I've never worked in that world, but I've covered enough from the outside to know it can be a hard fall. The kind of guys who run operations like this, they get where they are by being the smartest guys in the room, which is great until you're not the smartest guy in the room. And the thing is, they're so confident they don't even have an inkling of what's about to hit them until—bam! Enron. Bernie Madoff. The FTX crypto guy." He could see he'd lost her, and for a second realized what it must be like to be a frustrated parent, trying to get through to your hard-headed kid. "Be careful, is all I'm suggesting," he said.

"I appreciate your concern. *Dad.* But my employers are doing very good work. Very *important* work. Look, these aren't boom times for our country, right? We've got terrible leadership, we've got corrupt buffoons in charge, and we're still blowing up children with drone strikes. And for what?"

"Politics," he said.

"Right. My team versus your team. While we're all fighting over the idea of democracy, Congress is laundering money all over the world and Eastern European gangsters are driving policy. If they're not going to do their job of defending us, what do we need with government anyway?"

"What does this have to do with the dead Ukrainian?"

"Boldavich wasn't Ukrainian. He was Estonian."

"Whatever."

"Not whatever. They're two different countries," she lectured. "My point is, Boldavich was here to promote his country's interests. People are tired of hearing about Ukraine, but the entire Baltic is up for grabs. The energy companies are working both sides of the war, so my employers want to make sure Americans know what's at stake. It's time for us to get a slice of that money sloshing around."

"Using my newspaper."

"What are you here for if not to shed sunlight on the world's dark corners? You make this scoop, and it might get picked up by the *Washington Post* or the *New York Times*. They love a good Russian conspiracy."

He was speechless for a moment. "That's what you're peddling. A conspiracy about—what? Eastern European gangsters are laundering money out of U.S. companies?"

She held up the folder. "This makes it real. Allen is a real person, a former captain in the Navy. He has a real company, with a real ex-employee who ran a scam to rip off Americans. The employee working with some of the worst people on the planet. Take a look. Shine some light on it. That's all I'm asking."

Something in the way she said it made him think there was more here than she was letting on. She was too confident, brazen even, and he wanted to know what she was hiding.

"Who does this benefit?" he asked.

"Think of it as a form of justice. We let them know we're onto them. We're not here for them. We're here to fight corruption and promote what's best for our world."

"I don't buy it."

"All I'm asking is that you take a look. Make a few calls.

Run it by your editor. I'm not trying to make trouble for you. I'm not looking for parental guidance, or money, or any kind of bailout or apology."

"Apology for what? Until Friday, I didn't know you existed."

"Are you glad to know now?"

"I don't know. I mean, of course."

"You don't have other kids, right?"

He shook his head.

"So you're still processing."

He'd never felt the pull of parenthood, and seldom imagined himself with children, but in these past few days, something fierce and ancient had come dislodged inside him. His voice cracked, and he cleared some phlegm. "I missed it all," he said.

"All what?"

"Everything. The delivery. The diapers. All the fun stuff from when you were a little kid. I didn't even get the chance to be a dad when the boys started knocking. Or girls, I suppose."

"Boys," she said.

"All the stuff I was supposed to be there for, I wasn't. I'm not sure what to do now, to be honest."

"Well, to be honest, most of my friends had dads at home, and they missed a lot as well. Working too much, traveling for business."

"But they were there for the important things."

"I had my grandfather to show me what I needed."

"That's something. He set you up in this business?"

"He tried to leave me out of it."

"Your mother was strong-willed like that too. She never wanted to join the family business, but if she had, well."

"There was no stopping her."

"Right."

"There must have been a reason for it," Molly said. "What happened between you and my mother?"

"Long story."

"So? Look, I'm not here to dig that up or make an accusation, but I'd love to know."

He might have pointed out that by mentioning the potential for accusations, she was, in fact, making passive-aggressive accusations. And for what? Mary Grace had dumped him, for going into business with Harry. And now this girl was continuing her grandfather's line of business and seeking Wyatt out as an ally. He suspected Mary Grace would be appalled to know the path her daughter had taken, and he could almost feel her voice in his ear, begging him to re-direct Molly toward something, well, normal. Mundane. Even patriotic.

"I don't know," he said.

"You don't know, or you don't remember."

"I said your mother was strong-willed. She got it in her head that we weren't right for each other, and that was that. I would love to have been there. I mean, I would have married her if she would have had me."

"I should get back to work," Molly said. "You have what you need to get started on an article?"

"I'll look through the material you gave me."

"That's all I'm asking."

"Listen. Anything else I can do? You know, are you doing all right? In life?"

"Everything's peachy," she said, but he didn't believe her. After twenty years of interviewing people, he knew when someone was giving him a public relations line rather than something authentic.

"Maybe we could meet again. Have dinner or something."

"I'd like that."

Now that she was packing up, he felt a powerful sense of fear, premonition perhaps, that he would never see her again. *Don't do this to me,* he thought. *You can't come into someone's life, disrupt it like that, and just up and vanish.*

"What about Thursday?" he asked. "In case I have other

153

questions, for the article," he added quickly. "I'm sure it's fine, in which case you can just tell me about your life. Or I can tell you about mine. We can compare notes about your mother. Whatever."

"You've got my contact. Why don't you send me a message in a day or so."

They left it there. She gave him a presumptive peck on the cheek and left the folder on the table, his heart hammering like a caffeine high. He was in too deep and out of control. His mind didn't get the message of reason, his cerebral cortex flooded by neurochemicals from other parts of his brain, from deep recesses of the amygdala, where some rusty old pipe had burst.

He refilled his tea and spent an hour reading through the material, googling to see what he could validate out of the gate. She was right: there was a hell of a story in all of this, if he could obtain secondary verification. The way she'd approached him put him off, but either she knew him well enough to know how to craft the story for maximum appeal, or the story was the real deal. He would need to contact this Captain Allen, to hear a voice say *yes, yes, this happened.* Maybe the investigating officer could offer him a *no comment* with enough emphasis to confirm without confirming that Wyatt was onto something. And he would need to sell Bonnie, who would need to sell it to Reece.

But the story had legs. This much he believed.

Outside the Panera, another blustery day had all but disappeared. He was checking his emails on the sidewalk, the wind ripping through his hair and sticking his pants to his legs, when he once again felt someone's eyes on him. He looked around and saw a door close to a Starbucks at the other end of the shopping strip.

A brown Camry was in the parking lot. Ever since his

experience in Madrid, he'd been waiting for such circumstances. The mysterious car that kept reappearing. The half-open blinds. The door that shut too quickly. He felt as though a shadow had been chasing him half his life, quietly wrapping a noose around him, tightening the rope ever closer so that now, when the shadow finally came into sight, there was no escape.

He walked down to the Starbucks and peeked through the car's windshield as he passed. Nothing there but a Chick-fil-A cup in the passenger cup holder and a windbreaker in the back seat. Dirt and grime on the wheel wells. In the Starbucks he saw a couple splitting a Frappuccino, a mother eating a croissant while her son in a baseball uniform scrolled through his phone. No one looked up when he came in, but the girl in the couple looked over her glasses at him after a moment. The baristas bustled behind the bar. Fffrrrrttttttt went the milk wand. *Can I take your order?* into the headset for the drive-thru. He went to the men's room, found it unlocked and the light off. He pursed his lips and looked back through the coffee house. Nothing out of place, nothing you wouldn't find at ten thousand Starbucks across the country right now.

This was the beauty of a rendezvous in a North Charleston shopping strip, he supposed. It could be any place, and was therefore no place, which perversely implied that anything could happen here. As if Molly had chosen to meet in a black hole where time (and therefore events) did not exist. This was why some people thought of these places as hell. The thought made him shudder, so he buried the feeling of being watched, scurried to his car, and headed back to the peninsula.

Chapter Twenty

JARMAN HUDDLED in the women's restroom of the Starbucks for ten minutes and debated whether he should call someone to do a drive-by to see if Brewer had left. The longer he waited, the odder it would appear when a man—a tall black man at that, Kenyan by birth—came out of the women's restroom, and Brewer would definitely make him, if he hadn't already. Jarman was not the type of spy to blend naturally into the background. Bert had pulled him out of a sort of freelance analyst's pool many years ago now, when he'd needed someone on the ground in Florida to dig up what there was to find on Everett Archer. Jarman Nzuve, living it up in Miami, was the closest researcher available. He was an excellent analyst, but subtly was not his first gift. He wasn't sure what prompted Brewer to come into the Starbucks, but he made a note to be more careful going forward. Whatever Brewer was up to, he'd learned at least some elements of tradecraft.

Finally, when the second person tried the locked door, he flushed the toilet and made a swift exit, grateful that Brewer was not among the Starbucks patrons who eyed him scuttling out.

He returned to the offices on King Street and found Bert

and Penelope in front of a messy diagram on the whiteboard.

"He met with our girl again, but almost made me," Jarman said.

"The sleeping giant awakens," Bert said, and he paused.

"What do you think?" Penelope asked.

"I'm wondering if we might be dealing with an old pro who's been pulled back into it. Molly Keagan is picking up her grandfather's line of work, and she's called up Wyatt Brewer. If so, this is our chance. If we're going to find the center of it all in our agency, now's the time."

Bert stared at the whiteboard, where he and Penelope had sketched out connections between Brewer, Harry Cope, Molly Keagan, and Everett Archer. In the center of the board, he'd drawn a circle with a giant question mark. The identity of the question mark, assuming it was one person or team within the agency, would bring Bert's life's work to a close. What he'd not shared was a plan B in case the question mark was not a single person. What if the whole system was corrupt?

"So what do we do next?" Penelope asked. "You want to bring him in?"

"I don't think we're there yet. Not until we figure out what he's doing and if he's working for anyone."

"Figure out the job, disrupt the job, and unravel the thread to get to the center?"

"Exactly. Let's not lose this thread. Jarman, you have any idea where he went after he left you?"

"Couldn't tell you. It shook me up when he followed me into the Starbucks."

"Any chance he just wanted a cup of coffee?"

"It's possible, but that would be a coincidence."

"Got it. Okay. Penelope, you're on Brewer for now. Check the paper and his home. When you find him, just hang back. See what he does. Who he interacts with. Whatever they're planning, he's going to have to make a move soon. Meanwhile, Jarman, you're on Molly Keagan. What do we know?"

"Just the basics," she said.

"How old is she?"

"Nineteen, twenty?"

"Find out where she's been for the past three to four years. I don't think Harry would have pulled her in too deep before she hit about fifteen or sixteen, but you never know. See where she went to high school. Interview a few of her friends, but do it discreetly."

"You got it, boss."

"Where are you off to?" Penelope asked.

"One of Brewer's colleagues is an old squash partner. I'm going to buy him lunch and see what else our reporter's working on these days."

She gave him a curious look and thought of the call from Diane the other night on her way back from the upcountry. "You play squash?"

"Oh yeah. It might not look it now, but I was great at it until a case of tennis elbow brought me down."

Bert looked like he wanted to tell her more, but that was the life of a spy. You had a fascinating story, but you couldn't tell it to anyone. Some of her law school friends had found work as in-house counsel and grumbled about what went on inside corporations, and the stories they could tell if it weren't for the non-disclosure agreement. She bet none of it stacked up against what Bert had seen in his day. There were moments, in her career with ISD, where she thought she may have staked a claim on infertile land, that she'd invested her prime development years in a dead-end branch of the agency, but what kept her here was Bert—his passion for the work, his intelligence in getting the job done, and his haplessness when it came to fighting the bureaucracy. He wasn't James Bond, super-spy, yet he kept secrets from her. She feared they might be approaching the end of a good thing, but for now he was just Bert, burying his activities into complaints about tennis elbow and his squash days, and she loved him for it.

Chapter Twenty One

"The first thing you need to know about Wyatt Brewer is
he's too disorganized to be playing your games," Fitz told Bert
over a wine-and-hors d'oeuvres lunch the next day at a French
restaurant off North King. "I mean, I love the guy, don't get
me wrong. Great colleague. Smart. But there's a reason he's
still on the Metro beat and never settled down to have a
family."

"You never settled down to have a family," Bert said.
"What's your beat these days?"

"I didn't say I was any more organized than Wyatt is, but
for your information, I was married once. Twenty years ago."

"You never told me that."

"You never asked. I figured you had it in your file book
somewhere."

"What happened?"

"Didn't take. She wanted to build a house, and I got
anxious and fled the state for a few years."

An outside observer might question whether Fitz was
Bert's contact or vice versa. They'd mutually acquired each
other's friendship at a party celebrating Charleston's Spoleto
festival. Fitz was covering the event for the *Dispatch*, and Bert's

wife had been on the planning committee representing her library. The two men had spied each other spying on the crowd, and Fitz had mistaken Bert for a fellow reporter. Bert let that play out, never acknowledging who he secretly worked for, but Fitz was a professional observer. He had Bert's number by their second meeting, and ever since the two had passed each other occasional tips and contacts, usually over a vigorous game of when Bert still had his athleticism. Now they met for lunches.

"Maybe you've been considering Wyatt from the wrong angles," Bert suggested, thinking that maybe Brewer seemed disheveled because he'd been running two parallel operations his whole life. "Do you know much about his past and his private life?"

Fitz ate a few papas frites and thought about it. "No. I mean, he might have something in his background, before he came to the paper. I know he used to drink too much."

"Used to?"

"He doesn't talk about it, but he's in AA now, with one of our managing editors."

"Do you know where he goes?"

"I could find out."

"Don't rock any boats."

"No, no. I'll talk to Bonnie. She's more open about this kind of stuff. She'll volunteer the information without even knowing I've asked the question."

"Do you know how long he's been in the program?"

Fitz shook his head. "A while now. It's been since he's worked at the paper, but he orders ginger ale when he goes out with us. Asks the bartender to put it in a glass so people don't harass him about not drinking. I couldn't say when he quit, though I know ten years ago he would leave a bar just hammered. Couple times I drove him home myself because I thought he might wind up with his car in the Ashley River. If you'd asked me about him back then, I might have wondered what all he was up to, but you have a lot of rope in your twenties. Know what I mean?"

"Oh, I remember," Bert said.

"Sure," Fitz said. "When you're twenty-eight, you can drop a few balls and get away with it. When you're forty, you are who you are. You don't get to have this other life on the side where you're figuring things out."

Bert suspected they were no longer talking about Brewer, but he wasn't here to delve into Fitz's psychology of regret. He said, "So you're telling me Wyatt is who he is."

"He's a very good reporter, but he's also a recovering drunk. He can't hold down a relationship. He drives a beat-up truck. And he's about two rounds of layoffs away from having to find a real job in corporate America, where I believe he'll make a fine living. But right now? I'd be shocked if he had any secrets that would interest your people."

Bert smiled and thought for a moment about how much to divulge. On the one hand, Fitz was right. Wyatt Brewer was innocent in all the wrong ways, not so much unreliable as unstructured in his life. He would do well in a corporation that demanded much of him, but that offered a north star to get him through the day. All of that said, Bert couldn't deny the hard evidence he and his team had dug up: the murky finances, the coincidental encounters with Harry Cope and Molly Keagan, the manic flights from work to the funeral to the Panera in North Charleston. The man was up to something, and if it was unrelated to Cope and the agency, then Bert truly had been wasting his life.

"Tell me about his work these days. What's he up to?"

"His big case right now is the Folly Beach body."

"Refresh me."

"You didn't hear about that?" Fitz grinned. "And we like to think our stories reach everyone in the city. They found a dead guy on Folly last week."

"Drowning?"

"Looks like it, only he didn't have any ID on him. No wallet, no keys. Nada. Like something that would have come out of your shop, come to think of it."

"We're in the business of observation, not violence."

"Uh-huh. It's got a news hook, but it had about faded from everyone's mind because no one knew who the guy was. No one reported him missing, the police had no leads. Then Brewer comes in this morning with this secret source."

"Oh?"

"Someone he knows in the Navy. Or a contractor, something like that. Supposedly hired some Estonian gangster without realizing it. Real bad dude, using the shipyards for smuggling, I don't know, guns or something. The contractor's convinced the body is his employee."

"Now that's interesting. Do you know the contractor?"

Fitz shook his head. "I've already told you too much. I don't think our editor's going to go for it. It's a bit thin, even by muckraking crime rag standards. It is strange, now that you mention it, because Wyatt's never been a tabloid scandal kind of guy. Makes you think the thing has legs, which, of course, would be a hell of a scoop."

Captain James Allen's shipping company—E & J Enterprises, a nonsense LLC as far as Bert could tell—was located off 585 near the airport, in a part of town with rusty chain-link fences, overgrown grasses, and squat utilitarian buildings that looked like they might belong near an EPA superfund site. All that land eerily unpopulated. Robots working in warehouses, truckers coming under cover of darkness to deliver supplies, managers Skyping in from out of state as though South Carolina were some third-world outhouse, home of non-union labor and nuclear waste. In that light, Charleston itself was like a first-world resort on an impoverished island, or a cruise ship carefully designed to offer tourists an *experience* rather than a dose of reality.

Well. Bert had news for the rest of America: the whole country was a carefully designed theme park. He could say this, as one who trafficked in global reality.

Global reality was a rusty fence with overgrown foliage.

Allen's office was as empty inside as it appeared outside. The front room had a video camera in the corner and a bell on the front desk, and a few moments after he rang the bell, a stocky receptionist came out and asked, "Help you?"

"I'd like to talk with James Allen, if he's in."

"He expecting you?"

"I don't know. I doubt it."

"You ought to call first."

"Next time," Bert said. "I'm here now, so."

She looked at him like *So?* and then asked his name. "Hold on," she said, and she disappeared to the back again. A moment later: "He's in a meeting."

"Thanks, I can wait," Bert said, and he leaned against a wall and pulled out his phone, began ticking through email.

He felt the woman staring at him. Let her stare. Bert needed some information from Allen. He couldn't do his next thing without it, which meant he was here until Allen showed up.

"Bert. What can I do for you?" Allen said a few minutes later.

"You didn't have to break up your meeting on my account."

"Oh no, we were just doing some planning for the year. Meetings never stop."

Bert shook his hand and reflected that anyone who was too friendly and accommodating likely had something to hide. "I won't take too much of your time," he said. "I just had a few follow-ups from our dinner the other night."

"Of course. Come on back."

The receptionist gave him the stink-eye as he wormed his way into E & J Enterprises. Allen's office was cluttered with folders and paperwork stacked on every surface. He cleared a chair for Bert and sat on his throne across the desk. "So."

"So. Right. The other night when we met, I mentioned I had a contact disappear."

"You did."

"You said you didn't have any contact with any Estonians. No information for me. No names."

"That's right."

"Well, the thing is, Jim, a contact told me something today about one of your ex-employees. A guy named Boldavich?"

Allen looked confused for a moment, but recovered quickly. "Who told you about Stepan? I guess it doesn't matter, but yeah, Stepan really ran a number on my business last year. Embezzled funds, wasted company time, tried to use us to help his buddies in whatever-stan evade customs. He was a real mess."

"Why didn't you mention him the other night?"

"I didn't think he was relevant," Allen said. "Look, Bert, I'll be glad to tell you about Stepan Boldavich, but I don't think it's going to be much use to you. I fired him before I heard anything about an Estonian airfield, and quite honestly don't know where he's holed up. Is he your man who flew the coop? Jesus, if that's the kind of contacts you're running, I can't say I have all that much confidence in our intelligence service."

"You never know how people can help you."

"Even evil little rats like Stepan?"

"What made him so bad?"

"You can read about him in the paper soon. I sent in a testimony about his character. Allegedly, he had all kinds of nefarious connections. He's the kind of guy who would be collecting money for the bookies, not the kind of guy making the deals. Always trying to get rich but no line to actually make it happen. Then again, maybe he would make a fine contact for you. Could hook you up with everyone in the underworld without your having to deal with the real bad dudes."

"Did you know he might have washed up on Folly Beach?"

"A reporter from the paper called me with the same question a couple days ago."

"Wyatt Brewer?"

"That's right. He seemed very concerned about it all."

"And did you know?"

"First I heard about it was from the reporter. Like I said, I fired Stepan and hadn't thought about him in months. Years, even. I can't say I was surprised though, given what I learned about him."

"Any idea who might have done it, in particular? Or why?"

Allen shook his head. "Far as I know, it could have been anyone. The Russians, the whatever-stan gang he let down when I fired him, or even someone out of your shop. I spent long enough in the Navy to know government agencies don't coordinate. Your agent could have been on the hit list for someone else who didn't think to fill you in."

"Oh, I don't think it was our work," Bert said, not because he didn't believe that kind of thing went on, but rather he just couldn't see the motive. He needed more information, and hoped Penelope or Jarman may have dug up something.

The next evening, Bert found himself mired in a minor dispute with his neighborhood HOA. He'd joined the board during one long winter shortly after he'd gotten married, believing himself on the way to the civic establishment, and here he was, seven years later, somehow elected president and overseeing a discussion over one of the neighbor's flag poles. He should have gotten off the board long ago, but he believed it gave him a certain amount of cover. No matter how much he obsessed over his work, he still had this domestic outlet he could point to when Sylvia said she was worried about him.

"I wouldn't be going to the meeting if things were all that bad at work," he'd told her this afternoon.

"You've been at it every night when I've gone to bed, and every morning when I've gotten up. Do you even come to bed for a few hours of sleep in between?"

"It's not so bad," he said.

She tried to give him a look, but he could tell she wasn't genuinely mad at him, only putting on frustration as a way to tell him he needed to slow down soon.

"A big project's wrapping up soon," he told her. "And when it's through, we'll take a trip. Go up to Asheville for a long weekend."

"I'd like that," she said, and he was off to the HOA meeting at the local library. Living in the domestic sphere for a few hours, buying himself coin for another night of work.

He and Sylvia had bought their house at the right time, when interest rates were still low and builders were giving away incentives. The neighborhood had closed out with seventy houses starting to show a little bit of age. Most of their neighbors were either young couples making babies or retired seniors who had followed grandchildren to Charleston. The seniors had yippy dogs and questionable finances. One of those seniors, Colonel Barclay, had decided to erect a flagpole on his corner lot where he could display the American flag.

Although the HOA lacked a formal architecture review board, they did have stringent by-laws and a disgruntled young housewife who insisted the old guy needed to take the flagpole down.

"It isn't that I don't like vets or support the troops," she'd said on the phone to Bert. "It's just that we have rules. We want to keep home values up, and the flagpole is kinda unsightly."

Now here they were, an emergency meeting to give the old guy a chance to speak up.

While he half-listened to his three colleagues on the HOA board bicker with Colonel Barclay and Barclay's attorney, Bert tried to puzzle out his recent discussion with Allen. It all made him agitated, the whole situation was what his military friends called FUBAR. Allen had all but confirmed Fitz's story, that Brewer was nosing around and had somehow stumbled onto information about Stepan Boldavich. Much of what Allen said aligned with what Jarman had gotten out of Stepan —the money laundering, the Eastern European connections. Stepan had approached Jarman through a friend of a friend of an acquaintance, eager to deliver what he knew about some Very Bad Dudes in the Russian oligarchy conspiring to expand its sphere of influence. The plan, according to Stepan, was to allow the U.S. to build its silly airfield in Estonia, and then use it as a provocation to continue Russian expansion beyond Ukraine, with sights set on other former Soviet satellite states.

What surprised Bert was Allen's casual dismissal of Stepan. First, his primary contacts were Estonian, not "whatever-stan." Allen should have known better, and it was not like him to exhibit such ignorance of world geography. Nonetheless, what truly troubled Bert was that he'd not known of Stepan's connection to E & J Enterprises. Charleston was a small world, so it wasn't outside the realm of possibility, yet the extreme coincidence had him on edge. Like an animal with an instinct for danger, Bert's hackles were up, and he felt uncertain as to whether he was the hunter or the hunted. He believed his old friend had been forthright with him: that Allen had not made any connections between Stepan and the Estonian airfield contract, and had no idea that Stepan had been Bert's mole.

But if Allen hadn't been running Stepan on the other side, who had? Who was behind the Navy's contract in Estonia?

Jon Sealy

Who had the back-channel to the Russians? Who deemed it expedient to kill Stepan?

And who stood to profit from it all?

When the meeting broke up, he realized he'd not absorbed anything that was said. One neighbor left in a huff, while two others conspired in the library breezeway over some minor point of contention.

"See you later, Bert," the community manager told him.

"Hey, you too, Dave."

Then it was just Bert and Barclay in the conference room, Barclay's lawyer having absconded to make a phone call. Bert was ashamed to admit he didn't know how the board had left it, whether it had been a successful night for the old man.

"I never thought I'd be fighting at home to fly the American flag," Barclay said. "We were supposed to be fighting for freedom, and now…"

"I know," Bert said.

"You could have spoken up in there. I come into this meeting thinking all of you are against me, sitting there writing rules about what I can put in my yard."

"Well, I didn't write the rules."

"I know that," Barclay all but shouted at him. "I know that. It was that developer who put in the rules so the houses would look spiffy while they were slapping 'em up and trying to sell them. But the developer's packed up and left us to live our lives. What do you people think we're about? I'm on a fixed income, money for my service to the country. That flagpole cost money."

"I know," Bert said again.

"This is why we need to reelect Trump, you know," the man said out of nowhere. "You liberals don't get it, you just think we're all a bunch of racists, but what we are is fed up. We're fed up and ready to make a change, but you and your

168

media friends couldn't even allow that. Just more of the same."

Bert didn't know where to start with the old guy. Personally, he hadn't voted since he joined the agency in the mid-eighties and caught his first glimpse behind the curtain. The president was largely irrelevant to his world, though some of his colleagues in D.C. would give him an earful about it if he let them. He let Barclay rant on, but stopped the man when he said something about Eastern Europe.

"Come again?"

"I said we just leave our allies holding the bag. We gave Iraq to the Iranians. We gave Afghanistan back to the Taliban. Now we're dropping support for Ukraine. Is it any wonder no one trusts us? The Russians have always been what they are. It's our people who can't hold the line. Just like that developer, up and leaving us with an untenable set of regulations."

"That's right," Bert said.

"Yeah, that's right," Barclay echoed. "You think I'm old and not paying attention, but I haven't changed. I'm still holding the line. It's you people making a mess of the world."

That night, Bert sent a message to Penelope and Jarman to meet him in the office early. Then he sent a text to Fitz, thanking him for his help this week and giving him a lead on Colonel Barclay's American flag fight.

You can thank me later, he said.

Chapter Twenty Two

"So what do we know?" Bert said, standing in front of the office whiteboard, marker in hand. Jarman and Penelope sat like pupils at the conference table while their boss went into lecture mode. He began to draw a family tree.

"We know Everett Archer was running a numbers game in the agency from maybe the seventies into the nineties. Contractors or NGOs would give a kickback to Archer, and then he would have his operatives cook up global security reports to justify investments in U.S. military infrastructure. That's point A.

"Then we know he eventually hooked up with Harry Cope's law firm to act as the middleman between contractors, foreign politicians, government administrators, various NGOs —everyone an intelligence operative shouldn't be seen mingling with in the open. Our old friend Judge Cope would broker the deals, say a million-dollar payment to Archer, and then thanks to Archer's intelligence analysis, the government delivers a billion-dollar infrastructure project. It's straightforward corruption but with national security at stake. That's point B.

"Now, both of those guys are dead, so the first question is:

were they acting alone, or was there someone else in the agency pulling the strings? Did someone inherit Archer's scheme? I believe he did, or else our work is done and we can shut Project Gravy down.

"So, points C and D lead us to Molly Keagan, Cope's granddaughter, and then Wyatt Brewer, who we know has worked for Cope in the past. Neither of those facts would be of interest in themselves, if we hadn't seen these two conspiring of late, first after Cope's funeral Saturday and then yesterday in North Charleston."

Bert drew a divider line down the center of the whiteboard and stared at it for a moment.

"Question?" he asked Penelope, who must have been showing a tell. She'd been thinking of her call with Diane the other night, and it unnerved her to consider who was running what here.

"I understand the theory here," she said. "You have someone in the agency fabricating intelligence reports and getting kickbacks from military contractors, but don't we still need someone inside the agency? If Archer's long gone, who's been running things from inside? And why aren't we looking inside?"

"That's where we're going eventually," Bert said, "but we have to tread carefully. I'm sure whoever it is has plenty of tripwires in place, so if we pull the wrong file, or bump into the wrong officer, they'll pull the plug for a year and we're out. It's not an accident that Diane sent us all down to Charleston. That lets us do our work without raising questions in Washington. And as long as we appear to be looking for corruption *outside* the agency, we're fine."

"Unless they get wind of who we're looking at."

"Outside this room, only about half a dozen people know what we're up to. Diane, her boss, Congressman Jones on the Armed Services Committee. Maybe a couple of his staffers."

"You trust all of them?" Penelope asked.

"Look, Penny, we have to start somewhere, and we're making progress here. The three of us have done more in eighteen months than I was able to do in ten years on my own. We're close, but we need to stay focused. We get evidence for who's running what outside the agency, we set up a sting, and we use them as bait to draw out whoever is on the inside."

She relented. "What about the guy on Folly?"

"Ah. Here, we have our friend Stepan Boldavich that Jarman has been running. Over the past few months, he's been filling us in on a concerted effort by someone to get a handle on Russia's relationship with Estonia. Now, depending on who you talk to in our sister agencies, Estonia is most likely a non-entity while the Russians are focused on Ukraine. On one hand, there's some cultural ties between Eastern Ukraine and the Russians, so their interest could be about that as much as geopolitics. It's doubtful the Russians would risk a full-on hot war with NATO over the Baltic states."

"So why build an airfield over there?" Jarman asked.

"Precisely," Bert said. "We know the Russians have generally the same capabilities we do. They don't need to set up an air base in, say, Newfoundland, because if a hot war ever broke out between us, they'd be sending us ICBMs. A military base would be pointless except for the optics. Who benefits?"

"Everett Archer's contractors," Penelope said.

"Or the Russians themselves," Jarman added. "Make it look like we're the aggressors in the area to give themselves cover for escalating in Ukraine."

Bert stood back and looked at the whiteboard with his hand covering his jaw. Penelope thought he looked tired, like a man spending late nights or early mornings in a hospital ward with a loved one.

"Then there's the financing," he said, returning to the board. "Someone set up a shell company that owns an LLC that opened Capital PAC as a pro-capitalist, pro-business fundraiser. None of the money has gone anywhere yet, or at least it hasn't gone to fund any political campaigns. We don't know who's donated, or how much capital they have, but our Estonian friend seemed to think it's a lot, and that it was designed to lobby for the Navy to build an airfield in Estonia, ostensibly to defend oil installations in the Baltic Sea. But we suspect someone in our agency is getting a massive kickback for identifying the threat in the region. Our target makes it known there's a threat in the Baltic, the Russians are getting more ambitious than Ukraine, and Capital PAC dumps enough funds in the system for Congress to appropriate the expense. Then the Navy issues an RFP, Captain Allen gets the contract, jobs are created, the airfield goes up, and someone in our agency makes a mint. A million dollars in, a billion dollars out, and the U.S. taxpayer is none the wiser.

"Which brings us to Captain James Allen," Bert went on. "I've met with him a few times this month, and he and I go back long enough that I think I trust him. I *think* I trust him. When he tells me he doesn't know who's behind it, I believe him, for the most part. At least, I believe he's not driving the agenda. His company might stand to benefit if it gets the logistics contract, but I'd look elsewhere for the driver. The wrinkle is that Boldavich was a former employee of Allen's, and it seems he has some real ties to Estonian mobsters."

"How do you know that?" Jarman asked. "Nothing came up when I was digging into him."

"Our friend Mr. Brewer is working on a news story about it as we speak."

"How'd he get word about it?"

"Who knows. Brewer's been a reporter for a long time, so maybe he's got some local sources we don't have. Though I doubt it."

Penelope wondered what Bert was thinking. Although he was laying out the whole story on the whiteboard, he obvi-

173

ously was holding something back. Then it hit her. "You think he's working PR for whoever is running this whole scheme?"

"That'd be my guess. If you can build a credible case that Estonian mobsters are plotting with the Russians, you can put that into an intelligence report and suddenly you've built a case for why the U.S. needs more defense infrastructure in the Baltics. Our agency has a long history of doing this kind of thing. You call up NBC or the *Washington Post* and tell them what we need them to put out. It's sort of small-time to target a local reporter, though. They usually pick up what the big dogs are running. Still, we ought to pull Brewer in to see what he's got to say. What about this Molly Keagan?"

Jarman said, "She's an interesting case. We've had a granddaughter in our files for years, but just in the 'friends and family' category. Born Molly Cope, raised by her grand-parents. Father unknown, mother died in a car accident when she was four." Jarman paused.

"What?"

"Harry Cope was a judge by that point, so the accident made the news. Anyway, Molly graduated with a 4.0 from Ashley Hall and might be the only one in her class not to go to college. Never even put in an application, though she was talking a lot online about the Thiel Fellowship. We don't know if she applied for one of those grants, but if she did, she didn't get it."

"Remind me what that's about," Bert said.

"A Silicon Valley billionaire created a fellowship for high school kids to skip college and come work for him. He seems to think the whole education system is a sham, and judging from her social media posts, Molly agrees with him."

"Did she just think she was a shoo-in for that program and not even bother with a backup?"

"Don't know, but she's consistent in her contempt for the traditional system. Let's see, she's nineteen years old, officially changed her name a year ago, moved into a rental house near the Citadel, and makes her money as an independent consultant. We don't have a record of her clients, but she's developed quite the following online for anarcho-capitalist blogging."

"What exactly does that mean?" Bert asked.

"Her Substack is all about overthrowing the government and letting corporations take over. She regurgitates a lot from Reddit about Bitcoin and how governments enrich themselves without creating value."

"And corporations are the answer?"

"Decentralization is the answer," Jarman said. "She's got a long rant about how companies that don't create value would go bust overnight if they didn't have government rent-seeking holding them up. It's all Ayn Rand, end the Fed, the usual talking points."

"I get it. She's smart and has a political philosophy. Where does all of this get us?"

"The thing is, bloggers will say anything for an audience. She created Molly Keagan as a persona, so who knows how much of this she truly believes. I'm sure there's a piece of her that buys into what she's spouting, but she's also making a good living pushing content that the true believers want to hear. An attractive right-wing girl is a hot commodity on social media these days."

"You think she's a fraud?"

"Wouldn't be the first in America," Jarman said. "I don't know. She is her grandfather's granddaughter. People have a way of shifting their beliefs when it's economically convenient."

"So if she's working with Brewer, she could be the public relations arm of the system."

Bert wrote Molly's name under Capital PAC on the board and drew a circle around them both. He said, "Whoever's running Capital PAC pays her to send the signal out about the Russian threat, the Navy goes and builds its airfield, and what?

How does that serve her, what did you call it, anarcho-capitalist agenda?"

Jarman threw up his hands. "I don't know, boss. Big oil and the Russian threat aren't usually the purview of the Bitcoin anarchy crowd. Maybe she's just in it for the money."

"Or maybe she's a realist," Penelope said. "If the airfield is designed to protect oil operations in the Baltic, maybe she thinks she's bending governments to serve the market. That would be consistent with her position. When I was in training, I had this instructor from MI6 say you can't topple the government, but you can use it to your advantage."

"Was that Winston Shields?" Bert asked.

"Yeah."

"He's been like that forever. His name might be Winston, but he didn't have any Churchillian notion of saving the world. He said our job was just to further the interests of our empire, the rest of the world be damned."

"Spoken like a true MI6 agent," Jarman said.

"To get us back on track," Bert said, "we're looking for three specific individuals: the man on the inside, the broker, and the customer. I'm thinking the customer might be related to Mr. Boldavich and the Estonian mob. Assuming Ms. Keagan is our middleman with Capital PAC, our target now is the person inside the agency. How do we get to them?"

"What do you think the connection is between Brewer and Keagan?" Penelope asked.

"I don't know. What are you thinking?"

"Well, last week is the first time either of them showed up on our radar. She's got a paper trail going back a few years, you can see how she got where she is."

"But Brewer's the anomaly."

"Exactly," Penelope said. "Where's he been for the past twenty years? He's been working down the street at the *Dispatch*. He's not an anarcho-capitalist, and outside the one job twenty years ago, he's not been making steady money out of scams like this."

"So why now, you're asking."

"Yeah. Why now?"

"There's the funeral. Harry Cope died, and Brewer makes a surprise entrance back in the business. Could Keagan have brought him back in?"

"Maybe. He's not hard up for money, but maybe he felt sentimental about her grandfather."

"Or maybe she's blackmailing him," Bert said. "Whatever job he did twenty years ago, it couldn't have been legal. Maybe she knows about it and is calling in old favors."

"That would explain why he went to the funeral," Jarman said. "And why he hasn't touched the money in twenty years. He might have been hoping the job was closed out, and she put him back to work."

"If she can blackmail him," Penelope said, "it means he's vulnerable."

Bert drew a circle around Brewer's name, and then an arrow pointing to Keagan, and then an arrow pointing to the agency target. He said, "So Brewer's our point of leverage. We get to him, we get to her. We get to her, we find our target."

Chapter Twenty Three

WYATT HAD a dinner date with Molly Thursday evening. Just one week since he'd seen her on King in front of the Francis Marion Hotel, and his entire life had changed. They met at the Rutledge Cab Company near the Citadel, a quiet neighborhood he wished he frequented regularly. The restaurant was a brick-and-hardwood former gas station with alligator skin on the door and oxidation on the sign. It all felt authentically "New South," a look back at the city's rusty heritage and a look to the future with breakfast all day.

He arrived early, just after dusk, and got a seat and a beer at the bar, the temptation to drink something he would fix on the other side of this transition in his life. For now, he had good news for Molly. The article on Stepan Boldavich would be a Sunday feature, a feather in both their caps despite his reservations. Bonnie, Reece, everyone on staff, really, had been impressed with the scoop and excited by the prospect of selling a few extra copies thanks to a breathless headline about the Estonian mob. He told himself the story was compelling, the sources were solid, everything was confirmed, but it still troubled him that he didn't understand Molly's agenda. He suspected he'd been played, and recalled Warren Buffett's quip that if you don't know who the dummy is at the table, you're the dummy.

"Why don't we sit in a booth?" Molly said from behind him.

"That works. I was just—"

But she was already scampering away. He let the bartender know he was moving and followed her to a quiet corner of the restaurant. Sitting across from her, he felt a surreal sense of déjà vu, remembering how he used to sit across from her mother at the sandwich joint in Spartanburg. Molly had the same round face, the same waterfall of hair, the same blue eyes as her mother. The same brightness.

"Did you have a good day?" he asked her, and saw immediately it was the wrong thing to say. Too pedestrian. He'd dated plenty of women since Mary Grace, but the stakes had always felt manageable, as though he knew none of them would live up to the girl he yearned for, which paradoxically helped him relax and enjoy himself. Now he remembered the dating life pre-Mary Grace, when he'd been awkward and fumbling, and drank too much to loosen up enough to be wittier than *did you have a good day*. A week into fatherhood, and he'd already been reduced to a teenager again, nervous around girls and nothing in his brain but filler.

Fortunately, Molly took control of the conversation. "I had a great day, but I think the better question is, how was your day? Any luck with the article?"

"Actually, yes. You want a drink? Are you old enough to drink?"

"I'm not but I have an ID if you wanted to get me a glass of Riesling."

She looked at him as if daring him to say no. Less than a week, and not only was he reduced to a sputtering mess, she was acting the rebel. He was wrong the other day when he said he'd missed it all. He'd skipped all the worthwhile parts of parenting and landed right in the space where most parents fail to comprehend their own irrelevance to their children's lives.

"You can do what you want," he said. Then he felt stupid for worrying about it.

Just then, the waiter walked by accompanied by Ashley with some other dude. She wore tight jeans and a flowy black shirt. She caught eyes, including Molly's, who then looked at Wyatt with amusement. He took a swig of water and chomped on a piece of ice.

The dude was rotund and balding but floated through the room with the confidence of a swan.

Wyatt hadn't seen Ashley since he'd left her at the Francis Marion Hotel restaurant last week. They usually went a few weeks without contact, but so much had happened in Wyatt's world that he flinched as if bitten. Molly didn't seem to notice.

After depositing Ashley and her gentleman, the waiter returned to take their orders. Burger for him, salad for Molly. Drinks for both of them. The waiter didn't ask for Molly's ID, and Wyatt wondered what the waiter thought of them: a man with a younger date, father-daughter, or what?

When the waiter was gone, Wyatt said, "I've got good news about the article. My editor's blowing it up to a Sunday A1 feature."

"That's great news!"

"I thought you'd be pleased. I submitted the final copy today, so they're probably laying it out as we speak."

"Excellent work, Pops."

Pops?

The waiter brought their drinks—Ashley was glancing their way, trying to catch Wyatt's eye. He deflected and tried to focus on Molly. They toasted. He pulled out his phone and mumbled, "Quick work note, sorry," as he texted Ashley.

It's not what you think. I'll call you later.

He wasn't sure why he sent this. They weren't an item and she was here with her own date, but he nonetheless felt guilt simmering. It was a comfortable emotion, one he thought he might have been numb to by now.

He looked back to Molly. "Maybe you can fill me in now."

"About what?"

"This article. I did all the research, made the calls, and feel okay about what we're running, but I want to know the angle."

"Angle?"

"The why. Every PR hack has a why. Something they're trying to sell, or a scandal they're trying to contain. You said your employer was looking to ferret out miscreants. Shed light on dark corners. I applaud the sentiment, but you didn't actually give me a reason why. What's it matter to your employers?"

"What's it matter to you?"

"It's my name attached to it."

"Can you accept they stand to benefit by doing valuable work?"

"Benefit how? Who's paying them?"

She took a sip of wine, held the liquid in her mouth for a moment before swallowing. "I don't know. Like-minded individuals who believe capitalism is bigger than national borders."

"You mean like libertarians or business tycoons?"

"Maybe both. People who are asking the big questions. Could you have a corporation headquartered as its own nation-state at sea? Does the U.S., or any nation, really need a president? Could an AI system replace our federal bureaucracy?"

He smiled.

"What?"

"It's been a long time since anyone's brought up the big questions without irony."

"Why'd you stop?"

181

"Petty problems of adulthood get in the way. I don't have kids—well, I didn't have kids—"

"I get it."

"My friends who are parents, that's their life. They could be asking *what is life?* but instead they need to shuttle their kids to gymnastics practice. Or find a new eye doctor. Whatever. And when you get into that phase, politics becomes nothing more than property taxes."

"Spoken like a person of privilege."

"Maybe, but it's scary how that happens. You just wake up one day and find you are the system."

"And you don't think it's worth pausing on occasion to think about what you're doing?"

"Oh, I do," he said. "I used to think being a journalist somehow mattered, but instead it's just content creation to sell advertising. If you told my twenty-year-old self what I'm doing now, I'd be so disappointed."

"That was back when you were dating my mother."

He nodded slowly.

"Tell me about her."

"What do you want to know?"

"I was so young when she died, I never knew her. My grandparents told me a few things, but not enough to build a picture. For them, she went from being this carefree teenager to careless college student to, well."

"She wasn't careless when I knew her. I don't know. I suppose both of us were ordinary for college students. She had a charming sense of irony about being at an all-girls school. You would have liked her. You have a similar sensibility about you."

"Are you saying I'm ironic?"

"I'm saying you have an awareness of life's absurdities. Your mother had that. Converse was founded basically as a nunnery for the daughters of rich Carolina mill owners who wanted to keep their daughters pure, and even in the early

2000s they kept some old southern traditions alive. I think Mary Grace was the only girl on campus who didn't own a ball gown. She wore Chuck Taylors and would occasionally dye her hair pink with Kool-Aid."

"Really?"

"She never took herself too seriously, which is what drew me to her. I probably took myself too seriously, so we were a nice counterbalance."

"You wanted to be a journalist. What did she want to do?"

"You know, I couldn't say. She was a psychology major, which is one of those things you do when you don't know what to do. I think she had it in her head that some job would be waiting for her after college, and everything would work itself out. By the time she would have been applying for jobs, we were broken up. She was great with people, so I always pictured her doing something like what you're doing."

"Which is?"

"Public relations, event planning. Something concierge-focused. That or teaching."

"What if I told you she taught high school biology?"

"I'd say that sounds like something she might do."

"I'm kidding, alas. She worked at Starbucks for the health benefits, but as far as I know, she never sought out a real career or met a man to marry. Maybe she would have married you, I don't know. I don't think she ever got over you, for whatever that's worth."

The waiter saved Wyatt from shock by bringing out their food. "Everything look all right?" he asked.

"Looks good," Molly said. "Could I have another glass of Riesling?"

"Absolutely. You okay?" he asked Wyatt, who gulped the rest of his beer and nodded for another.

Ashley walked by again, and Molly definitely noticed her this time. Wyatt's phone buzzed a moment later. He glanced at the message.

Who is she?

"Will you excuse me a moment?" he asked, and he eased out of the booth.

The restrooms were tucked away behind the bar, in a long hall, and he found Ashley there waiting for him.

"Hey," he said.

"Look at you," she said. "The girl's young."

"It's not a date."

"You don't owe me an explanation," she said. "I'm not here on a date either, by the way. Doug's a client."

"So."

He couldn't say what had agitated him this evening, why he felt guilty here with Molly. In the years after Mary Grace, he'd never found another confidante. Because Bonnie was his editor and sponsor, he felt closer to her than anyone else, but there had never been a spark between them. Only friendship. Ashley had inhabited some hybrid space, which perhaps had run its course. Like he'd been at sea for twenty years and was ready to find a port.

Ashley gave him a quick kiss on the cheek and said, "We have a good thing, Wyatt. I'll call you. If you want."

She wiped it away before leaving him in the corridor. He blinked a few times to clear his thoughts before returning to the booth.

After he sat down, Molly asked, "Ever thought about leaving the paper? Trying to go to New York or somewhere bigger?"

"I did at one point, a few years ago," he said, remembering how he felt renewed at thirty-five. Newly sober, joining the Catholic Church, ready to take on the world.

"What happened?"

"I don't know. I feel like I missed my window. When you're my age time starts to speed up, and when you focus on taking one step after another, it's easy to say, oh, I'll get started after the summer or oh, I'll get started in the new year. Then five years goes by and you're past your sell-by date."

Wyatt had never fully analyzed his existence, but what he was saying, three beers in, felt right. His life wasn't a wide sea of gray, but it was also nothing to write a memoir about. It made him sad to think he'd amounted to a big fat nothing, a statistic for the census bureau, but the girl appeared interested enough. Perhaps this was what parents understood that he'd missed all these years. You bred yourself an audience, so that even if your world remained small, all diapers and grocery shopping, you'd raised your own approving witness for your life. He felt ashamed for not being a larger-than-life father for the girl, someone she could impress her friends by talking about, but she was engaged tonight. Perhaps that was enough.

"Maybe it's not too late," she was saying.

"Too late for what?"

"A fresh start. Go to a bigger paper, write for a magazine, I don't know."

"I lost the ambition, over the years. I like my little life here in Charleston."

"Why don't you tell me what's going on between you and that woman?"

Wyatt started. "What woman?"

"The redhead you've been eyeing all night. You followed her to the bathroom."

"You don't miss much, do you?" he asked. He chose his words carefully. "She's an old friend."

She waited for him to go on.

"Well, Jesus, you don't expect me to go into the sordid details, do you?"

"It doesn't bother me if you've got a friends-with-benefits situation, though I'd rather see you happy with someone."

"What makes you think I'm not happy?"

"As you said, I don't miss much."

"I've never been a permanent relationship kind of guy.

Not since your mother, anyway. I'm fine with my life the way it is."

"Whatever happened to the money you got from my grandfather's job?" she asked without missing a beat. Although he'd never sat through a police interrogation, he thought he understood what it might be like, under the bright lights, thrown off guard by your interlocutors. This girl had a gift. She'd make a fine journalist.

"It's sitting in a brokerage account," he said.

"Accumulating interest? Why not use it? Cash out and go to San Miguel for six months and figure out what you want to do with the rest of your life?"

"A fine idea," he said, and he drained another beer.

"What if you had another job opportunity?"

"I have a job."

"I meant something that had a little more money attached to it."

He sat back and thought for a second about the last time a Cope had offered him a job. The image of the body in Madrid had never left him. Those few moments in Oliva's apartment had defined his life: poisoned his relationship with Mary Grace, driven him to unhealthy habits, destroyed any personal ambition he might have held, forced him to become a guarded, paranoid man with a limited capacity for trust.

Yet he'd trusted Molly, as Bert and Penelope would point out in their interrogation of him in the following days: trusted that she was his daughter, trusted she was playing a straight-forward game of media relations with him, trusted she was the follower rather than the instigator of whatever scheme or hustle she was working. Afterward, he wouldn't be able to explain it. The bond of blood kin somehow transcended character.

"Once was enough," he said. "You should be careful with whatever game you're playing. I told you the other day, the kind of people who are into whatever you're into, well…"

"They're the kind of people who wind up dead on a beach somewhere?"

"You got it."

She looked away.

"What?"

"Nothing."

She took a sip of wine, picked at her salad.

"What?" he asked again.

"I might have a problem."

Afterward, he would replay the conversation, trying to poke holes in it, looking for an out for him and for Molly. He'd been right to fret, whether as her father or merely a bystander, for she was in more danger than he believed she knew. What's more, his article would make things worse, because it would cover the tracks of the people responsible for Stepan Boldavich's death. The first draft of history would show the man lived in an underworld of violence and cast the blame for his death on Estonian gangsters. There was no reason to dig too deeply into Stepan's finances, into his associates, and into whatever work he was doing here in the U.S.

Wyatt felt like an idiot, an accomplice to thieves and murderers.

"You're more worried about this than I am," Molly had said after she laid out the whole story, or what Wyatt believed was the whole story.

"Tell me what I'm missing."

"I agree there's risk here. I'm not denying that."

"Okay. Then?"

"Everything has risk," she said. "You took a risk taking that job for my grandfather. You took a risk keeping the money. And your money manager is taking risks every day with the money in the market."

"Yeah, but the worst that happens to money in the market

is I go broke. I'm not going to get strangled and dumped in the ocean."

"Neither am I," Molly said. "These people don't want to be dumping bodies in the ocean. The Estonian, sure, but that was different. He wasn't a U.S. citizen."

"I thought your ideology didn't care about national citizenship."

"He didn't have a network of friends and family members who missed him. No one reported him missing. You know why? Because the only people who might have cared were the same people who wanted him dead."

"Y'all want any more to drink?" the waiter asked from out of nowhere.

Wyatt sighed. "Yeah, another beer."

"I have to get going," Molly said.

"And also the check," Wyatt said.

"Be right back," the waiter said.

Wyatt could feel himself talking too loudly, leaning into the conversation too aggressively, but he had a point and wanted to impress it on her before she skedaddled. Same old Wyatt, never one to let something go once he'd got it into his head. It made him a reliable reporter, the reason he'd stayed on the Metro beat all these years rather than trying to slither up the corporate food chain.

"I know you're a smart kid," he said. "Much smarter than I was at your age. But there are some things you just don't know until you've been around the block a few times. I was an idiot in Madrid, both for taking the job and the money. It was sheer luck nothing happened, but I wasn't in nearly as deep as you are. You're like the lawyer I found dead in his apartment. You're *managing* the transactions. You can bet if my money manager lost all my savings, he'd be cut loose." He snapped his fingers. "Cut loose in business doesn't mean killed."

"Look. *Wyatt*. I didn't bring it up for a lecture. I've done fine without a father the past nineteen years. No offense, but I don't need your help."

"Well, why the hell did you bring this job up?"

"I only brought it up as an opportunity," she said quickly. "I guess I felt sorry for you. I feel like I rocked your world by letting you know I exist, and now you're over there moping around like you want to get to know me and be the father you never were. I thought maybe you could help me out a little."

"Well, my advice is you need to get out."

"I don't need advice. I was thinking co-sign on a loan, or maybe you knew someone in, I don't know, the Chamber of Commerce who might know of some startup fundraising opportunities."

"That's really not my area."

"I can see that now."

The waiter brought Wyatt's beer and the check, and Wyatt fumbled with his wallet and dropped his card. His hands were shaking, but he couldn't tell if it was the alcohol or a simmering anger. He'd not dug into an argument like this since the passionate days with Mary Grace, and he didn't care for the way he felt, the combination of frustration and self-loathing. No wonder his friends with children had all gone gray and fat.

"I appreciate the drinks," she said, softening a little. "And the article. That's going to be great, and I hope it works well for both of us."

He was silent a moment. Then he said, too loudly, "I don't know where to go from here. I don't know what you want, but I don't think I can help you. I mean, do you understand how foolish you're being?"

He was sputtering and felt hot in the face. Then he said a few more unkind things—later, he wouldn't remember exactly what—but he would remember how she looked at him with pity, which enraged him unlike anything he'd ever experienced.

Then she was gone. A wisp in the wind. A waterfall of blonde hair.

He still had his last pint in front of him to drink, and when the waiter brought his card, he said he'd take his drink to the bar. Ashley and her client had left. Another couple now sat at the booth, and they stared at Wyatt with malice when they saw him gazing their way.

He thought about himself here, a middle-aged alcoholic fallen off the wagon. Another night of bad decisions. Fumbling with his keys, night sweats on the horizon. He somehow maneuvered his car back to James Island, and somehow made it home without stopping at a gas station for more beer, and somehow managed to sleep until dawn, when he woke dry-mouthed and cloudy, with an overwhelming sense of free-floating guilt and amnesia.

Another day to face.

Another reckoning.

Chapter Twenty Four

BERT LANDED in D.C. at seven-thirty Friday morning, a pre-dawn flight out of Charleston's cozy airport, and by the time he'd rented a car and grinded his way to the agency's head-quarters in Bethesda, it was after nine and he was ready to get his meeting with Diane Neubecker over with so he could go back south and get on with the operation. In the years since she'd created ISD and Project Gravy with Bert, Diane had moved up to a directorship and oversaw the Office of Agency Insights and Special Projects (OAISP), under which fell a host of operations Bert neither understood nor cared to under-stand. What he knew was that even though Homeland Secu-rity funded ISD, he still had a dotted line reporting to OAISP, and Diane needed to sign off on any operation beyond data gathering.

Well. After more than a decade of data gathering, Bert was ready to bring the whole network down.

He drank a cup of coffee and waited in the agency's sun-drenched lobby for Diane to get out of her morning staff meeting. It had been more than a year since he'd been to D.C. He'd never had an office in the new Bethesda HQ, and wouldn't know his way around the building even if he had the right security clearances to wander freely. Which he doubted he did. His impression was that everyone here operated in a silo, quietly ushering along their slice of the intelligence apparatus, head down while one president after another undermined their work and brought in a merry-go-round of appointed leaders.

"Bert. Sorry to keep you waiting."

Diane click-clicked across the marble floor and held out a hand.

"You haven't aged a day," he told her. In fact, she looked better than when he'd first met her. Her hair was still a beautiful iron, but her skin was clearer and she must have dropped twenty pounds over the past year or two. The same, alas, could not be said for him. A junk food diet, a puffy face, two weeks with little sleep and twelve-hour days.

"Aw, thanks, Bert. I'm running a parade of cleanse diets."

She led him swiftly through the turnstile and toward the bank of elevators.

"It's chaos here, as you can imagine. Lot of our colleagues are just beside themselves. I feel bad for the thirty- and forty-somethings. The twenty-somethings can leave any time with a great line on their resume and get into something else. Me, I've got my thirty years, so I'm just riding this wave to bump up my pension, enjoying six weeks of vacation a year and a state-of-the-art gym downstairs. But those people in the middle, they've got families and ambition. The agency's no longer a very welcoming place if you're saddled with either of those."

"I'm not sure it ever was."

"It's always been political, but not everyone ends up with the wrong file on their desk at the wrong time. But it all worked out for you, Bert, didn't it?"

"We'll see how today goes."

"I'm excited to hear what you're onto. Might be a nice final report for both of us before we retire to somewhere sunny. Well, you're already in somewhere sunny, but I need to get out of this mess. They're expecting another nor'easter this weekend. I hope you've got an early flight."

One of the elevators binged, and they joined a crowd of folks coming from the basement. Bert held his briefcase in front of him and stood somberly as if in prayer while they rode up to ninth.

Diane's floor was standard corporate design: a fractal of low-walled cubicles across the center of the floor, with director's offices ringing the wall. The directors' offices had floor-to-ceiling windows and a view of pine trees, generic office buildings constructed in the last ten years, and the 270 spur connecting to the Beltway. They had glass walls, the thinking being that the ability to see into your director's office was more inviting and thus better for morale, but from Bert's vantage, no one on the ninth floor had any privacy. No space to think. OAISP may be in its silo in the bureaucracy, but someone near the top of the food chain had decided collaboration was king. No wonder the intelligence services were so dysfunctional. The enforced extroversion made him want to hurl himself out that beautiful window and onto the freeway.

"If you're where it sounds like you are, you might be coming home to one of these offices," Diane told him. "They're not so bad. Most people keep their heads down and leave everyone else alone. You can put a bunch of introverts in an open office, but you can't make them open up to each other."

"If we nail what I think we're about to nail," he said, "I may just put in my papers and call it a career."

"That good, huh?"

"I think this it," he said. "The white whale I've been chasing all these years."

Diane's phone rang and she held up a finger. "I want to

hear about it, but let me just," and she picked up the receiver, mumbled "uh-huh" a few times, and then said, "No, that sounds terrific. I'll meet you after I finish here." She hung up. "Sorry about that, Bert. So, tell me about what you're onto."

She listened and took notes on a yellow legal pad as he laid it all out: the intel about the Estonian airfield, the murdered contact, the partnership between Wyatt Brewer and Molly Keagan. "I spoke to an old Navy captain who put a bid in for the contract, and he all but confirmed we've found the people we're looking for."

"He told you that?"

"Not in so many words. I wonder if some of his Navy contacts might be the new Everett Archer. I could tell from my interview with him that he was uncomfortable. I think I was close."

"So now you have everything but the names and the evidence," Diane said without malice.

"Right, but I think we've got some leverage with the reporter. He did a job for Harry Cope twenty years ago, and he's got more than a million in the bank from it. Hasn't gotten a parking ticket since."

"You think the job was a one-time thing?"

"I do, at least until now. I don't know what happened. Maybe he just ran into Molly Keagan by chance one day, or maybe he went to the funeral hoping to get back in. Either way, I think he's in over his head."

He explained his plan: to pull Brewer in, give him a hard time about the money in the bank, find out what he knows, and then set up a sting using Molly to get to…whoever. Captain Allen, the Navy contacts, the agency conspirator.

"What do you need from me?" Diane finally asked once he'd finished laying it all out.

"I might need some additional surveillance support," he said, "but that's it. I just wanted to give you a head's up in case this thing blows up and we have to answer to the Secretary of the Navy."

She looked at her notes and thought for a moment.

"How confident are you that our conspirator is in the Navy?"

"I would have thought he was in the agency, but Allen's contact has all been through the Navy. I'd give it fifty-fifty. After construction, they stand to benefit the most from the airfield. I don't believe we maintain much naval presence in the Baltic."

"And the secretary's been lobbying for more ships and an expanded Navy for years." She paused, tapped the table. "Great work, Albert. You've shown quite some patience here. How many years is it now?"

"More than I'd care to count."

"From what you've told me, I think you're about to earn some kind of commendation. You let me know what you need, and we'll clean house."

She stood, and he took a moment to stare out her window. All the neighboring office buildings had reflective glass windows, masking what went on inside, and he knew the agency's headquarters was no different. Everyone operating behind a prism. The greater D.C. area had grown up so fast around the city, and with so much money thrown into the infrastructure, even the landscaping was artificial. He would be glad to retire, maybe take up teaching.

Diane walked him back to the elevators, with empty chatter about their building's construction, the security problems they had even getting contractors in to take out the trash. "I honestly don't know how anyone gets any work done in this town," she said. "We're all too busy filling out paperwork."

"Much of America might agree with that assessment."

"Yeah, well, most of America doesn't understand how the world around them operates. You know this better than anyone."

The elevator binged, and Winston Shields got off.

"Hey, Bert!" said his old colleague from MI6. "Nice to see you."

"I didn't know you were still here. I thought you were in New York."

"That didn't take."

"So you're here now. It's funny, I was just reminiscing about you with one of my officers. She went through your training seminar a few years ago."

"Wonderful. I wish I was still doing that, but alas the Company had other plans. I'm in Arlington now but came up for a meeting."

"Yeah," Diane said, "I'll be back up in a moment. Let me just check Bert out."

"Right-o," Winston said with his cheery English lilt.

"Good to see you, man," Bert said, wondering if perhaps Shields had taken his old spot in the Arlington field office. The last Bert heard, Shields was in New York negotiating financial ties and keeping an intelligence plant inside Wall Street and the World Bank. Not that anyone in the agency was planning to put a stop to malfeasance on Wall Street. Instead, they were leveraging some of the smartest brains that had chosen finance rather than government service as their field. Strange, then, that Shields was here with Diane, because OAISP had always shown little interest in the private sector.

In the elevator ride down, Bert hoped Diane might fill him in, offer some explanation for Shields, some bit of gossip about Wall Street, but she was silent, perhaps already thinking of her next meeting. The trouble with being a director, he thought, was you never had time to do your own work. Someone always wanted something from you, and there was always some new decision to make. He could never make the psychological transition, close out one meeting and snap to another, as though work fit neatly into file folders. His was a mind that lingered, turned over problems, thought through the angles.

The elevator pinged again at floor one, and Diane smiled and stuck out her hand. "Best of luck to you," she said. "Keep me posted."

"We'll get them," he said.

In the parking lot, he looked up at the iridescent windows of the ninth floor and thought about the departments siloed by floors, the floors open and collaborative, everything operating as though the agency were just a money-making operation, whose purpose was to engage employees and deliver returns to shareholders. The trouble was, society had no other model for how to build a web of people and marshal them toward some mission. It hadn't struck him until now just how ready for retirement he was. He was tired of chasing shadows, tired of the hamster wheel, tired of the smoke and mirrors. He'd recently seen an old guy wearing a t-shirt that said: *I've got a retirement plan. I plan to paint.* Sounded like a great plan to Bert. Pull out the old watercolors and jazz around until he lost his mind to dementia.

Still, he wondered: What was Shields doing here?

Chapter Twenty Five

THE WEEKENDS COULD BE dangerous times for someone on the edge, without a family to distract him or a job to do. Friday, after Wyatt's evening out with Molly, he sent a few texts to Ashley (no response) and agreed to attend an AA meeting with Bonnie on Saturday night—a distraction on arguably the most treacherous night of the week. He sat in the back with her but didn't speak. She held his hand to let him know she was there and proud of him for going. When it was over, they went out for waffles at a Huddle House in Mount Pleasant and caught up as colleagues.

"What do you think of the paper's re-design?" he asked.

Reece, their editor-in-chief, had recently made a public announcement about covering more local news in the A section and sticking national news into the B section.

"I think it means you'll get more prominent placement throughout the week," she said. "It could be job security, if that's what you're worried about."

"I'm not, really. Reece's editorial had the public relations spin, you know?"

"I do know," Bonnie said, and then in a mocking voice: *"Readers want local. Engagement. Connection. And we're poised to deliver.* If you'd told me that twenty years ago, I would have said it was parody, but those are the times we're living in."

Wyatt had been hearing about the collapse of media his whole career, but he knew eventually the fall would come. He said, "Yeah, but readers do want real stories about real people. They don't care about the canned content. Which would be great if our editor didn't sound just like the canned content we bring in."

"Hey, you've got a great article coming out tomorrow. Cheers to that," she said.

"I guess."

He had a tough time getting excited about the piece given how it had come to him. Of course, Bonnie knew nothing of that, so had every reason to believe it was a fine piece of investigative journalism.

It was late when they said their goodbyes, even later by the time he made his way through traffic across the peninsula. Highway 17 had a lane closed due to an accident, so to avoid traffic he exited onto East Bay and found himself cruising slowly by the waterfront. Past the market he turned onto Broad toward the "four corners of law," the courthouses and city hall.

As if on autopilot, he pulled over in front of the palm-lined cathedral. It was a couple hours past the vigil mass and everything appeared shut for the night. Yellow lights from the street radiated upward, and the top of the cathedral was out of sight inside Wyatt's truck, as if the building indeed reached up to heaven.

When he'd joined the church's RCIA program years ago, he'd gone through all the rites including his first reconciliation, but he'd not confessed to the stolen money from Spain. He couldn't say why, then or now, but he suspected one reason he shied away from confirmation at the end of the program was because he wasn't sure what crime he'd committed, so he couldn't clear his conscience. How do you atone for something you don't understand? Likewise, he'd not touched the money. It had doubled twice in a brokerage account, but he knew it wasn't his to spend. He'd always thought he would tap it at some point, and maybe now was the time. He felt run down from the last ten days and thought it might be best if the paper laid him off to force his hand.

Confess, act, or accept the money for what it was.

In his truck by the cathedral, he crossed himself and said the Our Father. He only knew a few prayers by heart, and this one crossed over from his Presbyterian childhood to his Catholic flirtation. Maybe another reason the conversion hadn't stuck is he'd never learned how to talk to God. He could recite a prayer but couldn't open his heart, not since he'd been a teenager.

Lead us not into temptation, but deliver us from evil.

He felt something release inside him, so he resolved to go to Mass in the morning and try again with the Lord. He would confess the money and consider whatever Father Jim had to say. Even if he couldn't keep it, he still believed he might put in his notice at the paper, offer to build a relationship with Molly, and remain sober. Salvage something of his life for the back nine.

The next morning, he woke at seven but stayed in bed until eight thinking about his life and what might be in store for him if he could put the past behind him. A new career, either freelancing or changing fields altogether. Fatherhood, perhaps. Maybe he could find a relationship that would work. He felt poised in a way he had never experienced, as if his prayers had changed something metaphysical in him. Like water was about to start flowing downhill in his life.

For the kingdom, the power, and the glory are yours, now and forever.

He put on his clothes from last night, splashed some water on his face, and went out to get the newspaper. The paper was wrapped in a translucent yellow bag and lay at the front of his sidewalk. He picked it up and pulled it out and saw his A1 article, accompanied by a desolate photo of Folly Beach, blue lights flashing out of the frame.

Skimming the lead in the paper, he didn't notice the black SUV in a visitor's space across the lot, didn't see the man and the woman get out and stroll toward him. Only when the man said, "Good morning," did Wyatt look up, and he understood he was not free, that his material reality was the same as always.

His past had caught up to him, and his life's reckoning was at hand.

"Good morning," he said.

"I wonder if you might come with us," the man said.

Part Three

Chapter Twenty Six

THE DAY DARKENED and cooled around the house on King Street South of Broad. Wind rattled the old antebellum home, the same ancient force that had been lashing against human civilization since the first hunter-gatherers set up roots and established an approximation of community. Inside the house, while darkness settled over the Holy City, the two agents and the reporter continued their interrogation. Deep into Sunday night, Wyatt explained as forthrightly as he could his connection to Harry Cope, the Madrid operation that had led to his fortune twenty years ago, his falling out with Mary Grace, and his chance encounter with Molly Keagan at the funeral.

The agents asked again and again about the events from ten days ago, incredulous that a person might act on impulse with no grand design. No, he'd not known about Molly before last week. No, he hadn't known she was his daughter. No, he didn't have any plan when he set out to attend the funeral.

"It was all just random chance," Bert said. "We're hearing you correctly?"

"Random, implausible chance."

Bert smacked his lips a few times and did his eye-squinting

thing. "I take it by now you've figured out I don't hold a lot of truck with chance."

"I've wrestled with it myself over the years."

"I bet you have. And where have you landed?"

"You write about enough dead bodies, you find it hard to believe there's order in anything."

"Not a conspiracy theorist then."

"Are you? I would think you've run into your share of dead ends and miscommunications. Enough to see sometimes people just let you down, not because they're part of some secret cabal, but just because they're human."

"What are we doing here, Wyatt? If it's all random chance and humans being unreliable, what's the answer to the big question? Why are we here?"

"Do you need an answer?"

"I supposed not," Bert said. "Just wondering what a smart man such as yourself had to say about it."

"I don't know. I can tell you I haven't left anything out of what I've told you. It sounds random and it is, but there you go. I can also add, I know the types you're trying to catch."

"Oh?"

"Whoever the big fish is, they're not ones to play around with."

"They're the type of people who murder lawyers in their homes."

"Or gangsters on the beach," Wyatt said. "I can tell you I'm not embedded with them, and I doubt Molly is in too deep with them."

Bert scoffed. "You hardly know the girl, daughter or not."

"I get a sense of people pretty quick, and can tell you she doesn't fully understand the type of people she's in with."

"What makes you say that?"

"She's an idealist. She believes she's somehow saving the world with whatever she's doing. Promoting capitalism, defending against tyranny, making the world a better place."

"You're not an idealist?" Bert asked.

"No, and I don't think you are either."

"I'm shocked!"

"What do you think you're doing—saving the nation, here, or merely shutting down one criminal in one little postage stamp of the big wide world? You and your partner strike me as down-to-earth, methodical, and skeptical. Not the type of people likely to be persuaded by some random screeching out on Facebook. Am I wrong?"

Bert looked at Penelope, who smiled and shrugged her shoulders.

"Right. Whatever," Wyatt said. "All I know is Molly doesn't understand her precarious position, whoever she's working for."

"Which is why you've agreed to work with us instead," Penelope said.

Wyatt nodded.

"You do understand that we're not investigating you, and we're certainly not arresting you. Yet."

"Yeah, yeah, I get it."

"This isn't a plea negotiation. We can go that route if you want, but…"

"But right now I'm just cooperating. I get it," he said again.

"We may have some paperwork for you to fill out, to that effect."

"Of course you do."

"We don't like it either," Penelope said. "Everyone likes to rail against government red tape and mindless bureaucrats, but it's not like we're here pushing for useless paperwork to keep ourselves busy. There's a reason for doing it the way we do."

"I work for a huge conglomerate. Private industry's no better than government."

"Will you excuse us a moment?" Bert said. "Do you need

207

a restroom break? Something to drink? I think we're almost done here."

"I'm fine."

Wyatt coughed. Somewhere during the day—he wasn't sure when—his sinuses had thickened like a mask had been placed over his system. He felt a long and unpleasant chest cold coming on and wanted only to finish up this interrogation and get some rest, praying another bout with Covid was not in his near future. He hoped he'd impressed on the agents that his daughter was not the ringleader they were looking for. She was less innocent than Wyatt in all of this, but she was naïve all the same. He wondered if the agents accounted for relative awareness, and feared they did not. If their agency operated like any other organization, Bert and Penelope's boss was looking for a big fish, and didn't care about the collateral damage. If a big fish was not forthcoming, he suspected they wouldn't be above inventing one. Wyatt's job, then, was to make sure they found the real person they were after, to try to salvage something of Molly's life. It startled him how much she'd gotten under his skin in the past week. All those years of careering along, drifting from woman to woman in the off hours, he never believed he was missing anything. Children could come or not, some day, but he was busy. Now he was beginning to suspect he'd been an idiot, one more failure to add to the litany.

When the agents came back, they set a folder in front of him. Rather than sit down, Bert said, "I think it's late enough, and we'll all be in better shape if we reconvene tomorrow. That okay with you, Wyatt?"

"I worried you were going to keep me here all night."

"It's been a long few weeks for our team as well. I think fresh is best. We've taken the liberty of booking you a room in the Mills House up the street. Why don't you get checked in, have a drink on us if you like, enjoy a nice big breakfast, and come back refreshed late morning. Say around eleven?"

"I'll have to check on a few things at work."

"That won't be a problem," Bert said.

"It won't be a problem for me to check on work, or work in general won't be a problem?"

"We have some connection to your company. We'll get word in that you're on a special assignment with us."

"Do you think that's best? Newsrooms love gossip, so it won't take long before someone starts snooping where they shouldn't."

"And what will they find?"

"Look, we all leave a paper trail. Where we've been, who we've met. If my pal Fitz sees I'm missing the day after the Folly Beach scoop, he might start wondering and look into it himself."

"Fitz won't be a problem."

Wyatt took that in for a moment. Replayed his recent conversations with Fitz for any indication that the man was not on the up and up. He was a good actor if nothing else.

"Do you at least have a toothbrush for me at the hotel?" he asked.

"You'll find a change of clothes, toiletries, everything you need," Penelope said.

Wyatt walked down the steps and onto the quiet strip of King Street a few minutes later. Even in winter, this part of Charleston maintained its mystique, dark foliage sheltering old houses, a few lamps and porch lights to indicate life but nothing to indicate riffraff were welcome. South King Street was like a wealthy southern matron: friendly and open on the surface—public street, all welcome—but with an icy edge that somehow let you know you were not one of them. Perhaps the area's reputation preceded it, and all Wyatt felt was the myth being confirmed, but he nonetheless felt like a boy trespassing in his neighbor's woods, the sheriff one short ride away. The air was cold, and the wind blew up from the harbor like Confederate ghosts rising from the mist, here to retake the

Jon Sealy

peninsula in the night. He scurried onto Broad like a man under fire, and felt relief as he hoofed it to the Four Corners of the Law at Meeting and edged his way through the bite to the Mills House.

After he checked into the hotel, he skipped the bar and went up to his room on the fourth floor, where he was surprised to discover not only had the agents delivered toiletries and a change of clothes—but they'd delivered him his own belongings. The bag was not his own, but the under-wear, socks, jeans, and button-down were from his closet. He coughed out a scratch in his throat—definitely a virus settling in—and checked his phone. He had no messages, and he thought about who he might call. He thought the agents might have a listening device in the room, but that was okay because after staring at his screen for a few mindless moments, he understood he had no one to call, no reason he needed to return home, nothing on his plate at work that couldn't wait.

His life, it seemed, was a big fat nothing sandwich.

His life except for his newfound daughter.

And he wanted to protect her.

He went to bed steeling himself for what he would need to do in the coming days to keep her out of trouble, both with her unnamed employer and the agents from the unnamed agency.

Chapter Twenty Seven

BERT WAITED at the house on King until he received a text from Jarman that the subject had arrived at the hotel, and that audio was up. Then he shut down his computer, checked the windows were shuttered, and locked up for the night. In the dark he sent an encrypted message to Diane on his phone, saying they'd had a good interview and were on schedule with their target. Now all he needed was a few hours of sleep himself before they laid the trap tomorrow.

Unlike Wyatt, Bert had no hang-ups about life in South of Broad Charleston. He was a non-native and a non-southerner, so the sense of manners and decorum had always struck him as something of a show. It was beautiful down here, for sure, and he did prefer the Lowcountry weather to that of D.C. or, heaven forbid, Pennsylvania. That said, the show of the South was too much for him. He would always be an outsider here, he knew, no matter how many homeowner's boards he joined or southern belles he married. He was okay with that, though his wife preferred the fiction that they were one invitation away from high society. If the agency wanted to transfer him after this case closed, he would most certainly have to retire rather than move elsewhere. He would miss the history of this neighborhood and the access the agency's house gave him, but he was ready for it to be over.

He got in his car, headed up Meeting, and crossed the Cooper River Bridge to reach his neighborhood. He took the long way in and rolled past Colonel Barclay's house, the old vet's flagpole still standing, the flag whipping in the night air as if in defiance not to the silly rules of the HOA but against the very nature of decay. An emblem of something permanent fighting today's whims, something future generations could look on with pride when Barclay, Bert, Brewer—all of them were dust. Stand tall against the injustice of death, he thought as he coasted around the bend and into his driveway. His house was quiet and dark like all the others, the anonymous suburbs. His neighbors were in "IT," or "business," or "sales." Generic occupations in which they made small fortunes by historical standards but which today only served to keep them on a level playing field with each other. They knew he worked in "government," or at least they knew if they'd paid any attention, but when you tell people you work for the bureau-cracy, they quickly wonder what else of you might be worth conversing about. Sports, the weather in winter, ailing lawns in the summer. What would they say if they knew what he was really doing with his life?

Would any of them care?

Should they?

The next morning, he woke a few minutes before Sylvia left for work. She was in the bathroom, fiddling with creams or cosmetic supplies, he never knew what. He could have slept another few hours but had grown accustomed to taking what he could get.

"What time did you get in last night?" his wife asked from the bathroom.

"You don't want to know."

"You're working too hard again."

"A few more weeks, this big project will wrap up. I was thinking about retiring afterward."

She quit what she was doing and came out to him, shirtless and with a curling iron in her hair. "Not sure I heard you," she said.

"I think you did."

"I didn't think you'd ever talk of retiring. I'd long since resigned myself to taking cruises on my own, in my seventies."

"It's been a long winter," he said. "I don't think it'll be too long before the powers that be start looking at my line item and cutting our budget to the bone, and they're not going to want to hear why it's imperative they leave us alone. Same as you're dealing with."

"It's not fun," she agreed. "But everyone's got oversight. It's part of society."

"I've been wondering whether society is worth it."

"I surely hope you're joking," she called from the bathroom.

"You know I am," he said, even though he was not.

She came out fully clothed and ready for anything library patrons—or county administrators— had to throw at her. "I'll be glad to have you at home," she said. "You've been working hard as long as I've known you, so whenever you're ready, you've got my support. Just make sure you're not storming out over something temporary."

"You know me."

"I do," she said, and she kissed him on the top of the head. "I have to run."

"Go to it."

"Coffee's ready for you."

"God bless you."

And she was out the door, down the stairs, nattering in the kitchen. They'd settled into a comforting rhythm together, he thought, and he believed they would make it to the end. When he'd first asked her to marry him, he'd been irresponsibly in love and felt as though he were jumping out of the burning building of his old life—but into what? Sylvia had been thirty-eight then, so it had been conceivable they might try for children even though Bert had been upfront about his lack of interest in a family. She'd said she understood, she was in it with him, but a part of him had wondered nonetheless. Each year had slid by—thirty-nine, forty, forty-one—and now they were definitively past it. Childless. This was it. This was their life together. He was delighted now to discover his love had not been irresponsible at all, but had turned into the most responsible thing about him. He was safely anchored, which gave him the courage to be reckless in his work—to stake his career on what happened over the next few days.

Wyatt was sitting on the steps of the King Street office when Bert arrived an hour later. The reporter stood and shook a cramp out of his leg as he walked over to greet Bert, who told him, "I'm glad you remembered the right address. People don't take kindly to strangers on their stoops in this neighborhood. I'm told."

"It's a tourist district," Wyatt said. "They'll get over it."

He wore jeans, a t-shirt, and an unbuttoned flannel shirt that hung loose on him, straight out of the nineties grunge scene. Given the reporter's age, that made sense. You have your cool years, and then you freeze in time while the rest of the culture moves on. Same reason Bert tucked in his polo shirts and why Penelope still had a pair of giant sunglasses from the twenty-tens.

"You sleep okay?" Bert asked as he unlocked the door to the house.

"Like a log. You didn't have to book a room for me." The man cleared his throat and took a few moments to cough. "I'm a fifteen-minute drive away," he croaked.

"We like to take care of our friends," Bert said, pausing. "You all right?"

Wyatt sniffed. "Yeah, just developed some bronchial distress overnight."

"Not from the hotel, I hope?"

"Maybe the late night."

Bert led him into the house and clicked on the lights.

"Well, I'm sorry to have kept you out. But with these things, you never know who's watching. We went through several steps to get you here undetected. It saved us some time."

"Undetected by whom?"

"Probably no one, but you never know," Bert said again.

"I couldn't help but notice you rummaged through my drawers to pack a bag. Isn't that some kind of Fourth Amendment violation?"

"It's only search and seizure if you're a suspect, which of course you're not."

"I'm not sure that's quite right."

"You're welcome to make a complaint. I can give you my supervisor."

"What am I doing here today, Bert?"

"Ah, here's Penelope pulling in now," Bert said from the window. "Listen. Maybe we can take a walk. It's so nice outside, nice to have a break from the January gloom."

"We can walk or we can talk here, doesn't matter to me. What I'd like to know is where this is going. Where do we go from here?"

"Come with me," Bert said, opening the door. "Morning, Penelope. We'll be back in a bit."

"Of course," she said to Bert, and to Wyatt, "Good morning."

They headed east onto Tradd Street, Bert in the lead, Wyatt hacking away like a dog with kennel cough.

"How about we head down to the Battery?" Bert said.

"Enjoy the warmth and the water view. I've been here a decade now and still haven't gotten tired of it. You know what I mean? I grew up in central Pennsylvania, so this still doesn't feel like real life. Did you feel like that, when you first came here?"

"It took a long time for me to get acclimated."

"Of course, you've been here half your life now. Practically all your adult life. You ever thought about leaving?"

"No," Wyatt said. "I had a decent job offer out of school and didn't have any reason to go somewhere else."

"Never thought about trying to find a bigger paper? Heading for New York?"

"It honestly never occurred to me. I mean, I had a number of colleagues move on up to bigger papers, but I like what I do. I like the local beat. I'm comfortable here."

"Plus, you didn't need the pay raise."

"There's that as well."

"We haven't told you a whole lot about who we are and what we do," Bert said. "But you might find we have quite a bit in common."

"Oh yeah?"

"Most of my colleagues in the agency have spent their careers trying to move toward the center of the action, which means D.C. or a foreign posting. Get to the action and build an empire. Some of them have done very well for themselves in that regard."

"I don't believe you ever said exactly which agency you work for."

"I don't believe I did," Bert said. "What I think my colleagues never understood—which I think you and I understand—is that no matter how much success they see inside the system, they're still inside the system, subject to its whims and flaws."

"Cog in a wheel, huh."

"Cog in a wheel," Bert agreed.

"You think I've stayed at a small-town paper because I understand, what, the existential nature of the media machine and have decided to opt out? I recognize the machine, but I'm in it. A small-town paper owned by a national conglomerate is a national conglomerate, so you can't 'shop local' your way out of the system."

"What I'm saying is you recognize the issue. The futility of ambition. You might be in the system but you're not a part of it. I listened to you talk for hours yesterday, and I can tell you most certainly see yourself as outside the wheel. Because of what happened in Spain, if nothing else."

"And you?" Wyatt asked. "Do you think you're somehow outside the wheel?"

"I have no illusions. My department is still part of the system, but we're operating on a different wheel, if you like. Like a training wheel running beside the master. And like training wheels, our job is to make sure the system doesn't collapse."

When they reached the Battery along East Bay near Rainbow Row, the wind kicked off the water and pelted them with spray. The sun burning above them, it felt pleasant to be out here. Amazing that it was January, and that ten days ago they'd been dealing with sleet. In Pennsylvania, Bert's family would still be crunching through twice-frozen snow and looking at the sooty banks on the roadside. Everyone would be coughing like Wyatt.

"So how can I help you keep the system from collapsing?" Wyatt asked.

"Well, to be frank, we do have a plan for you."

"I'm all ears."

"I have to tell you, Wyatt, you're not going to like it." Bert quit walking and leaned against the railing to look over the water. "But it's the only way you'll be able to avoid charges of treason."

．　．　．

217

Wyatt listened to his pitch, and when Bert had finished, he left the reporter at the end of the Battery to weigh his options. Bert had given him a prepaid cell phone with a number programmed in. "Send a text to that number—a simple *yes* will do—and we'll get everything in motion. You have your next steps, and we'll be in the background, with you every step of the way."

"And if it's a no?"

"Nothing you've told us could be used in evidence, but most of the details could be accessed by any investigator."

"I haven't broken any laws."

"Maybe, maybe not. At least not yet. But whether you like it or not, I'm certain Molly Keagan isn't through with you. And if you're correct that she's in over her head with someone, she's going to bring you into her morass. It's only a matter of time, and we'll be meeting again on the other end."

Wyatt was silent, so Bert left him with his final trump card.

"If you truly believe she's not at the center of this thing, the best thing you can do for her is help us find who is at the center. Text the number when you're ready, Wyatt. But don't wait too long."

Bert ambled his way back up King, where Penelope met him at the corner of Broad.

"Jarman's on him?" he asked.

"As we speak," she said. "How'd it go?"

"I think he bit."

Bert grinned and offered Penelope a fist bump. Now all they had to do was wait.

Bert suggested she take the rest of the day since she put in so many hours over the weekend for the interrogation. "Have a nice dinner, get some rest," he said. "Once we're ready to move, this thing is going to go fast."

"Will do, boss," she said.

"All right, I need to get a cup of coffee. I'll see you in the morning."

When he headed east, she turned down King and went back to the office. It had been a dizzying twenty-four hours since they picked Wyatt up, and she'd not been able to think about what kind of reports she might file on this. She'd not spoken to Diane since Bert's supervisor had called her on the way back from the funeral, ten days ago now, but she had an encrypted message in her inbox with a single question: *Status?*

What was the status on Wyatt Brewer? In some ways, they were no closer than they were when she'd spotted him at the funeral. He and Molly Keagan were involved with something, but did it relate to Harry Cope and Everett Archer? Did it have anything to do with the team's dead source on Folly Beach? She had nothing to tell Diane that wasn't already in the paperwork a week ago. More importantly, she had nothing to say about Bert. He was the same disheveled operative who had hired her two years ago, maybe more animated now that they appeared to have a new lead on whatever fraudulence there was to uncover, but if Diane had been fishing for something unbecoming in Bert's conduct, there was nothing there.

Still.

Penelope let herself into the office and took in the empty room where they'd spent the bulk of yesterday interviewing Wyatt. A sheaf of papers lay on the table—Bert's notes that he'd used to guide Wyatt through twenty years of history.

The office was a three-story home the agency had owned since the seventies. The top floor had been padlocked for as long as Penelope had been here. The second-floor bedrooms were filled with case notes and legal documents, box after box destined for a shredder one day. Downstairs, the team had a trio of desks in what used to be a master bedroom. They had an understocked kitchen and an interview setup in the living room.

She went through the living room and kitchen to their

offices and scanned Bert's desk. She'd never rummaged through his belongings before and didn't trust herself to dig beyond what he had in the open. He was an old-school operative at heart, and although she'd yet to have training on counterespionage, her instincts told her to touch nothing.

On his desk he had a few handwritten notes about someone named Barclay. *Check the covenants,* he'd written, whatever that meant.

There was a printout of a ticket for a booze cruise leaving Charleston harbor in a couple of days, a fundraiser for a group called ROI Charleston. She pulled out her phone and did a quick search but found nothing about the group. She did see the touring company's web page, but there was no events calendar. The company said to call for details and pricing.

She took a photo of the notes about Barclay and the cruise ticket. She opened the email from Diane, and her finger hovered over the reply button.

The front door opened, and she jumped, nearly dropping her phone on Bert's desk.

Quickly, she shoveled it into her purse and met Bert in the living room.

"Oh hey," he said. "I wondered why the door was unlocked. What's up?"

"I forgot my phone when I came to meet you, so I needed to get it before heading out."

"You all right?"

"Just fine," she said, and she tried to remember if she'd had her phone out at all when Bert met her on the corner of King and Broad. She didn't think so, but everything was happening fast. The house was warm, and Bert was giving her a cryptic look.

"Got your coffee, huh," she said stupidly.

"Fast and French. I would have brought you one."

"No, no, I'm on my way out."

"Well, see you tomorrow."

She tried to act casual as she walked down the steps and turned up King. It was only mid-afternoon, but the sun was already low in the sky. The winter light bit into her eyes and blinded her as she shuffled up the street. At the corner of Tradd, she glanced back and saw Bert standing on the stoop of the office.

Watching her go.

Chapter Twenty Eight

WYATT AND MOLLY were meeting at the Rarebit. Another dinner, two days after his sickening interviews with Bert and Penelope. In a way, he felt better knowing his past debts had finally come due. This was the only way for him to take a tally of his life and begin the messy process of squaring the books. Over two days, he'd experienced everything from rage at the nerve of those agents (their smugness, their certainty, their professed good nature) to fear of a looming indictment (though he couldn't say for what, exactly, only that he was certain the Patriot Act extended enormous liberty to a government hell-bent on declaring you an enemy of the state) to acceptance that this was his moment. He was in the trench between yesterday and tomorrow, and what happened over the next few days would determine where he would spend his tomorrows going forward.

He was already seated when Molly arrived a few minutes late, wearing dusty Chucks, jeans, and a gray sweater that made her look more like a down-to-earth high schooler celebrating an A on a calculus exam than an international public relations mover and shaker running in circles of bribery, espionage, and murder.

"I could get used to these dinners out with Dad," she said. "It's a lot better than my usual Panera or Great Wall takeout."

"It's a crime to live here and not enjoy a meal out every so often. I was talking to a friend recently who said he still couldn't get over living in Charleston, even though he's been here ten years."

"He's bought into the tourist propaganda."

"I don't think so. He's pretty cynical."

"Even cynics need their fix," she said.

"I'm glad you agreed to join me. I haven't tried half these new restaurants on Upper King."

"Aw, you've bought into the tourist propaganda too."

She said it with a smile as she opened her menu, so he had the good sense not to be Mr. Pedantic and said nothing.

The Rarebit was the kind of New-New South restaurant that had emerged in the twenty-first century, as the youngest Gen Xers and oldest Millennials decided they wanted to reclaim the food of their grandparents—the blue-plate specials, the greens, the chops, the stews, the fries—but served up in elegance and with flavor beyond lard. Hence, farm-to-table. Hence, *Garden & Gun*. They each ordered the chicken and waffles.

She asked for a glass of wine, and he told the server water was fine.

"Not drinking tonight?" she asked.

"No," he said. "I thought you said you seldom drink yourself."

"This is a special occasion," she said.

"Well, you're young. You can handle it and still be productive. Once you hit twenty-five or so, it's all downhill."

"Uh-huh."

He coughed a few times, held up a finger in apology.

"You all right?"

"Yeah, just some allergies."

"Little early in the year for that."

223

He sniffled. "Anyway, the truth is, I sort of had a problem with drinking when I was younger. Not much older than you. I finally had to quit for a while."

She took a careful sip of her wine, and then asked, "Are you an alcoholic?"

"I suppose I have to say yes. The programs tell you to be honest about that if nothing else. I don't have it like some people"—and he could feel himself sliding into the old, dangerous lie, and corrected course—"but yeah."

"So you're off the wagon? Or is it on the wagon?"

"Off, when you're drinking. I'd call it a few slips lately."

"Because of me?"

"No, before you. A constellation of things."

"Now there's a description. You want to elaborate?"

"Not particularly."

She surprised him by saying, "That's fair enough. I've got a few updates for you, if you want to hear about them."

"That's actually one reason I wanted to meet up this week."

"I had a feeling when you texted so quick after the way we left it last week. I thought I'd either hear from you right away or never again."

"I couldn't just write you out of my life," he said. "I was angry with you because I'm worried about you, but I'm working through it. I actually wanted to apologize. I'm new at this, but it wasn't my business to pry into your work. I don't know what you're into, but you do, and I crossed the line trying to tell you how it was. I'm sorry for that."

"Thank you," she said. "I'm sorry too. I mean, you're right, some of the people I work with are into dangerous business, but that's the world we live in. You can't live on the sidelines in good conscience. At least I can't. But I was being defensive, because I wanted you to approve of what I'm doing."

"I do admire your engagement. It seems to be common among young people today. They're *woke*."

"Ha! That term is turning toxic. Anyway, you didn't grow up with TikTok to show you the world."

"Or connect me with people outside my Podunk little town."

She looked surprised.

"What?"

"You said that with a little more bitterness than I expected."

"Don't get me wrong, there were a lot of advantages to growing up in a small town."

"All fireflies and drinking from garden hoses?"

"Well, that's a little…"

"It's an internet meme," she said. "Don't worry about it."

"Right. Fine. I don't know what I was going to say. We knew all the neighbors. Kids maybe had a bit more freedom than they do today. And I think it helped me hang onto some innocence a little longer than I might have."

"You didn't have the big bad city to corrupt you?"

"No," he said. "It was more that, my impression from friends who have kids here in Charleston, they're exposed to a lot, and a lot younger. The pressures are on them to perform a certain way, so they can, I don't know, get into the right school. I have friends whose kids are starting actual nonprofits at fifteen, sixteen years old. That would never have occurred to anyone I grew up with. To build an organization, or march for a cause. The big bad world was *out there*, and we were in our innocent little bubble, causing local mayhem but not fully participating in the world. Your generation's different."

"You can join us any time."

"Well, that's what I wanted to talk to you about today," he said. "But you said you had some updates for me?"

"No, go ahead."

"You sure?"

225

"I'm curious."

"Last time we met, you asked what if someone offered me a job opportunity."

She slapped the table. "You do want back in!"

"I didn't say that," he said.

"After all that ranting about how I needed to be careful, you've thought about it and decided you wanted to come over to the dark side. That makes my job a little easier tonight."

"Why?"

"Because one of the things I wanted to talk about was another writing job. My boss could use someone with a reporter's skillset."

"Doing what?"

"Stakeholder interviews. We need a white paper about the Baltic states, the Lowcountry energy sector, and the declining Charleston economy. We want a local angle to sell an infrastructure project to Congress. Give our representatives a fig leaf to hide behind when they vote to approve funding. It's all kind of tedious, but naturally, I thought of you for the writing."

"What exactly would the paper's position be?"

"That we're going to create jobs."

"And are we?"

"Of course we are. They might not come from Charleston, but we're asking for a multi-billion-dollar investment. That money's got to go somewhere, and raw materials are only a small part of it."

"You want me to help defraud the U.S. government."

"It's called lobbying," she said. "Everybody does it."

"I don't know any lobbyists."

"Not the point," she said.

"I presume the job pays well?"

"A whole lot more than a reporter's salary, I would think. I'll have to put you in touch with a colleague for specifics."

"I'd like to meet your boss."

"My boss?"

"Whoever's running all this. I want to meet him."

"Or her," she said.

"Or her," he corrected. "Whoever it is, they've roped my only daughter into their orbit. One thing I did grow up with, pre-internet, is I like to know who I'm in business with. I like to look people in the eye and see what they're about."

"You and my grandfather," she said. "I'll see what I can do. One thing I'd like to know, though."

"Sure."

"Why'd you change your mind?"

He thought for a moment. "I don't know. Don't get a big head about it, but having you show up in my life has kind of rocked my world. I was perfectly happy humming along in my day-to-day, but now it all feels so pointless. I'm a cog in the machine," he said.

"I sold you on my vision of the world, huh?" she said.

"Not exactly. I'm glad it's fired you up, but I still think you might also be a cog in the machine. A different machine, maybe a better machine, but you're still working in some kind of system."

"So why join me?"

"It's tough to explain. You ever heard of James Dickey? Author of *Deliverance*?"

"I've heard about the movie."

"He worked in advertising and said he spent his days selling his soul to the devil and his evenings buying it back writing poetry. Maybe I've been thinking about the two halves of my life and want to do something different for the back nine."

"You've got the money to retire and golf whenever you want."

"You know it's not my money," he said. "Anyway, I thought if I'm going to keep working, it might be nice to be in business with my daughter."

227

Chapter Twenty Nine

DIANE STILL HAD NOT RETURNED Bert's calls or texts letting her know the operation was a go. He had Jarman and Penelope working sixteen-hour days to try to keep tabs on Wyatt and Molly, but right now they were operating without a plan and without backup, which in his world was like an astronaut bobbing around the spaceship without a tether. You could move around the craft, hold onto the handles, and quite possibly make it back inside the ship after the job was complete. But the risk was very much there that you would jettison into orbit away from the craft and get lost in the void. Bert had stared into the void before and knew little good ever came from operations like this.

He needed Diane to break her silence.

While he'd been waiting, he'd hired a local investigator to let him know what Captain Allen had on his calendar this month, so when Diane finally sent her cavalry, he would be able to direct them to all the players. It turns out Allen had been invited onto a private charter booze cruise in the harbor Wednesday night, the same night Wyatt was having dinner with Molly. Allen's cruise was something of a fundraiser for a local group of investors, ROI Charleston, seeking out feel-good places to put their clients' money. Judging by the crowd, the economy was so overstuffed with cash from the past few years that an investment in some no-name housing projects looked like a golden opportunity to the Lowcountry's business class, even if interest rates had spiked. Bert didn't understand it, but he didn't understand much about the mindset of financial wheelers and dealers—at least those who operated within the law. They seemed to be a mercurial, largely foolish, but also largely benign group of citizens.

"ROI Charleston's a great organization," his wife said when he suggested the two of them sign up for the cruise together. "We've applied for grants from them for the library, and everyone we've ever worked with has been just delightful. I would love to go!"

"I may have a little business to conduct while I'm there, but nothing much. I thought maybe you might enjoy a night out."

She stood on her toes to give him a kiss, and he felt like a real hero. He'd bought another night of work on the case while also arranging goodwill with his wife.

So on Wednesday night, the two of them met after work and took a Lyft to the dock on Ashley Point, near Wappoo Creek and the James Island Connector to the peninsula. Bert didn't own a tuxedo but wore a dark suit he'd had specially tailored for an uncle's funeral a few years ago, brightened up with a white shirt and a springy green tie. On the ride over, Sylvia suggested it might be time for some shoe polish. "Those are pretty scuffed," she said.

"You embarrassed to be schlepping around an old government bureaucrat?"

"Absolutely not. But I just thought you should look your best."

"Hey, Jarman left a catalog on my desk the other day. There was an advertisement for some kind of contraption that's supposed to exercise your chin. I asked him about it and he said, 'You want to have an executive chin, don't you, boss?' I told him if I'd wanted an executive chin, whatever that is, I'd have become an executive. I *think* he was kidding around, but."

"It sounds like your team is comfortable with you. You're a good boss."

He thought for a moment about their life and how little he'd been able to tell her about his work. Then he thought about Penelope returning to the office the other day. He'd not believed her when she'd told him she'd forgotten her phone, but he couldn't figure out what was what. A good boss ought to know what was going on with his team, but in his line of work, you had no team. You only had people in your orbit. You never knew about them. Perhaps the same could be said for Sylvia's world. She'd gotten a dud director over at her division in the library. It was taking a while to fire the guy or find a new home for him, so in the meantime, half his staff had quit. Sylvia's team had been picking up the slack for six months now. He said, "I know you haven't had it so easy at work."

She waved a hand. "I just work my eight hours. But if they were asking us to work the kind of hours you and your team put in, I'd need better leadership. Hey, did our HOA ever get things squared away with that colonel?"

He laughed. "You know how those things go."

"I thought I saw a professional photographer out there taking pictures."

"Of Barclay's flagpole?"

"Yep."

"Huh," he said, and she squeezed his hand.

They walked up to the charter boat and presented their tickets. The boat must have had eighty people on it, all white and on the younger side, with just a touch of gray in their hair and an aristocratic bearing to their strides.

Bert and Sylvia found a spot on the starboard side of the

boat, each with a glass of wine. It was not an ideal night for a boat ride. The cold front had passed, but the air was chilled, amplified by the wind chopping at the water. Waves lapped against the bow of the boat, and they stood there and rocked and drank their wine and braced against the wind while the rest of the guests boarded the ship.

"See anyone you know?" he asked.

"Couple faces I recognize."

"We don't get out enough," he said.

"That's okay."

"It's not my crowd."

"I understand."

"If we had more free time—"

"Bert, it's fine. I'm just happy to be out here with you."

The boat honked and drifted away from the port, the motion so insignificant that it was tough to see they were moving. People were yelling now to be heard, carrying wine and mixed drinks around, rubbing elbows, aggressively talking about the market in general, this or that development or the city government.

You remember the city before they started letting in the riff-raff from commercial cruise ships?

Mayor Joe's days, he really cleaned up the city.

I remember what it was like as a kid, you didn't come into downtown.

It took a while, but Bert finally spied Captain Allen standing with his wife, a short-haired and lean socialite in a striking black dress. "Ah, there's my guy."

"In the Naval uniform?"

"He's a retired captain."

"And what's your interest in him?"

"I just wanted to see who he's mingling with. What type of crowd he runs in. See if he's got any unscrupulous connections. You know, running afoul of the USDA," he said quickly.

231

"Have you brought me out with a boatload of criminals?" she asked. "What do you know about ROI that I don't?"

"As far as I know, these are all upstanding citizens making the world *sustainable for the future*."

"But the captain?"

"Let's go say hello."

He led Sylvia over to the captain.

"Bert Wilson, how are you?" Allen shouted.

"Just fine thanks. This is my wife, Sylvia."

"Pleasure. Is ROI your cause or Bert's?"

"Maybe a little of both," she said as she shook Allen's hand. "I've worked with ROI some through the library system."

"You're a librarian?"

"I am."

"Well! This is my wife, Jane. You two would have some things in common."

"I manage an after-school reading program," Jane said.

"No kidding. Which one?"

While the women talked about the local education system, Allen asked Bert to follow him over to the bar for another glass of wine.

"So, you just happened onto this boat by chance?" Allen asked.

"I have my philanthropic side," Bert said.

"Uh-huh. Well, I saw your article in the paper the other day. About Stepan."

"Wasn't my article, but what'd you think?"

"I'm glad someone's finally telling that story. Exposing him for the liar and the troublemaker he was."

"You weren't upset to see your name in it?"

"Oh no. If anything, it's been a boon for business. Shows I'm willing to take a chance on anyone hardworking, and it makes me look like the benevolent victim. My clients know I never charged them a dime more than I said I would, and I never let on to any of them I was having problems. This makes me look like Hercules to them. A lot of contractors would have slipped a surcharge into all their bills to cover their losses."

"No one was worried you were in business with an Estonian national?"

"Bah! Everyone in this business relies on foreign labor. It doesn't matter where you're from in our line of work, so long as you get the job done. It helps if you have papers to prove you're legal, if you want to work on any government contracts. Otherwise, it's a meritocracy."

"How noble."

"It's business," Allen said. "Hey, if it wasn't your article, whose was it?"

"The reporter's, I guess."

"And where'd he get it?"

"I thought it came from you."

"Huh. Well." Allen took a healthy sip of wine. "You find out, I wouldn't mind your sharing that with me. For old times' sake."

"What's your next step?" Bert asked.

"Tonight? This is Jane's organization, so I'm here as the token veteran." He grabbed his lapels and shook his uniform. "Truthfully, I intend to drink as much of my entrance ticket as I can manage and then take tomorrow off to tend to my hangover."

"What about the airfield?"

"Still waiting on the call, but rumor is it's kicking back up soon. We need to defend ourselves in the Baltic against those Russians."

"Is that why you're in it?"

"Of course not, Bert. I'm in it for the money, same as every other American. But you have to have your ideals to back up your income. Don't you know that? Ideals have been justifying our political economy since we brought smallpox blankets in for the Indians. Creative rationalization: that's the American way."

The captain laughed as they returned to their wives, wine in hand, and Bert put his arm around Sylvia. She was warm against the cold air blowing over the boat. She put her arm around him in turn, and soon enough the two couples parted ways. The ship lurched on into the black sea, bearing against the wind in the late January night.

Chapter Thirty

Wyatt had taken the week off for vacation, explaining to Bonnie that he needed to pull himself together.

"Hey, take care of yourself," Bonnie had said. "We'll get the paper out while you're gone."

Which is how, Thursday morning, he was able to nurse a pot of coffee and scroll mindlessly through his various news feeds for a few hours before Molly and her colleague picked him up. Today was job interview day, a hastily arranged meeting with her mysterious boss. If it went well, the gig would help Bert and Penelope bring down whoever they were trying to bring down. He hadn't seen the agents since Monday morning, but he knew they were watching him. Could feel their eyes the same way he'd spotted that dark brown sedan last week.

What he tried not to consider was who else might be watching him.

At ten-thirty, his phone buzzed with a text from Molly saying they would be pulling into his complex in a few minutes. Be on the lookout for a black Volkswagen hatchback.

He put on his coat and locked up just as the hatchback pulled to a stop. Molly was in the passenger seat, so he got in the back. "I'm too old to be riding around in a car like this," he said.

"Old is a state of mind," she said.

The driver said nothing. Wyatt tried to catch his eye in the rearview, but the man—a bullet-headed dude with a sober disposition and sunshades—appeared oblivious to the new passenger.

"We've got a little dance to get where we're going," Molly said. "To your point, we have to be careful."

"Absolutely," he said.

"It'll be worth the wait. I think you'll have fun with this job, and who knows, it might lead to some more work."

They headed north across the Wappoo Creek into West Ashley and out toward Citadel Mall, Molly chattering about the weather and the driver saying nothing.

"You like these suburban outposts, don't you?" he asked.

"I told you, no one expects international business transactions out here in the safety of retail land. There's a reason drug dealers love these places."

After circling the mall, the driver pulled up in front of the Dillard's.

"This is our stop," Molly said, and she opened the door.

Wyatt didn't dare look around to see if the agents had tailed them here, or if they would be able to park and continue tracking them. Wyatt had left the burner phone at home, not wanting to risk a search, so he had no way of alerting Bert and Penelope to his location. He wasn't fully on board with the plan Bert had outlined Monday morning—the risk both to him and to Molly—so perhaps it was better that Molly's crew had some evasive tricks up their sleeves.

He followed her into the department store, swiftly through the women's clothing section, and then out the perfumed front of the store and into the mall proper.

"Do this often?" he asked.

"Just enough to stay on our toes," she said as she led him

toward the center of the mall, past Rue 21 and a diamond dealer and then out an employee exit, some forgotten corridor no shopper would ever venture through. They burst into the sunlight of another parking lot where a PT Cruiser awaited them.

"You know, there's still a market for Lincoln Town Cars," he said.

"You're in front," she said.

When he got in, he was stunned to see Lillian Cope at the wheel, wearing a pantsuit and looking like she'd been dragged away from a standing bridge game.

"Lillian," he said. "What are you doing here?"

"Wyatt." She smiled subtly and looked around.

When he and Molly were buckled in, Lilian wordlessly piloted the car out of the mall and onto 526. He studied this woman more closely than he had at the funeral—hair going gray but with enough strands of black to recall what must have been a violently beautiful youth, skin mottled with freckles and scars, the bones in her jaw jutting out fiercely. She'd lost the softness he remembered, but as they made their way onto the highway, he was already rewriting history. When he'd been twenty, Lillian had been the mother, the domestic backbone of the family, the quiet appeaser. It had all seemed very old-fashioned, which made Mary Grace a mystery to him. How had this force of nature come from such a traditional family? Perhaps now he had the answer. Perhaps Lillian had been the quiet force of nature in the family all along.

He caught Molly's eye in the rearview mirror, but she merely raised an eyebrow and then looked out the window, where the land had turned marshy and underdeveloped. It was an overcast day, a day that accentuated the factory smoke and paper mill side of Charleston, the industrial ring around the tourist enchantment. Lillian remained silent as they continued north and crossed the Ashley River, and then she took an exit and parked them in a Wal-Mart shopping center.

Jon Sealy

She pulled out her phone and dialed a number. On speaker, it rang twice before a British man picked up. "I'm here," he said.

"Great," Lillian said, and she put it on speaker and set the phone on the armrest in the center of the car. "We're all here as well. I've got Molly in the back seat and Wyatt Brewer here beside me."

"Wyatt, great," the Brit said. "I'm glad you could join us. I apologize for not being there myself, but it's the best we could do on short notice when Molly said you wanted to meet the team."

"Right," he said. "Well. She mentioned an interesting job, but I like to get to know who I'm working with."

"Of course. Client service at its finest. I hope you don't mind that I couldn't catch a flight. I manage our operations here in London, though of course, Lillian is the brain behind it all."

Lillian smiled at that. "Thank you, Winn." To Wyatt: "We run a tight core team. You know Molly, of course, and obviously we've met. Winn is our liaison with different governing bodies. We have a few other operatives and administrators, but I presume you weren't trying to meet everyone Molly works with?"

"I have to say, it is a pleasant surprise to see you here."

"You're not a very competent liar," Lillian said. "I could see the wheels turning the whole ride over. You thought my husband was running the show, and wondered who replaced him when he passed."

"Well, it was his law firm that hired me."

"And I don't know if we'll ever find a better set of business partners than the people Harry recruited. Molly's doing a great job bringing a public relations angle to our work, but my Harry was something else. We were such a good team."

"I'm sorry, I'm still a little confused," Wyatt said. "Are you the one hiring me here?"

238

"I am," Lillian said. "Assuming we can come to terms. I'm sorry if you felt misled. Molly has a way of making our operation appear bigger than it is."

"Oh, I don't feel misled. Just…"

"Internationally lobbying and diplomacy don't seem like the forte of an old woman. I get it. But look deeply enough, and you'll find there's always a woman at the heart of the matter."

"You set me up in Madrid, didn't you?" It came out before Wyatt processed what he was thinking, but as the words came out, he understood they were true.

Lillian smiled as if she pitied him for his obtuseness, and he understood he'd been a useful idiot for her agenda. He started to speak, but the dry air caught in his throat and he started wheezing.

"I believe you were trying to ask for an explanation," Lillian said. "Why did I have Harry hire you all those years ago? What happened with Sr. Oliva? The details don't matter, but I can tell you, the deal was going to go bad one way or another, and I didn't want Harry anywhere near it. You happened to come along at the right time. I must say, I didn't expect you to be so…circumspect. You might be the only man in America to keep that kind of money quiet. Did you even spend a nickel of it?"

He shook his head.

Lillian smiled. "I never approved of you with Mary Grace, but I must say, you have fortitude. It's a shame it never would have worked out between you."

"Maybe it could have."

"My dear, no. If she hadn't found out about the money on her own, I would have told her and that would have been that."

"Why?" he asked

"That's difficult to answer for someone who doesn't have children," she said. "I understand you and Molly have gotten to know each other a little bit, but that's two weeks. I'm talking about a lifetime of parenting. I watched Mary Grace's personality evolve from day one. I knew my daughter, and whether you believe it or not, I knew she wouldn't be happy with you."

"Maybe you didn't know her as well as you thought."

Lillian smiled again. "I thought about having you caught with the money in Madrid, but I saw how you looked at my daughter and guess I felt sorry for you. Poor boy, you were about to get tossed away by the woman you loved."

"You were buying me off."

"If you'd spent the money, someone would have found you. I thought perhaps you deserved some time to enjoy yourself. I certainly didn't expect you to be so disciplined. It made me think I'd misjudged you."

"Did Mary Grace know about you?"

"Let's say I found it convenient to remain the loving housewife. For everyone."

"You could have just left us alone," he said. "Left us to live our quiet lives."

"What kind of life would that have been?"

"We could have been happy. Mary Grace might still be alive."

Lillian shot him a look. "That's a strong assumption on your part," she said acidly. "As I said, I knew my daughter. But you: I've kept some tabs on you all these years, and when you showed up at Harry's funeral, I knew you'd never gotten over it. You poor man. Maybe now that I'm experiencing my next wave of grief, I wanted to offer you a second chance. Earn some money you can spend. Do something fun. Travel."

"Connect with my daughter."

Lillian paused. Molly was silent in the backseat, and Wyatt wondered how much of a spell this old woman had cast on her granddaughter. He suspected Molly had her own designs, just as he knew Mary Grace did. Lillian could talk all she wanted about knowing her daughter, but he detected a strong blind spot in her and wondered how he might use that to his advantage. Whatever he brought to Bert and Penelope after this, it would have to be enough to entrap Lillian while exonerating Molly.

"The work remains the same," Lillian said, "regardless of who's behind it all. Harry and I had a partnership, a good one. My Uncle Everett was the one who encouraged me to marry him, and he set Harry up in the family business. He had great foresight, my uncle did, and now my life's work is almost complete. I don't have all that long here, but I'm excited to see how Molly's brought in a new energy, and I'm curious to see where she takes it. I see a lot of Mary Grace in her, as I'm sure you do, and I think with the right people around her—someone like you, someone she can trust—Molly's going to take this business into brand new territory."

He looked at the phone, still sitting quietly on the armrest between them. "And him?"

"Winn and Harry go way back, to my uncle's days."

"I'm working on business continuity myself," the Brit said on the phone. "I've got a line on a few contacts here in Britain. We'll all get together soon."

"But first let's start with the one job," Lillian said.

"Molly's told me a little about it. Sounds like you need a writer more than anything."

"Yes, but one with your skillset of interviewing people and drawing out their stories. We've got a few contacts here in the Lowcountry who will be valuable sources for you."

He turned to his daughter. "What do you think about all this, Molly? Did you know your grandmother could be so ruthless?"

"She raised me," Molly said.

Wyatt was quiet for a moment.

"I'm glad we met up today," Lillian said, "because what I don't want is for you to do some one-off job for us and call it a day. I want you to know we're looking for someone who could join us on a more permanent basis."

"I don't understand anything you do."

"Then we both have a job for the coming weeks. Why don't we take this first project as a test. A chance for you to show us what you're capable of, and for us to show you what we're about. If we both come away satisfied, we'll see where it goes."

"I think we have a lot more to talk about, you and I," he said. With a final glance back at Molly, he asked, "Where do I start?"

Chapter Thirty One

"WELL, SHOOT," Bert said when Wyatt and Molly got out of the car in front of Dillard's. "Pull over here."

He got out and scrambled toward the entrance, but by the time he made it inside the department store, the targets had vanished. The store was quiet and musty, with Muzak on the radio and a besuited sales clerk coming his way. He waved her off and found his way to the mall—where he spotted Molly and Wyatt boogieing down the main path. He watched them duck into an emergency exit and sent a text to Penelope.

North exit.

He waited a moment and followed them out, in time to see them piloting out of the parking lot. He called Penelope, who answered on Bluetooth, static in the air around her.

"They're in a white PT Cruiser, heading out now," he said.

"You want me to pick you up?"

"Tail them if you can."

"I don't see them."

"Should be taking the exit toward 17. By the light."

"Nothing," she said.

He cursed.

"You want me to keep driving?"

"No, come get me. I'm by the east employee entrance, next to the old Penney's."

Need more surveillance, he texted Diane. Where was his boss this week? It was not the time for her to go missing, and she'd been nearly MIA all week. She'd replied to a couple of texts with a *Got it* or *Roger*, but wouldn't return his calls, hadn't commented on the particulars of their plan, and had refused to engage when he talked about needing resources.

When Penelope pulled around and Bert got in, she asked where to.

"Back to the office, I guess," he said. "I'll text Jarman to see if he can stake out Wyatt's house. I want you on Molly this afternoon when she shows back up."

"You think he's going to land it?"

"I don't know," Bert said. "I'm sure he left the burner at his house. We'll see what he says when they get back from wherever they're going."

"Assuming they get back."

"Yes, assuming. But if they don't let him go, we're out of a case."

That evening, after receiving texts from Penelope and Jarman that they'd each spied their charges, Bert closed up shop at the office and sent another text to Diane.

Target still in hand. Need surveillance team. Is one coming?

No response.

When he pulled into his neighborhood, it was full dark and cold outside, a front coming in from the sea and settling over the Lowcountry like a virus in the lungs. He felt a scratch in his throat and remembered Wyatt hacking away in the office the other day. Illness was just what the team needed right now. Get sick and limp across the finish line of his career.

Colonel Barclay was out in the yard, his garage door open,

and he appeared to be struggling with something in the bed of his pickup. Bert pulled into the drive and cut the lights.

"Help you with anything?" he asked through his window.

"I'm putting in some vegetable beds for the spring," Barclay said. "Trying to get a jump on it."

Bert saw the man had a truck full of two-by-eights and about fifteen bags of potting soil. He got out and said, "I can give you a hand. It's too cold out here to be messing with all this."

"Took me longer at Home Depot than I thought," Barclay muttered as he wrestled another bag of dirt from the truck.

"It always does. Let me help you."

The bags of dirt weighed fifty pounds apiece, and Bert didn't see how this frail old dude was hauling those around like they were bags of air. He felt his spine bending as he lugged the first bag to the garage.

"You can set it anywhere. I park outside."

"Got it," Bert said through his teeth. "Hey, you heard anything more from the HOA about your flag?"

"My lawyer's writing up something."

"I saw you in the paper the other day."

"Yeah, I don't know how that reporter got my name, but I appreciate whoever gave him the tip."

Bert waited, but the man genuinely seemed to have no idea he was the one.

When they'd unloaded the truck, Barclay thanked him for the help.

"What're you growing?"

"I don't know. Tomatoes, maybe some hot peppers. I grew zucchini last year and the suckers took over my yard."

"Oh yeah?"

"Big as my arm. I couldn't give them away. Thought I might try coriander this year."

"That sounds fancy."

"I used to have a gal working for me, and she'd bring in

fresh cilantro from her garden on occasion, in the summers. This was back before Mexican food was everywhere, so it was a real treat. I thought maybe I could recreate it."

"What line of work were you in?"

"Oh, I did all kinds of things. When I got out of the Navy, I had an early McDonald's franchise. I got bored with that, so I got into real estate. Got a couple of properties and some income coming in from that, and used it to buy a Volkswagen dealership."

"You don't say."

"First one in South Carolina."

"This was back when they had all the fun ads?"

"We had people coming in from all over. They'd see the commercial about the snow plow driver, and people who had never seen snow in their lives wanted a durable vehicle. In case it ever happened, I reckon."

"What happened to your dealership?"

"Oh, I sold that after the gas crisis. Shored up my finances and more or less retired, though I've always had a little something going. I still have a few properties out on John's Island I rent out to tourists. Keeps me young."

In the yard, when the wind picked up, his flag rattled against his flagpole.

Barclay looked up to contemplate the flag. "People wonder why I can't just put it on my porch like a normal homeowner. You can't get that same sound from a flag on your porch. It reminds me of being out on a ship and having the wind tear at your masts. When you get old, those little reminders come to mean more to you. Where you've been, what you've done. I'm not looking for another adventure here. I just want to live out my days in peace."

"I can understand that," Bert said.

"See if you can't convince your colleagues on the HOA. They sure are dense."

"There's no getting around people sometimes," Bert said.

His phone buzzed, and he saw he had a message from Wyatt. "Well, I got get on," he said.

"Go to it," his old neighbor said. "I appreciate the help."

Bert left him there, staring at the bags of dirt and the lumber in his garage, flag rattling overhead, and it appeared the old man was trying to figure out what he should do next.

Chapter Thirty Two

PENELOPE WAS WRUNG OUT. Everyone on the team was drained, Bert had picked up Wyatt's infection and was hacking away, and she felt a little scratchy in her throat as well. It had been a long week following Wyatt around with no support from Washington, meals in her car, Dunkin' Donuts coffee and the occasional Wendy's salad, and now it was Friday morning and she'd trailed Wyatt to the airport. She put in a call to Bert to see if they could get a line on his credit card purchases this week, but he told her they were on their own.

"I'm sure the FBI could get the data," he said, "but we'd still need Diane or someone to get us in front of the FISA court before they'd hand it over."

"You heard from Diane yet?"

"Not a word."

"You worried about it?"

"Not yet. I don't know what other operations she's got running, but even if she were just focused on us, she'd still have a pretty big bureaucracy to navigate. We'll get what we need, when we need it."

"I hope you're right."

"You just worry about Brewer."

"He parked in the 24-hour lot, and I'm following him into the departures area now."

"Keep your distance."

"He's not paying any attention."

"Still."

"I know. Look, could you do a search and see what's taking off in the next couple of hours? Specifically, from United?"

"I've got it up now," Bert said. "You've got Charlotte, D.C., Miami, and Philly."

"Hang on."

Penelope followed Wyatt to the self-check-in counter, saw MIA on the screen over his shoulder, and proceeded to the agent. If he'd noticed her, he didn't show it. He seemed to be puzzling over his options. His only luggage was a briefcase.

"Are there any flights back from Miami tonight?"

"Um, yeah. A late arrival, nonstop, leaves around ten."

"Got it. I think he's making a round trip."

"That's only a few hours in the city."

"He's only got a briefcase with him at check-in. Maybe he's got a meeting set up. You think this is it?"

"It can't be. He texted to say they were on for next week."

She set the phone down and asked the ticket agent if there were any seats left on the Miami flight.

"Let me see," the woman said, and she started the click-clicking of the process.

"Do we have anyone in Miami?" Penelope asked Bert. "Anyone we can lean on?"

"You're it, if you can get a flight," Bert said. "Jarman said Molly's at the gym, so I doubt this is it. Stay on him if you can, but be careful."

"Always am," she said, hanging up.

"Good news," the ticket agent said.

. . .

Penelope's seat was in the back of the plane, giving her a clear view up to Wyatt in the center exit row. While everyone finished boarding, he scrolled through the news on his phone, and then he shut it down and took a nap during the bulk of the flight. Penelope paid for Wi-Fi so she could stay connected, sent a series of encrypted messages to Bert and Jarman—but heard nothing from either of them.

In the Miami airport, she tailed Wyatt as he navigated the throngs of people, briefcase in tow, down to the arrivals exit. She felt reasonably confident he had not spied her in Charleston, nor had taken note of her on the plane, but now this was the gamble, trying to blend in with a crowd of Jersey bros at a bus stop while they all waited for a ride into town. Miami had a thick and swampy heat, even for someone used to muggy Charleston. Her cotton shirt clung to her. Her head throbbed. She was not cut out for equatorial climates.

At one point while they waited, Wyatt glanced around nervously but passed over her. Penelope had her hair pulled into a tight ponytail and was wearing sunglasses and a baseball hat. She tried to affect a thousand-yard-stare, just a bored Millennial waiting on the bus. Then she pulled out her phone and ticked through her Instagram feed, decidedly not looking at Wyatt. She followed weightlifters and recipe bloggers, so her feed was clogged with images of Herculean women dead-lifting four hundred pounds, dudes snatching more weight than she could add in her head, and chefs showing off their techniques for preventing hollandaise from curdling and making pancakes with Greek yogurt.

The bus approached and came to a halt with the sound of a drum set dropping out a second-floor window.

Penelope took a seat in the back, kept her shades on and her phone handy, and eyed Wyatt out of her peripheral vision. He looked up and down the bus before sitting near the door, and held his briefcase to his chest like it contained nuclear secrets.

The bus wended through the swamps of South Florida and then into the smoggy city. She'd never been here, never been south of Savannah on the east coast, but Miami seemed built like any other city. The slum-like exurbs, the moneyed skyscraper district, the tourist draw by the water and the construction economy keeping Florida solvent.

Somewhere amid the skyscrapers, Wyatt pulled the string and hopped off the bus, 2nd and Flagler. Penelope headed toward the front of the bus, but Wyatt was looking around too carefully for her to risk following him here. She waited a block and pulled the string and got off at 1st Street. From fifty yards away, jogging down the avenue, she saw Wyatt enter a financial services tower, and she slowed.

By the time she approached the building, Wyatt was long gone from the lobby, and the security guard asked if he could help her. She took off her hat, conscious she was not dressed for such a place. Schleppy yoga pants and a T-shirt.

"I'm running a few minutes behind," she said. "I was supposed to meet a colleague here. Wyatt Brewer?"

"He just went up. I'll have to call Mr. Robinson to have someone come back down for you, Ms.?"

"You know what, I'll send him a text," she said.

The guard had his hand on the phone. "I can call them up. I'm sure they won't mind sending someone for you."

"Let me just text him," she said again. "I think it was going to be a quick meeting, so I may not need to be there."

She backed out onto the sidewalk, phone in hand. She looked up at the building and googled the address to try to find out who Mr. Robinson was and what he did in the great city of Miami.

After meeting with his long-time advisor and setting up a trust with his assets, Wyatt shook Robinson's hand and gathered his papers.

251

"Always a pleasure," Robinson said. "And congratulations on your growing family."

"I appreciate it, Dan."

"What's next for you?"

The two men headed toward the elevator. The twelfth floor had floor-to-ceiling windows, and blinding light reflected off glass from neighboring buildings and lit the floor in a dazzling array of sunshine.

"Travel, maybe? I don't know. Things aren't all that stable at the paper."

"It's nice you're able to do it out of love rather than having to pay the bills. Our local paper's falling apart, and I know it's because they don't have the same advertising dollars they once did."

"For us, it was the big retailers. Macy's and Dillard's quit buying those full-page ads, so all you had left was the car dealers, and most of them have pulled out. A few colleagues have joked we need to get the financial advisors buying ads."

"Because we have the money?"

"Because your clients are older. They're the last people reading a print newspaper."

"That's interesting. I'll have to talk with some of the partners about that."

Robinson hit the button for the lobby, and they ran out of small talk a few seconds before the doors opened and his advisor was able to usher Wyatt back to the security desk.

"Great to see you, Wyatt. Thanks for coming down. Have a safe flight back."

"Thanks, Dan. See you next time."

Wyatt turned in his security badge to the front desk, and the guard thanked him and then said, in an afterthought, "Were you able to catch up with your colleague?"

"Who's that?"

"The young lady. Came in just after you got on the elevator."

"Was she blonde?" Wyatt asked.

"Nah, brunette. Pretty girl, but not really dressed for a business meeting, if you know what I mean. Looked more like a tourist."

"We must have missed each other," Wyatt said.

He remembered seeing the girl earlier today at the bus stop. She'd looked familiar under the ball cap, leaning against a light post and flipping through her phone, but he'd quickly put her out of his mind. He tried to picture her more completely, but only had a shadow in his mind. Spooks everywhere. He thought now that she could have been Penelope, but she was already fading in his memory. The stress of last Sunday night and Bert's intense stare were his abiding impressions from the interrogation. And if they were following him? Well, he'd not told them everything about his meeting with Lillian, or about his contingency with Molly Keagan. It made sense they would want to keep tabs on him, yet he took note that he would have to proceed with caution. He'd spent the past twenty years looking over his shoulder, and if he came through this operation with Molly, he understood he would be spending the rest of his life looking around corners. His fate was set, the board arranged, so all he could do was play the next series of moves and hope for a checkmate.

Chapter Thirty Three

WHILE PENELOPE WAS SKULKING around after Wyatt in Miami, Jarman was cramped in the driver's seat of a little Hyundai Accent, his temporary replacement to the big brown Camry he'd forfeited after Wyatt made him. He'd been staking out Molly's rental house near Hampton Park and the Citadel, but the girl didn't have a life. Watching her for the week, you'd think she was an independently wealthy hermit. All she did was go to the gym and eat at a little café near her house.

She stayed on her phone full time, but while her digital life may have been wide and rich, her analog existence was confined to a few square blocks. The one time she left her neighborhood, she ended up at a Piggly Wiggly, where she filled her cart with produce, cereal, and white wine.

As an immigrant, he understood what it was like to have a wall around you. He never believed Americans, white or black, understood him, so he bounced through his days with the assumption of being alone. It was what made him so well-suited for life on Bert's team. Whereas most of their colleagues in the agency rubbed elbows and scrambled for power, Bert set their focus on a few targets out in the world and encouraged them to remain otherwise invisible.

Molly was one of them. He could tell by the way she glanced up and down the street before locking her front door, the way she paid for her meals and groceries in cash, the way she always walked around the block before going back into her house. He'd been more careful this week than when he'd been tailing Wyatt. Kept his car at a distance, parked on the opposite side of the grocery store lot, stayed two aisles away from her while she was shopping. She may have picked up the shadow—most people who operated in the covert world were paranoiacs and always sensed a tail, whether there was one or not—but he made sure that any time she looked around, there was nothing but sunlight and an empty corridor.

On Saturday night, she broke her routine and drove down the peninsula, almost to Broad Street, and parked on Queen. He dropped his car around the corner on King. Saturday night but it was still winter, which meant even the tourist district was sparse. The Market was crowded, Meeting Street had enough people to remain invisible, but the side streets and back alleys were deserted. He made sure she was well ahead of him, nearly out of sight, as he trailed her to the restaurant 82 Queen, where she met her grandmother and a well-dressed man in his mid-forties who had a wave of dark hair and a friendly smile.

Now this was interesting. Wyatt had told him that after they lost him at the mall, Molly had brought him to a meeting with her mother and a British man on the telephone. Bert had flagged the information but held it close until he worked out whatever was gnawing at him.

Penelope had let them know Wyatt was back from Miami but there was no sign of him now. He texted her to confirm the reporter wasn't on his way.

He's at home now, she wrote.

Any sign of movement?

He's got a basketball game on. Appears to be cooking dinner.

Molly and her crew are at 82 Queen. Any word from Bert?

Nothing.

Then he sent a few messages to Bert, filling his boss in and asking if they had any new resources from Washington. At that moment, his boss was having a heated conversation with Diane over the nature of the operation and was sending messages to Jarman while he had Diane on speaker.

Not a thing

You want to meet me for dinner?

Hang back. Don't want to jeopardize anything.

Roger dodger. Want me to tail either of the others?

Stick with Molly. Until we know differently, she's the one we're after.

Jarman waited until he saw the trio had been seated. He couldn't see them from the street, and since he would be conspicuous going in for a table himself, he walked up to the Market to kill some time. A few vendors were set up in the center of the street, hawking everything from beads to baskets to bandannas. Tourists strolled arm in arm up and down the strip, and Jarman ducked into a little coffee house. The place had a French bistro vibe to it, wood paneled walls and a prominent pastry case stuffed with croissants. You needed that to stay in business in Charleston. The restaurant industry would spit you out if you didn't provide the right combo of ambience and hospitality.

He sat at the bar and made friendly small talk with the barista while she pulled shot after shot of espresso for a steady stream of college kids and tourists. A kid in a jean jacket and a brown cap sat down the bar from him, an unopened anthology of Kierkegaard in front of him and a TikTok feed pulled up on his phone. Jarman had never been one for scholarship, but he liked the physical world and mistrusted the internet. He'd long felt rootless in America, but these days, when he looked around, he was beginning to realize no one had roots in this country. Perhaps at one time Southerners were proud of the South, but now? Everyone seemed to belong everywhere they went, which meant they belonged nowhere.

After finishing his coffee, he walked back to the restaurant, poked his head in the door, and saw the trio still working on their meals. He buttoned his pea coat and returned to his car, where he waited another hour for Molly leave the restaurant. She came back to her car alone, got in, and drove straight back to her house.

Adventure over, back to her cloistered world for another night.

At the office a few blocks from 82 Queen, Bert was on a never-ending conference call with Diane, while she went over endless scenarios regarding the week ahead.

What if we—

Or how about—

Have you considered—

It was maddening, and he now understood how she'd achieved her promotion to the directorship, by being as methodical as an independent auditor and as paranoid as a corporate defense attorney. Men in the agency may have skated to the upper ranks on charm and a few solid returns, but women in leadership were in short supply. Diane made her mark by showing up prepared. Fine with Bert, but he'd been waiting on her preparations all week and was long ready for action.

Let's think about this—

I remember when we tried—

I need to ask Winston—

"Wait, what?" Bert asked.

"Winston. He needs to weigh in on this aspect."

"Shields? What's he got to do with anything?"

Diane's voice crackled on the line. Bert took it off speaker and held the phone to his ear. "I brought him into the department," she said.

"Since when?"

"He's been a part-time advisor for us for a few months. The other day he accepted a full-time placement."

"The day we ran into him by the elevator."

"Yeah. We met to discuss his role after you and I met."

"And what is his role, exactly?"

"Look, Bert, the department has changed since you and I set up ISD. Project Gravy is a one-of-a-kind operation, but I'm overseeing a number of internal investigations. Winston's brought his international network in."

"You mean MI6 specifically."

"Sometimes the best way to get a handle on life in the fishbowl is to have someone outside take a look."

"You've been using the Brits to investigate the agency. Jesus, Diane."

"They don't have anything they couldn't get through other channels. What's happening is that intelligence agencies around the world are scrambling to figure out how to operate. The tech companies have more information than we ever could have dreamed of. So while you've been investigating Archer and Cope, we've been trying to figure out how to navigate the public-private distinction when it comes to information. And that distinction has led to sharing across international borders."

Archer and Cope. Twentieth-century figures, old Cold War battles. She was too kind to say it, but he understood her inference that Project Gravy was a cold case investigation, a dead end researching dead men and their legacies. He recognized the world was not in the same place where he'd started his career, but it alarmed him to hear how cavalierly Diane was talking about things that would have been considered treason twenty-five years ago.

"Okay," he said. "So run it by Winston. I understand ISD

isn't the same organization we started ten years ago, but we've got a chance to land a big case here. Not a cold case, not Archer and Cope. Living people, who are sources of rot in our system."

"I hear you, Bert, and I don't disagree."

"So, can I get an extra surveillance team?"

"Let's talk about it Monday."

"The operation is Monday, Diane. It'll be too late then."

"My hands are tied. Winston's out of pocket, and we need to make sure MI6 is informed before we widen your operation."

"Is Shields working for you, or are you working for him?"

"I told you there are nuances," she said. "If I pull resources from one operation and give them to you, then what happens if that other operation goes south?"

"I understand competing priorities. What I don't understand is why Project Gravy isn't at the top of your list. If we've got corruption in the system, it follows that no operation is truly safe. We're all compromised."

Diane was silent.

"You don't agree."

"I don't disagree," she said again.

"But you're not going to do anything."

"Let's talk on Monday morning."

"We're in execution mode tomorrow," he said. "If we don't have a team en route tomorrow, then we might as well wait and I can tell you how the operation goes. Maybe I'll have great news for you Tuesday."

"Let's put something on the calendar Monday," she insisted.

"There's nothing to report on Monday. My team's going to be in full-on surveillance mode. We're pulling down twenty-hour days right now."

"I'll send a meeting invite," she said, and he hung up on her.

Chapter Thirty Four

THE JOB LILLIAN and Molly had in mind for him went beyond simply writing a white paper about Eastern European immigration, though that might have been their cover for stakeholders who were funding the operation. The real thrust of their agenda was fuzzy, like a magic eye puzzle that wouldn't slide into view, but his general sense was that a white paper would only be the first step, evidence showing a demand for capitalist freedoms among ex-Soviet citizens—evidence that would help them raise funds to further whatever agenda they had beyond promoting capitalism beyond the old Iron Curtain.

Unfortunately for Wyatt, the job was not simply aggregating and organizing data into a clean report. Rather, his job, as he understood it, was to manufacture the data by contacting certain underworld figures.

"Didn't you just have me write an article disparaging the Eastern European underworld?" he asked Molly on Sunday evening over dinner. They were at an Indian buffet in West Ashley this time, a quiet, white-tablecloth kind of place with more reasonable prices than the downtown fare. "Didn't my article about Stepan Boldavich do enough to show how dangerous and, well, un-American those underworld connections are? And you're asking me to make friends with those people?"

"Facts on the ground are changing every day," she said. "Stepan was a key contact for us."

"Do you know who killed him?" he asked.

She didn't reply.

"Was it one of the people I'm supposed to be introducing myself to? Or was it one of your people?"

"My grandmother and I aren't in the business of murder," she said.

He'd insisted she take him to her boss, and instead she'd brought him to Lillian. He believed her when she said Lillian was running her little area, but he also believed there was someone beyond Lillian who was running the whole operation. Harry—or Lillian—had been the middleman, not the orchestrator, of the Madrid debacle. Lillian may or may not be in the business of murder (the death of Sr. Oliva was still unsolved, as far as Wyatt was concerned), but the orchestrator, whoever that was, might be.

"What about your guy on the phone?" he asked.

"Winn? Winston's all right. Besides, I don't think he's ever been to South Carolina."

"Doesn't mean he didn't hire a hitman."

"No one's forcing you to take this job," she said. "If you don't trust us, we can call it a day."

"It's not that I mistrust you. It's the circumstances. If I met a friend in a bar and told him about the past few weeks, his best advice for me would be to get out. Think about it: you show up out of nowhere and ask me to look into a murdered Estonian and his underworld connections. I publish an article about how big and bad these people are, and now you're offering to pay me to get to know them. Befriend them. Write favorably about them so—what? So you can convince donors that only capitalism can save the new world order."

"Not just capitalism," she said. "We're trying to promote economy over politics. A system over national borders. Action over identity. What you do is more important than who you are or where you live."

"Yeah, yeah," he said.

He stared at the carpet beside the table, unsure how to unstick the conversation. The restaurant was warm and smelled of cooked paprika and garlic.

"Don't be like that."

"Like what?" he asked, though he knew exactly the problem, sulking like a child placed in time out, knowing some truth but unable to communicate it.

"We didn't come out here to argue. It won't hurt my feelings if you decide you don't want to go through with the job."

"I do want to do it," he said. "I just want you to acknowledge it doesn't make a whole lot of sense."

"Let me explain it to you."

"I get what you're telling me."

"You hear me, but you're not comprehending."

"What am I not getting?"

"Stepan Boldavich's contacts weren't the problem," she said.

"I'm sorry?"

"If I understand you, you're worried about Stepan's underworld contacts. You believe they're shady and dangerous."

"Aren't they?"

"Of course."

"There you go."

"But they're no more dangerous than the U.S. military. That guy you interviewed, Captain Allen? He's into way worse than whatever Stepan's Estonian friends are doing

down at the docks. I didn't ask you to write about the Estonians to show how dangerous they were."

"Well, that sure was my article's thesis."

"That's fine," she said. "But I asked you to write it because
of Stepan. We needed to discredit him, because he was
working with the U.S. government."

A waiter came over to refill their water glasses. "Help
yourself if you want another pass at the buffet," he said.

"Oh, we will," Molly said. "Thank you."

The man nodded austerely and vanished back into a back
corridor of the restaurant.

"What do you mean he was working for the government?"

"I mean, he was a spy for some security agency. CIA
maybe, we don't know."

"What's the harm in that? It was an American firm?"

"Yes, and we'd love to work with whoever he was working
for. But not like that. Not covertly."

"What makes you think he was a spy?"

"Winn has some contacts in MI6. They share intelligence
with some of our agencies, and vice versa. He got word of an
informant in Charleston, and it didn't take long for us to
connect what MI6 had with Stepan Boldavich."

"You *did* have him whacked."

"I did nothing of the sort. We merely cut him off, which
might have jammed him up with his underworld friends."

"Same difference."

"It's not the same," she insisted. "If he was promising
something to a bunch of gangsters, and we were the product
he was selling upriver, we're the victims. We merely shut the
door in his face. What happened after that isn't our concern."

"But you hired me to slander him. Surely, you take respon-
sibility for that?"

"You didn't write anything untrue. All we did was tip you
off."

"Again, you're splitting hairs."

"I don't think so," she said. "I don't think so at all. My point is that the real threat isn't the Estonian immigrants Stepan was mixed up with. Some of them may be bad apples, but they're not a threat to you, so long as you're not financially entangled with them. I wouldn't be sending my long-lost father into the lion's den."

"You're still asking me to operate on faith."

"I am."

"Tell me again what it is you're looking for me to do."

"One of Stepan's old contacts runs an association, Good Will Refugees. It's a tiny little operation off Church Street. They're expecting to meet you tomorrow."

"For what?"

"To talk about what they do, and give you the lay of the land. Eastern Europeans in the Lowcountry. How many, how they got here, how they make a living."

"These are the same people who killed Stepan Boldavich?"

"We don't know. It doesn't matter. Look," she said quickly, "I understand on some cosmic scale it matters, but as a matter of safety, you're fine. They see you as an ally. You're going to draw attention to their plight—and help us get some American development in their homeland."

"Tell me about who these people are."

"I told you, they're Eastern European nationals. Mostly Estonian."

"What does that mean? What do they want?"

"They're looking for a nice life here, and working for liberation in their homeland. Do you know how the U.S. screwed all those nations in the 2000s? When we canceled the defense grid? They got a raw deal, so the Estonians at large have been cozying up to the Russians. We didn't help them, so they've turned to the other great superpower. I want to change that."

"You'd still call the Russians a superpower?"

"They are what they are. That's why we're trying to influence policymakers to build that airfield."

"I thought you were trying to defend the interests of the oil industry. Or, excuse me, *capitalism*."

"I am trying to defend it. The stability of the region is good for international business."

"And to build stability, you need to make friends with everybody? Gangsters in the underworld?"

"We're trying to build alliances. That's what we had with Stepan Boldavich, even if he was connected to some bad people."

"But he was also connected to the intelligence community."

"Yes, without our knowledge. That's what we ran into with him. He was playing too many sides, so we're starting over. Starting with Good Will Refugees. We want to make friends with the Estonians here in Charleston, write a brief on them so we can build some funds and make our case for the airfield. Which is, of course, where you come in."

"I'm just interviewing them?"

"Easy peasy," she said. "Same as you would for a news article. Take good notes and report back."

"I'm still having a hard time understanding how they'll trust me. I just wrote about how awful they are. Violence, nepotism, you name it."

"That was a splinter group of Estonian gangsters. These people run a respectable organization."

"I thought you said they were one and the same."

"They are, but to their mind, you didn't write about their association. You didn't write about Good Will Refugees. You wrote about some thugs smuggling drugs and skimming money off the docks. That's not what they're about, on paper anyway. They're eager to share their more benevolent operations."

"I'm getting a second plate," he said, and he stood up for another pass at the buffet. "You need anything?"

"I'm good," she said.

He filled a second plate with rice and a spicy grilled chicken with a deep red color he suspected was only achieved via dye. He'd tried to make tandoori chicken at home on occasion, but no matter how much paprika he put into the mix, the yogurt marinade always produced a lump of clay-colored meat that tasted fine but lacked panache.

He watched her from across the room. She was clicking through her phone, a study in elegance there with her free hand wrapped around her wine stem, her blonde hair tucked behind her ear to show off her visage. It still took his breath away to see her and remember Mary Grace, her striking blue eyes and rounded cheeks, and the way she made living appear effortless. She glided with ease through the world. Quick to laugh, always ready with a wry comment, she approached the world hungry. With appetite.

He saw that same hunger in Molly. She had a plan, he could tell. Regardless of whether the operation would prove as straightforward as meeting a few exiles, hearing about their refugee operation, and writing a white paper, Molly had set out the bread crumbs. She expected—no, knew—he would follow the trail. He would report all this to Bert tonight, and the agents would follow him to Church Street tomorrow. What happened from there depended on what Wyatt did not know —the collision of Molly's (and Lillian's) agenda and the agent's grand plot to entrap whoever or whatever they were looking for.

For now, as he returned to the table with his fresh plate, he was conscious this might be his last meal with Molly. He hoped they would both get away and enjoy another dinner out, but a knot in his chest suggested this could be it—that one of them would soon be picked up by gangsters, by federal agents, by the mysterious Person Behind the Curtain.

"I could get used to these dinners out," he said as he sat back down. "It's nice to have a dining companion."

Molly put her phone away and took a sip of her wine. A red zinfandel she'd ordered unself-consciously after he'd ordered an iced tea. "What about the woman from the other night? I thought she was your companion."

"I'm not sure about that anymore."

"Because of me?"

"Because of me," he said. "Because of her ex-husband. Because our relationship was never meant to be anything serious. I made the mistake of thinking it was more than it was."

"I'm sorry it didn't work out," she said.

"I appreciate that, but it's my own fault. For the last twenty years, I've done a fine job of never growing up. Always trying not to commit too deeply, and I fell for a companion who literally couldn't commit."

"You could talk to her about all this."

"I could," he agreed, "but that would take away what we had. The point between us was the in-between. The escape. I thought she might have seen us together and thought we were an item and been jealous. I misread her. She told me a long time ago she never wanted to remarry, and I guess I thought something might change."

"It changed for you."

"Maybe."

"Did you tell her I was your daughter?"

He shook his head.

"Have you told anyone?"

"I don't have anyone to tell," he admitted.

"What about your mother? I first met you at your mother's house, after all."

"I haven't talked to her either. I left the next morning before she woke up. I'm telling you, I've never been good at the reality of everyday life. The world most people operate in,

I haven't felt comfortable in ever since I took that job for your grandfather."

"I'm glad I've gotten to know you," she said. "I'm glad you didn't just run off screaming when I showed up at your door."

"I feel like you're the first honest thing that's happened to me in the last twenty years. I'm not sold on your grandmother. I don't trust her or her motivations, and I'm not sold on this job tomorrow. But you. I had no idea children could do this to a man."

She looked away, and he drained his glass of tea, chomped a few pieces of ice. He'd not had a drink in a few days and had not experienced the shakes, which he thought was a strong harbinger of his renewed sobriety. He did, however, feel emotionally vulnerable, and regretted being so nakedly honest with his daughter. He'd not spoken the word *love* in twenty years, since his trip to Spain with Mary Grace, but he felt it now, something unhinged and wild inside him. Out of control.

"Well," he said. "I'm sure we'll catch back up soon. But if anything happens to me tomorrow—"

She looked up. "What would happen?"

"Hopefully nothing. But like I told you, I don't fully trust this operation. If anything happens to me, check your email. I'm sending something your way."

"What is it?"

"Think of it as a get-out-of-jail-free card. Hopefully you won't need it, but your dear old dad is worried about you."

"There's nothing to worry about," she said.

"I hope you're right."

That night, after he'd paid the tab and they'd hugged in the parking lot and parted ways, he sat in his car while she drove off.

There's nothing to worry about, he repeated to himself.

The agents would be surveilling him, and they would use whatever he gathered to bolster whatever case they were building. He'd asked them to take care of Molly, to go after the person behind the curtain, but part of him knew there would be a double-cross and that Molly might be taking a fall.

In the parking lot, he pulled out his phone and sent an email to Bert updating him on the meeting and the next steps for tomorrow. He would be meeting the Good Will Refugees contact early afternoon, at their offices on Church Street. From there, he hoped to gather enough information to draw the agents' attention, clear Molly and himself, and get out of this whole mess. After sending the note, he saw he had an email from Bonnie, whom he'd not seen in more than a week.

Checking in — you okay?

She was surprised he'd taken the week off with no notice and wanted to make sure he wasn't drunk in a gutter some- where. His article had been a hit, she said. High traffic on the website, plenty of shares on social media, and an atmosphere of general kudos around the office.

I hate that you're missing it, she wrote. *Let me know if you need anything. I'll be out tomorrow, but stop by my office Tuesday.*

What could he tell her? He wouldn't be in the office tomorrow either, and likely not Tuesday. By Wednesday, he surely would have burned any goodwill he'd accrued, and if he wasn't back by Friday he might not have a job waiting for him the next week.

He cranked on his car and logged out of his Gmail. He assumed the agents had some form of tap on his *Charleston Daily Dispatch* and Gmail accounts, and he didn't want anyone but Molly to see what he was about to send. He'd created a Proton Mail address and logged into it now.

In South Florida Friday, he'd put half a million in a trust, matching the money he'd taken from Spain. It was never really his, so now Molly could access it with the right informa- tion. If something happened to him or if the agents moved in on her, the money would be there as a safety net to bail her out. He wrote out the details of the trust and the name of his broker.

Dear Molly, a way out for you.

He took a breath as he signed the email, *Love, Dad.*

Then he set it to send tomorrow evening. If everything went smoothly, he could delete the draft, but he felt like a gambler who knows, before asking for one more spin of the wheel, that his luck had run out.

Chapter Thirty Five

SUNDAY NIGHT the team gathered at the King Street office to plot out tomorrow's movements. For the past two weeks, they'd cataloged everything they knew about Wyatt Brewer and Molly Keagan, as well as the associates of Harry Cope— his wife, Lillian, Captain James Allen, Stepan Boldavich, and the Brit Wyatt had heard on the phone. Everything was laid out on a whiteboard, next to a series of messy circles and arrows showing the connections and touch points among them all. The most recent addition to the board was Good Will Refugees, an LLC owned by a series of nested shell companies, like layers of a matryoshka doll. They had yet to trace ownership out, but Jarman had discovered a series of financial payments between one of the shell companies and Capitol PAC, Molly Keagan's political fundraiser. They would be able to find out more tomorrow when the government reopened after the weekend. The missing data was likely handwritten in some record book in a neighboring county, not that it mattered.

"We know they're connected," Bert said. "First, because Brewer emailed us earlier this evening, and second because of the donation. The question we've been asking all along is *who*, and tomorrow Wyatt Brewer should be able to give us the final clue."

"Are you going to have him wired up?" Penelope asked.

"I'd love to, but I think that'll be too risky. We don't know what he's walking into. Plus, uh." He was unusually reticent here. Pinched the collar of his shirt together. "Diane hasn't come through with any additional surveillance. I think we'll need eyes from all of us."

"We don't have *anyone* coming?"

"I've asked every way from Sunday, but the last word I had from her, she wanted to have a meeting with Shields."

"The guy running infrastructure in New York?" Jarman asked. "Why him?"

"I don't know. Diane just told me there were nuances."

Jarman and Penelope looked at each other, the glance colleagues give one another when they're both thinking it's time to dust off their resumes.

It was late in the night. They had a few hours of sleep in front of them, and then they all needed to take up a post around Good Will Refugees. It was a standard surveillance operation, but they couldn't lose Wyatt. The minutes after the meeting ended would be the most important of ISD's existence. If Wyatt tried to disappear, or if something happened to him at the end of the meeting, or any other unexpected situation—the whole case could dissolve.

"Look," Bert said in his last effort to rally the troops, "it's not ideal, but we have a workable plan. We're not floating in the wind here, like we've been doing for twenty years. Our man Brewer is going to walk into Good Will Refugees headquarters, he's going to meet with whoever, he's going to take notes, which is what Molly's paying him to do, and he's going to report back the missing link we need to go in and make our case. With Brewer as a witness, we'll have enough to indict Molly and Lillian, and maybe someone in Good Will Refugees, and we should be able to leverage that so they give us whoever inside our agency has been running things. We bring this case to Diane on a silver platter, she won't have any choice but to bring it to the DOJ, no matter the nuances."

"I hope you're right, boss," Jarman said, a rare expression of doubt from Bert's number two.

"You've trusted me this long," Bert said.

Jarman nodded.

"We need to talk about where each of us will be," Penelope said, mercifully steering the conversation away from doubt and toward action.

"Right." Bert opened his laptop and put a map of the peninsula on the projector screen. "This is our target," he said.

After running through the operation, Bert dismissed them, but Penelope lingered after Jarman had said his goodbyes. "Got a second?" she asked.

"Yeah, hang on, I need to file this with Central."

"Hold on, before you do."

He paused and looked up at her from his desk. He glanced back at his notes on the screen of his desktop, and then he minimized the tab and hit "win" and "L" to lock his screen. He said, "Why don't we take a quick walk."

She opened her mouth but he held a finger to his lips, pulled his phone from his pocket, set it on his desk, and motioned for her to do the same. Then he put on his coat and nodded toward the door. On King, he took her elbow and steered her south toward the Battery. The night was frosty, and the wind coming up from the water soon chapped her lips. As they walked beneath palms rustling in the breeze, she waited for Bert to break the silence.

After half a block, he said, "Whatever's going on, I wouldn't trust our offices."

"You think someone is listening?"

"I don't know. I assume every word and every keystroke is monitored. The agency doesn't have the manpower to check all the call logs for every officer, but I would think AI could analyze the relevant data. So what's up? You've been dodgy for a while here."

She took a breath. "On the way back from Cope's funeral, Diane called me to ask about what was going on."

"And?"

"She was fishing for information."

"Did you tell her we were filing reports? We've got nothing to hide. Yet."

"Basically."

"But?"

"She asked how you were doing. I thought at the time she was worried about you, since you were maybe losing your life's case with Cope dying."

"But?" he prompted again.

Penelope took a breath, hoping Bert would absolve her. She wondered if this was what it felt like for Catholics to go to confession. "She told me to keep an eye on you, and the other day she sent a request for a status update."

Bert chewed his upper lip as they kept walking. They crossed South Battery and entered the waterside park with its memorials to the Confederates. At the harbor here, the Ashley and Cooper rivers converged and bled into the Atlantic. The water was black and choppy, and slapped against the seawall. They leaned against a railing, and Bert studied the water for several moments.

"I've been with the Company more than thirty years," he said finally. "People do this. Whether it's mistrust or ambition, they go around each other. You've been here long enough to understand information is our currency. She's probably thinking I'll put in my papers soon, so she might be grooming you to replace me."

That had not occurred to Penelope.

Bert went on, "Or she's lost trust in me and thinks I'm about to lead the team into something foolhardy. Which is possible. What do you think?"

"I think we've got a good plan for tomorrow."

"About Diane, I meant."

"I don't know. I thought she was worried about you, but now I'm wondering if she thinks, you know, you're the guy on the inside."

Bert smiled. "You think we've got a good plan?"

"I do, yeah."

"All right. It's too late to worry about what Diane is up to. I'm going to hold off on filing anything with Central. Will you do me a favor? She's going to be wondering why you haven't responded, but I'd like to think about how to land this plane. Will you give me a day before you send her an update?"

Chapter Thirty Six

CHURCH STREET. The oldest part of Charleston, with some of the oldest buildings in the United States at one end and St. Philip's Episcopal on the other. A narrow one-lane corridor with three stories of stucco and brick, cemeteries and palmettos. The Dock Street Theatre had a green iron balcony on the second floor, arches and lights. The architecture evidence you were in the old French quarter, a district filled with ghosts. Tourists bought into these legends, but you couldn't walk around this area on a warm summer evening, or on a quiet and sunny January afternoon, without feeling a presence from the spirit life.

Wyatt was in the neighborhood well before the meeting. It was a beautiful day, sunshine and Carolina blue skies to remark upon, so he parked near the waterfront and strolled through the park, readying himself for the performance to come. A few college kids were out with dogs and Frisbees near the pineapple fountain, and he shunted in along Queen. He dodged a bus as he crossed East Bay, and then the street narrowed to a tight brick alley where no sunlight ever penetrated. Ahead of him, in a splash of light on State Street, a horse and carriage clopped along and vanished by the time he crossed the intersection. There, an idling delivery van, parked illegally, blocked his way. He slid between the bumper and a palmetto tree growing out of the sidewalk and kept moving down Queen toward Church. He suspected the agents were somewhere nearby, but he couldn't see them. Hadn't seen them since his meeting with Bert on the Battery a week ago now. Well. They could photograph him and follow him all day. He only hoped they would come in packing if today's meeting took a turn.

Agents or no agents, the tourists had dropped away, and he felt alone with his thoughts—not a pleasant place to be this afternoon. He'd not slept easy since meeting Molly. He had money in the bank, a job he enjoyed, a life he'd liked until recently, but now, in these idle moments, some voice emerged and screamed that he'd done it all wrong. He'd wasted his life. George Orwell said a man got the face he deserved at age fifty, and while Wyatt still had a decade to get there, he panicked with the thought that he was too far down the wrong course. His was the face of a man who had never committed, had taken the money and run, and had kept himself so occupied he never actually had to grow up. Molly had changed that. She'd wrenched him out of himself, so here he was: changing his life for a daughter he hardly knew, risking his freedom to pull her away from the people she was mixed up with. He'd stepped over the ledge and could only trust his meeting with Good Will Refugees would break the fall.

Church Street was ominously quiet. A flock of starlings danced from the bell tower of St. Philip's and pirouetted across the sky, but no soul was here save Wyatt in a battered brown suit, newspaper reporter freelancing in a world of free market thuggery. No matter how long he'd lived in Charleston, he'd never gotten used to the mysterious alleys and quiet side streets. Still a small-town boy won over by the history and ghosts of a big city. Some people referred to spots like Church Street as *thin places*, where the border between the living and the dead was so thin as to become porous. Places where even the most obnoxious of tourists—or college bros—grew somber as they felt some connection to the afterlife. Wyatt had always wanted to be a religious man, but his upbringing had given him platitudes in place of mystery, easy stories in lieu of the true *this-ness* of the world. The churchgoers he'd grown up with had been happy to exist in the system. It wasn't prosperity gospel, exactly, but he'd felt their convictions were for this world rather than a City of God. This world, he'd discovered, was nothing but a playground for operatives.

He was early for the meetup, so he walked down Broad to the Cathedral. It loomed just as high as it had the other night, the wooden doors beckoning. He thought they might be locked but when he tested them the door opened. A few lost souls were scattered in the pews. No one looked his way as he crossed himself with holy water and sat toward the back. The pew creaked beneath him, and he held his breath to silence himself. He'd sat back here for months before the pandemic, a candidate for full communion undergoing a spiritual journey. He went through a first confession where he'd laid the sin of pride at the foot of the cross, prayed the act of contrition, and continued the process.

But he'd not laid everything out. He'd confessed things he felt guilty about but he'd not examined his conscience to fully unravel his past. He'd known this, on some level, so one day he skipped the mass, and then he skipped another, and then four years went by. Bonnie had asked if he'd wanted to talk about it, encouraged him to meet with Father Jim, but there was nothing to say. He was on his own before his ultimate reality, a coward who couldn't lay himself bare. Not then. Today he thought about that, and about his newfound daughter, and the money in an account for her. He thought about the job he would be doing for Molly and Lillian, Bert and Penelope. He said the Jesus Prayer to himself and tried to think what else he could say, but he had no words for what he was feeling. Whatever was coming, today was Day Zero of some new life.

He checked his watch and then got up and crept out of the sanctuary. Walking down the steps he saw the priest coming down the sidewalk and recognized Father Jim. He pursed his lips and gave a half-smile and nod.

The priest nodded in return but then narrowed his eyes in recognition.

"Hi, Father," Wyatt said.

"I know you," the priest said.

Wyatt re-introduced himself.

"That's right. The reporter."

"The reporter," Wyatt agreed.

"Did you come to mass today?"

"Not today. I was in the neighborhood so stopped by for a few minutes."

"Welcome home," Father Jim said. "Is there anything I can do for you?"

"Pray for me," Wyatt said, already walking away.

He'd been early for his meeting but now he had to hustle back to Church Street. The home for Good Will Refugees was a few blocks south of the Dock Street Theater, a plain white building that, out of context, kind of looked like an old-fashioned small-town bank wedged between two shotgun houses. Stucco construction, tall columns framing glass windows and doors. Palms towered overhead, and their fronds danced in a slight breeze. A *crime watch zone* sign was on the street, and a *for lease* banner hung from a fence near the building.

If they only knew, he thought as he walked up the steps to the double doors. He couldn't count the number of interviews he'd done in his work as a reporter, the number of strangers he'd called or approached cold. He was a confident man, he thought, but he felt a lump in his throat today that reminded him of being a young man, green and afraid of the world, a feeling he thought he'd lost forever.

He glanced around to see if he could spot Bert or Penelope, but the street appeared empty. Thin places, the membrane between the living and the dead. Perhaps ghosts of Charleston's slave market, or dead Confederates, or eighteenth-century aristocrats, or Lowcountry natives had their eyes on him, waiting. A shudder passed through him, and he turned back to the double doors and knocked.

Chapter Thirty Seven

AT THAT MOMENT, Bert was on a third-floor porch across the street, surreptitiously eyeing Wyatt and waiting for the moment of truth. Like many old towns with English provenance, Charleston's property taxes in the early days were based on the number of windows that faced the street, which meant builders over the years had developed long and narrow shotgun houses with few windows on the street and porches that disappeared into alleys. It was the perfect setup for a spy who wished to observe the street without being observed himself, and he now understood how Charleston was able to operate with its secret society hidden behind its tourist front. The old-money patriarchs were just like Bert on this porch, watching the city while secretly controlling its machinations.

From his safe perch in the shadows, Bert had the perfect view of Good Will Refugees. He'd arrived at nine, rang the bell of this house across the street, and, discovering no one home, marched up the stairs to stake out the street. He got a call from Penelope that said Wyatt was parked and heading his way from Waterfront Park. He dialed in Jarman and merged the calls. He knew from the sound of Penelope's puffing that

Jon Sealy

she'd disappeared somewhere around East Bay and was hoofing it up Market to set up in St. Philip's church.

Jarman was no doubt hunched low in a car to the south, perhaps puffing away on an e-cigarette. He'd answered Bert's call but said nothing. He didn't need to say anything. Just needed to be there in case Wyatt came tearing out of the meeting, or someone unexpected showed up, or they heard gunfire from the building.

A few minutes later, Wyatt hung a left onto Church. Bert watched him shuffle nervously along and whispered into his cell, "Target's approaching."

Wyatt looked drunk! He'd not shaved, and he appeared to be wearing something he bought at a thrift store, some moth-ball-laden outfit an old widow donated after her insurance broker husband kicked the bucket. They'd pushed him too hard, Bert thought. He'd been a man on edge for twenty years, and when he was finally caught, he'd relaxed his guard. Like a dam that finally burst, the trickle became a flood. Wyatt had become a wastrel overnight, a man in decline.

Bert ignored the flock of starlings overhead, instead keeping his eyes on the reporter as the man scooted down Church Street, paused, and then backtracked toward Good Will Refugees.

The reporter looked around him carefully, and Bert held his breath as he walked up and knocked on the glass door. The door opened to reveal a burly, balding man who looked like he belonged in a basement boxing ring.

And then, too late for regret or recriminations, Bert under-stood his mistake. His team had been so focused on the Eastern Europeans, the deceased Stepan Boldavich, Good Will Refugees, and the Estonian airfield that he'd not been paying attention to ISD, to Diane and Winston.

They'd cased the alleys and back streets around St. Philips for the right places to set up and watch Wyatt's meeting with Good Will Refugees, but they'd not taken note of who might

282

be watching them. Bert had no reason to ask who watches the watchers because ISD was an insignificant outpost, a group of nobodies known to almost no one, in the agency or outside.

Tell that to the Winston Shields, who materialized on the sidewalk behind Wyatt, and to the team of agents who emerged from—where? Alleys, sewers, parked cars along narrow Church Street.

A dozen agents descended on Wyatt, took him to the ground, and stormed into the headquarters of Good Will Refugees.

Why would anyone be watching Bert's team in ISD? The answer was clear as a mountain spring. They'd been playing a game inside the system this whole time, and now they'd reached the end game. Mom and Dad had come in to shut down the operation.

He watched the agents funnel into Good Will Refugees, bringing Wyatt in with them to clear out the street, and then an agent mounted the steps behind Bert.

Bert did not turn until the agent cleared his throat and said, "Mr. Wilson, will you come with me?"

Chapter Thirty Eight

STANDING AT THE DOOR, waiting for someone to let him in, Wyatt had the same feeling he'd had in Spain, when he knocked and then let himself into Sr. Oliva's apartment. It occurred to him that he had been here before, standing outside a door to the unknown, chasing after a dream. Years ago the dream had been for Mary Grace, the love of his life, and today it was his daughter, Molly. And as with years ago, he was still blind to so much in the world.

Still innocent, even if life had kicked him around some.

Unlike Madrid, if no one answered he would not be letting himself into the Good Will Refugees headquarters. He would not be stumbling onto a dead body today. Instead, he would jet away toward the Market to find safety in crowds, and he would send messages to Bert and Molly letting them know it was off. He still had the money in the bank. He could disappear at the first sign of trouble.

Then the burly man answered. Wyatt had enough time to register a few sad hair plugs, old acne scars, and cigarette-stained teeth as the man said, "Yes?"

Something caught the man's eye, and a look of panic flashed across his face. He took off into the building. Wyatt took note of a potted plant on a walnut table in the foyer. A chandelier overhead. A black and white tiled floor. No trace of the man down the dark hallway. No one with guns in there to seize him.

The guns were outside. Behind him.

Before Wyatt could turn, someone was on him. He was thrown to the concrete stoop, and a British voice said, "Stop! In the hall!" And there was a clamor around him.

He cursed Bert and the agency—they could have *told* him what was coming, he could have *prepared*—and then the man pinning him down pulled him up. His knee had been bashed into concrete, and he couldn't stand on his right leg.

"Let's go, Wyatt," the British man said. "We got to get off the street. Hey, Carlin. Help me out."

Wyatt knew that voice.

He studied the man—tall, rakish, but with a middle-aged loosening of his cheeks and waist, something Wyatt knew all about. This was the man on the telephone the other day. Had he been set up? Could he never see what was coming?

Still innocent, after all these years.

The British man and his colleague took hold of Wyatt's arms and led him into the musty building and set him on a set of stairs. Other men fled through the room, pistols drawn. There was some commotion from deep in the building, a series of thuds and a scream, and then the entryway was cleared.

Molly.

The email would arrive this evening. Assuming she stayed clear of the agents today, she should be able to access the funds tomorrow. From there, it would be on her to do something with them. Buy a new identity, flee the country, and start a new life for herself. For all he knew, the agents were at her house as well right now, pulling her into custody, ready to bring down whatever kingpin she was working for, but he prayed she had escaped the dragnet.

Jon Sealy

The British man ran a hand over his jaw. Then he closed the front door. He paused for a moment, listening as the sounds in the building quieted down. Wyatt's knee throbbed, and he was about to launch a complaint about the way they'd handled it, to ask where Bert and Penelope were, and when he'd be free to go.

But before he could speak, the Brit began to read him his rights.

286

Chapter Thirty Nine

ONE THING PENELOPE had learned from years of powerlifting is that you could tell when you were going to fail a lift before you ever touched the barbell. Perhaps it was a self-fulfilling prophecy, but that could only explain some of it. As you got to know your body, you learned how much gas you had in the tank. If you did five reps, you knew whether you could do one more, or three more, or if you would fail number six. You knew it by your respiration, by the way your heart thrummed in your chest and the arteries in your neck throbbed, by the twitch in your muscles, and by your mental exhaustion. If the world grew silent and a ringing filled your ears and spots appeared in your eyes and your head emptied of thoughts and blood, you were done with this set. One more exertion would finish you. Powerlifting gave you that sense of proprioception: of your body in space, and of your body's relationship to itself.

She'd never found a better way of looking inward than by stepping under a barbell, and she'd found, recently, that the benefits of the iron bled over to the rest of her life. She knew, for instance, watching Wyatt shuffle down Queen Street and racing to beat him over at St. Philip's, that something was off. It was no surprise when the first agents appeared—as though it were preordained, some psychic signal sent via the world to her blood to her brain—and she quickly maneuvered her way into a restroom inside the church, locked herself in a stall, and stood on the toilet so her feet would not be visible should someone sweep the room. After an hour in the stall, no messages from Bert or Jarman, she ventured into the warming afternoon, strolled north to the Market, and disappeared into the throngs of people enjoying a sunny day after Charleston's bleak month of winter.

By March, the camellias were in bloom and the sweet scent of jasmine perfumed the peninsula. She suffered a long bout of bronchitis, which kept her out of the gym for a month. When she finally returned she found, to her dismay, she'd lost thirty pounds of strength and had to struggle with squatting 185. There went a year's worth of progress, wiped out by a nasty bug. She pulled her resume together and had promising interviews with several departments around the agency. She expected an overdue call from Dallas or San Francisco any moment. Funding for ISD ran out in June, so by August she would either be in another city or knocking on doors in the private industry. Some days, in-house counsel didn't sound like a bad life. Banker's hours, a liberal salary, the chance to become part of the system, another anonymous suburbanite working the wheels of corporate America.

She told her brother, Eric, about her troubles at work, but not her parents. He was still working in IT in D.C., but he was living with a girlfriend now and on the verge of getting married. There was no room in Bethesda for Penelope, but he nonetheless offered an ear to complain to.

"I can't go into the details," she said, "but the details almost don't matter. My boss was fired, my colleague's in the wind, but I'm still on the payroll."

"Who're you reporting to now?"

"No one."

"What do you mean no one?" he said. "Who was your boss's boss?"

What was there to say about Diane? "She's the one who shut us down."

"There's still got to be a paper trail. You're on an org chart somewhere."

"I'm not sure I am," she said. "Bert got canned. The rest of us have showed up a few times, but no one's there. No one's contacted us. It's just silent. The way we reported in, we got our funding from one division and our assignments from another. They dismantled the group that gave us the assignments, but the funding's still there. They never had any oversight of us, though."

"So you're just getting paid because of a glitch in the system?"

Her brother had always looked out for her, proffering unsolicited advice since she was old enough to walk. She usually would roll her eyes, but today she felt sad as he went on a tear about how she needed to protect herself. There was nothing he could say to fix this, and the way her agency worked, her entire life was classified. There would be no recourse.

"Promise me you've got your resume updated for when they figure out what's happening. Do you have a good lawyer?"

"I don't have any lawyer."

"You can't rep yourself."

"I know, Eric. I'll hire someone if it comes to that."

"What a mess," he said.

What she didn't tell her brother was she felt lucky not to be facing any indictments. Before he'd disappeared himself, Jarman said agents had taken Bert into custody outside Good Will Refugees. Whatever bear he'd poked, they brought the roof down on ISD, and Jarman thought Bert may be facing some kind of trumped-up obstruction charges, maybe worse.

Wyatt had been released after a battery of interviews, but she suspected the federal government was not done with him. Without clearance from her agency, he potentially could be facing federal charges of treason. The way things worked in the bureaucracy, she believed that she, Bert, and Jarman might be the only people who knew the poor, alcoholic reporter was innocent, a pawn played by the agency to hook a bigger fish. The marlin had gotten away, and Wyatt was being fed to the sharks.

In late spring, when it was clear information would not be forthcoming from anyone in the agency about ISD and Bert's entire operation out of the house on King Street, Penelope arranged a meeting with Wyatt at a strip mall Starbucks on James Island.

He arrived first and was on the patio with a cup of tea and a yellow legal pad. He put the paper away when she walked over.

"Thanks for making the trek out to my neighborhood," he said. "You want anything to drink?"

"I'm all right. I appreciate you meeting with me," she said.

He shrugged.

"You working on another hot story?"

"No actually, I got laid off a month after, you know."

"I'm sorry," she said. "Because of us?"

"Yep. They had me on leave after the feds raided my office. Then someone from HR lined up a Teams call to suggest I take a package. More layoffs were coming, so it was only a matter of time anyway."

"I'm sorry to hear it. What are you going to do?"

"I've got a friend who does corporate event planning, and she's introduced me around some business groups. Who knew big companies needed research papers? That's keeping me afloat anyway."

Penelope wondered what he would think if he knew his whole life had been turned upside down thanks to a series of fraudulent research papers.

He took a breath. He said, "So here we are again."

"Here we are," she agreed.

"Where's Bert?"

"I don't know. He got canned too, and I haven't been able to get in touch with him."

She'd received a few encrypted messages from him, but neither of them had been able to talk openly. He'd reassured her that he was fine and reminded her to run the dishwasher at the office. In other words, clean up Project Gravy before she locked up. Hence, her visit today.

Wyatt whistled.

"I wouldn't worry about him," she said. "He had his thirty years with the agency, so I presume he's got a nice pension. Maybe even some contract work lined up in the private industry."

"In exchange for his silence?"

She said nothing.

"I thought so. So everybody gets away. Except me, it seems. Did you know someone has me under investigation? I don't know who. FBI, the attorney general, it's all very abstract. Don't suppose you're here to give me some good news today?"

"I don't know what's going on," she said finally.

"Well, don't look at me. I was living a perfectly comfortable life before you showed up at my door and said get in the car."

"That's not exactly true, though. You were sitting on that money for a long time."

"Right, but what would have happened if you hadn't shown up? Maybe Molly and I would have gotten to know each other. Maybe she would have offered me the job anyway, but I wouldn't have taken it. I would have tried to talk her into getting out of whatever scheme she and Lillian were running. Whatever the case, I feel confident I wouldn't be here waiting on someone like you to straighten everything out."

"Do you know where Molly is now?"

"Why don't you tell me?"

"I don't know," she said. "That's why I'm asking you."

He looked at her a few moments. There was a flash of something in his eye, but he tamped it down.

"Our people are looking for her," she said, "but it sounds like she's disappeared. They seized her bank account, but there wasn't enough in it to start over. I was kind of hoping she'd reached out to you."

"Not a peep," Wyatt said. "What about Lillian? She say anything?"

"I haven't talked to her, but I presume someone in the agency has. As far as I know, she doesn't know where her granddaughter is any more than the rest of us."

"Are you going to arrest her?"

Penelope was silent. There was nothing to say. She and Bert had boxes and boxes of evidence against Harry Cope but next to nothing on his wife. Lillian was a few pages of a dossier, a nexus between odious men and their dishonest dealings with the federal government.

"So she gets away with it," Wyatt said. "She sets us all up, wrecks your department, I'm under investigation, and she lives out into the sunset."

"Do you have a lawyer?" Penelope asked.

"Of course I have a lawyer."

She nodded. "They'll get it straightened out. To charge you, they'd have to dig up too much from my agency, and no one is going to let that happen."

"I know the charges won't stick," he said, "but that doesn't help me today, does it? I'm out of a job, and all my old colleagues think I'm some kind of criminal. If the paper had backed me up, that would be one thing, but my journalism days are over."

"I can't do anything about that."

"Of course not. You people just bulldoze your way through whatever it is you do, never mind the consequences. Not like the media's any better. Bunch of jackals waiting for wounded prey to show up. The system's FUBAR. So why are you here, Penelope? If you're not here to straighten it all up and get me out, what do you want?"

"I want to figure out what just happened."

"Ha! You and me both."

"My career is probably over, too," she went on. "My boss is gone, my other colleagues are fleeing the ship, I'm either getting transferred or out of a job, and the only reason I'm still employed today is a technicality around my department's funding. No one I talk to in the agency can tell me anything, so I was hoping you might be able to help fill in a few gaps. Maybe together we can see the whole story."

"I doubt it," he said.

"Maybe we can start with what happened that day. At Good Will Refugees. Did you have a sense of anything? From Molly or Lillian, or the guy who met you at the door?"

"All I know is I was supposed to interview him to write a white paper. Exactly what I told Bert the day before. The guy who opened the door was just as surprised as I was when federal agents barged in and arrested us."

"Do you know who killed the Estonian on Folly Beach?"

"Nope. East European gangsters, I presume."

"What you wrote in your article."

"Molly handed me that story, but I did my own research. Based on what people told me, it all held up. Stepan Boldavich was in deep with some shady figures."

Penelope thought for a moment. She assumed whoever Boldavich was working with had killed him. Someone had worked out he was funneling information to ISD and wanted to put a stop to it to protect the airfield scheme. It made sense to pin it on some Estonian mobsters, but she did wonder who else might have had an incentive.

"You think the people you were about to interview at Good Will Refugees had him killed?" she asked.

He shrugged. "I don't know who they were, but I wouldn't be surprised if they were responsible for a few dead bodies."

"What makes you say that?"

"That's what Molly outlined anyway. There are good gangsters and bad gangsters. The Good Will Refugees people, allegedly, are the latter."

"And you believed her?"

"Molly? She's my daughter."

"You believed that?"

Again, a look flashed across his face. Again, he tamped it down.

Molly was certainly Lillian and Harry's granddaughter, but her father's identity was speculation. Wyatt could be her father, but it was equally likely that Molly and Lillian had cooked up the story to manipulate him into publishing his article about Boldavich.

Penelope let it go and asked, "Why'd you agree to take on the job for her?"

"I didn't have much of a choice."

"You could have said no."

"To whom? You people would have hounded me over the job I did for Harry Cope. If I'd said no, I'd be right here facing some other investigation, only you'd be on the other end, funneling false information to the authorities, wouldn't you? I'd be fighting you rather than...whoever it is I'm fighting now. Who set me up? Was it someone in your agency, or another agency?"

"They were in my agency."

"What happened? Was Bert running a rogue operation? Was he dirty himself?"

"No, Bert was clean as they get."

He ran his tongue around his lips a few times and eyed her. Didn't look like a man completely on the outside. Looked like someone who knew a lot more than he was letting on. He said, "So the people we're up against are the bent ones. And they're high enough up that you can't do a thing about them, am I right?"

"You worked that out quick."

He leaned back and smiled, making her question her assumptions once again. Had she just confirmed a theory of his? Was he as innocent as he appeared? Impossible to say. Impossible to know someone else's thoughts.

"I've had nothing but time for the past six weeks," he said, "and I write stories for a living. Every night I just write one story after another to try to make this make sense."

"Did Molly or Lillian tell you anything about the people they were working for?"

He shook his head. "Only that they were pro-business, anti-nationalist types."

"Tell me about that."

"Molly's got it in her head that the nation-state is over. When more people are members of Facebook than are citizens of any single country, the idea of a *country* with borders and a common identity is no longer relevant. Kissinger said the U.S. doesn't have friends, only interests. Molly had that same view about international business, and whoever she was working for was trying to use the U.S. military to build an airfield in Estonia to further their business interests."

"But you don't know who her employer was."

"I don't. She said her grandmother was running the show the whole time, and Harry's law firm was just the agent. There was a British guy on the phone that day. I'm pretty sure it was the same agent who arrested me."

She sat forward. "Really?"

"Just a hunch."

"That's all we have in this business."

"Sure. Well. They called the guy on the phone Winn."

"Winston Shields," she said to herself. "Why didn't you tell us his name?"

Wyatt couldn't disguise the look on his face.

"What?" she pressed.

"We were moving fast," he said. "And I didn't know he was working for your agency."

"You were playing both sides," she said.

"I wanted to make sure I knew what I was onto before telling you everything."

Bert had told them Winston Shields was involved, and he'd been on the ground during the raid, but Diane had been running Shields. If Shields was in the meeting with Lillian and Wyatt, then there were two possibilities. Either MI6 was playing the Americans or Diane was behind it all—the target ISD had been looking for. It meant she'd been running the scam all these years and had created ISD with the sole intention of keeping an eye on Bert and his team. To make sure they never got too close to the truth.

Penelope felt sick. If Diane was running things as the new Everett Archer, then their entire operation—Bert, Jarman, Penelope, ISD—was nothing more than a front for Diane to control the investigation. They'd been funneling information up to the one person who could manipulate it to ensure her own survival. Wyatt was right. The system was FUBAR, and Penelope needed to get out of the agency altogether.

She cursed. "We could have avoided all of this."

"You think Bert would have called it off just because he had a hunch the man on the phone was one of yours?" he said. "I told him it was a Brit. He wasn't a dummy. If your Winston Shields is so well known in your group, the connection must have occurred to him. Yet he sent me in any way."

Wyatt was right. Bert would have sent him in regardless. What she couldn't figure out was why the reporter had suddenly decided to hold onto critical information right before the operation.

Molly. It had to be the girl. The reporter was a sentimentalist.

If she could find Jarman, she would suggest looking into Wyatt's investment accounts. That would explain his trip to Miami. If he'd made a funds transfer, Molly could be anywhere in the world, a new identity already in hand.

"Anyway," he was saying. "If one of yours was involved, that explains why I'm here and you're homeless. They're covering their tracks."

"They don't have anything on you," she assured him. "They know we flagged you as a known associate of Harry Cope, but Bert kept his reports vague."

"Lucky me," he said. "Sounds like he knew what's up. Where does this leave me?"

She waited another beat before crossing the line she'd come here to cross. She pulled a thick yellow envelope out of her purse and set it on the table.

"What's this?"

"That's the file we had on you," she said. "Or everything we had before we pulled you in for the interview. You'll see we didn't know much about you—you weren't really on our radar—but there are a few things you might find interesting about the Cope family."

"Why are you giving me this?"

"I don't know, Wyatt. I came here to try to make sense of what we all just went through. I know what we put you through wasn't fair, so I thought this might help, to see what we saw. If nothing else, it should help your lawyer clear any charges."

He drummed his fingers against the envelope but didn't open it in front of her.

She nodded and left him there with as much of the puzzle as she believed they would be able to assemble. The Estonian

airfield was a go. Someone, with reports from Diane and
Winston Shields, had deemed it good for defense, good for
business, good for the economy, good for America. The energy
companies would expand their operations in the Baltic, the
Russians would keep their focus on the Black Sea, and the
façade of American power would remain intact for another
day.

Penelope thought about how she'd almost turned on Bert,
almost spied on a man she did trust for the woman who might
have been their target all along. As she drove back to the
peninsula, she tried to come to terms with the end of something and what she could do next. It wasn't every day you
found out your life was a sham, that you'd been operating
inside a fiction all this time. Fitzgerald once said there were no
second acts in America, but that was just what she needed. Or
a third act. She and Wyatt both did.

She exited the James Island Connector onto Lockwood
and then Broad, heading back to the nondescript office on
King. She wondered if Wyatt had read through the file she'd
given him yet, and how he would take the news that Harry
had enlisted his daughter Mary Grace after college. From
their interviews on King Street, she assumed Wyatt never
knew his old sweetheart had gotten into the family business—
and that the story of her car accident, officially ruled a DUI,
was riddled with holes.

She believed him when he said he didn't know what
happened to Molly Keagan, but the file on Wyatt and the
Cope family might inspire him to look for her. If another
posting didn't come through in Dallas or Denver or even
Duluth, Minnesota, Penelope would have time on her hands.
She might keep an eye on Wyatt to see what he did next. Until
then, she parked on a palm-shaded side street near the office
and thought about how else she might salvage her own
fleeting life.

About Jon Sealy

Jon Sealy is also the author of *The Whiskey Baron, The Edge of America, The Merciful,* and the craft book *So You Want to Be a Novelist.* A South Carolina native, he currently lives with his family in Richmond, Virginia.

Subscribe to his newsletter: www.jonsealy.com

Made in United States
Orlando, FL
04 June 2024

47539064R00188